Beyond Big-g City

(Book Three in the Small-g City series)
By S. D. Matley

WolfSinger Publications ∫ Security, Colorado

Dedication

This book is dedicated to the Alaskan Way Viaduct (1953-2019), Seattle's double-decked elevated freeway that was part of State Route 99, home to Ralph in his structureling days, and the spark that made this series come to life. Rest in peace, old friend.

Acknowledgments

People make books. Lots of people.

Thanks to Margo Metegrano and Sienna Reid for sensory details about the Capuchin Crypt in Rome, Italy; to the Seawall Project Street Team, Seattle, WA, for information about the waterfront seawall; to Susan J. Tweit for recommended reading on climate change; to Carol Hightshoe and WolfSinger Publications for bringing this book to life.

I am forever indebted to Martin McCaw (whom I kindly refer to as the Line Editor from Hell) for his thorough critiques and revision suggestions on early drafts of *Beyond Big-G City*. Also to Bruce A. Matley (who left Earth on December 23, 2018) for his long and devoted history as First Reader, his love, and his unflagging support of my writing.

Author's Note

This is a book about Greek immortals. As you may know, they support the mortal world behind the scenes through the corporation Olympus, Inc. It is the third book in a series, preceded by *Small-g City* and *Big-G City*.

About Olympus, Inc.

Olympus, Inc., was founded by Zeus, a Greek immortal of mythic fame, thousands of years ago. Zeus served as CEO of Olympus, Inc., until 2015 CE[1], when he was succeeded by Veronica Zeta, the youngest child of Zeus and his wife, Hera. Olympus, Inc., is headquartered in the City of Mount Olympus, the capital city of the immortals, also referred to as Big-G City.

What do these immortals do for us? Lots of things, really. You may have heard of Demeter, the goddess of agriculture and harvest. Every year she and her daughter, Persephone, bless our mortal grown crops. You might also remember Poseidon, the God of the Sea, who looks after marine life and protects sailors and fishermen. Not so familiar is Clifford Essex, Director of Architectural and Computer Services. His job is to make sure ambitious but under-engineered mortal structures don't fall down on our silly heads.

In short, Olympus, Inc., is a vast civil service organization. Why do the immortals do this type of work instead of lolling around, consuming ambrosia and talking about the good old days? Because they were created by the Titans to look after us. And who are these Titans?

About the Greek Immortals

The whole flock of Greek immortals started with Gaia (Mother Earth) and Uranus (Father Sky). The twelve children of Gaia and Uranus were Titans, who were primeval deities. Two of these children, Cronus and Rhea, are the parents of Zeus, Hera, Poseidon, Demeter, Hades, Hestia and Stella. Cronus intended to keep control over all his children, but was overthrown by Zeus, Poseidon and Hades, who successfully conspired to murder him.

Due to the limited number of marriageable beings, brothers married sisters. Children came. Uncles married nieces, and so on. Almost any Greek immortal can legitimately call Zeus dad, uncle or

---

[1] Common Era, which is a more modern way of saying Anno Domini (AD). BCE stands for Before Common Era, the update for Before Christ (BC).

brother. When mortals were assigned to their care, the Greek immortals made children with them, too. Depending on the throw of the genetic dice, a few of these half-mortal children inherited the trait of immortality.

About Big-Gs and small-gs

The Greek immortals are divided into two types: Big-G Gods and small-g gods.

Zeus and his siblings are Big-G Gods, a type of royal family, as are all of their full-blooded Big-G children and some of their mixed heritage children. Again, it's a matter of how the DNA gets distributed. Small-g gods fall under the cheating definition of Greek immortals who are not Big-G Gods.

Until recently, Big-Gs typically ran the most important departments of Olympus, Inc. When Veronica Zeta took charge she reformed the corporation from a nest of nepotism to a meritocracy; now, small-gs can rise on the corporate ladder through talent, determination and a strong dose of luck. Small-gs also fill many support roles: rain gods and goddesses, robotics technicians, computer analysts, clerical workers, etc.

In addition, immortals of all ranks are deployed throughout the mortal world. Many work alongside us, undetected. They tend to be transferred a lot because they age the equivalent of one mortal year for every century. Not all immortals work for Olympus, Inc. Of particular note is Aphrodite, Goddess of Love, who runs her own adult-themed business empire, Love, Inc.

About the Big Twelve

Greek mythology names twelve Big-Gs as "major gods" who are sometimes disparagingly referred to by the others as the Big Twelve. All sources show Zeus, Hera, Poseidon, Demeter, Athena, Apollo, Artemis, Ares, Aphrodite, Hephaestus and Hermes in the membership. The twelfth position is sometimes given to Hestia (Goddess of Home and Hearth) and sometimes to Dionysus (God of Wine). In short, it depends on the personal priorities of the list-maker. Plato connected the Twelve Olympians with the twelve calendar months but whatever honor was originally intended by the designation has long been forgotten. Still, some of the Big Twelve are known to throw their weight around when they feel slighted by (presumably) lesser gods.

About Structurelings

A number of small-g gods work as structurelings. This vocation initially involved dispersing one's molecules into unstable architectural structures for reinforcement. Between 2010 and 2015, structureling work was computerized. Detailed descriptions of oldstyle structureling work appear in *Small-g City*, the first book of this series.

About Auras

Some immortals have the capability of seeing auras. This is particularly useful to those in the psychological counseling and medical professions. Immortals have purple auras and those who are Big-Gs have gold super coronas. Mortal auras are pink. When auras blacken or start to look moldy, illness is indicated.

About the City of Mount Olympus

In addition to Olympus, Inc., headquarters, the City of Mount Olympus is home to Athens U and Athens Tech. Hotels, shopping and cultural venues are in the center of the city. Residential neighborhoods and businesses make up the rest. Nearly all local transportation is by horse-drawn chariot. Immortals can travel to and from this city by flying in and out under their own power or taking a high-speed shuttle chariot to and from a charmed section of Athens International Airport, the same airport we mortals use.

Mortal and Immortal Synergies

With all this going to and coming from the mortal world, it's no surprise the immortals pick up our customs and fads. The immortals have devised methods of digital communication from Mount Olympus to the mortal world, which has greatly improved the flow of day-to-day operations. Immortal import agents regularly visit the mortal world to procure luxury items that aren't produced locally. However, citizens who spend most of their time in the City of Mount Olympus, where togas and sandals are de rigueur, have difficulty keeping up with mortal fashion.

The City of Mount Olympus is also home to The Power, a malevolent supernatural being who is incarcerated in a seventh basement cell at Olympus, Inc., headquarters. The Power, after tormenting Zeus and his family, was captured and imprisoned in the course of *Big-G City*, the second book in this series.

MONTH ONE

June 20-July 19, 2025

FRIDAY, JUNE 20, 2025

City of Mount Olympus
Hermes

Hermes, Director of Digital Devices and Robotics at Olympus, Inc., fretted as the elevator swayed up from his fourth-floor department to the CEO suite on the eleventh. He hated annual reviews, something Veronica Zeta had implemented when she'd taken over from Zeus. Once a year she met with her Directors one-on-one, to discuss performance and set goals.

Reviews annoyed Hermes and today he was downright edgy. Veronica had always sent his review file in advance. Not this time. The reason might be simple, a mere technical glitch or she might be running behind in her work? His gut disagreed; his gut strongly suspected Veronica was holding something back.

The elevator chimed and the doors rolled open. The vast CEO suite, a light and airy refuge studded with skylights and decorated with lush, green plants, appeared before him. The reception desk was vacant. Veronica's assistant, Alexandra, was nowhere to be seen. None of this boded well, nor the fact he was late.

Veronica, herself, sat at her own desk half-way across the suite. Her posture suggested an iron rod. Formal as ever, she wore the snow-white, gold-edged toga of a CEO. Her fingers drummed the desktop.

Forward he strolled. Hermes threw back his head to sweep the hair out of his eyes. "Hey, Ronnie." He flashed a slow smile and flopped into the chair across from hers.

Veronica extended her hand. "Thank you for meeting with me today, Hermes."

Her dark eyes studied him. She didn't say anything about his being late.

Hermes threw his hair back again. His shaggy surfer cut was longer than usual, no time or inclination to have a trim for two or three months. He set his digital tablet on the desktop.

"Didn't get your review file yet."

"Here." She tapped the screen of her own device.

His eyes shifted to his tablet. Hermes read in silence, scrolled back up and read the review again. He looked up. "And this is supposed to be my fault?"

"It's an old law, Hermes." Her face was stone. "When an immortal interferes with mortal technology—"

"Interferes?" He shot from his chair and started pacing. "They'd still be rubbing sticks together to make fires if it wasn't for my *interference*. How dare you—"

She rose and planted her palms on her desk. "For Dad's sake, control yourself! You're the one who taught them how to use fossil fuels and you know the law as well as I do. If an immortal interferes with mortal technology, said immortal must monitor the use of that technology and minimize whatever harm comes from it."

He glared at her.

She glared back. "Now, sit down and listen to me."

A white ray of sun shot through the skylight above Veronica's desk, bleaching the color from the room. Hermes understood the big picture. If the mortals succeeded in destroying their planet and went extinct, it would be the end of the gods, too. The gods had been created solely to take care of the mortals. Their worlds mirrored each other in many respects. Temperatures were rising, slowly but consistently, in the City of Mount Olympus, too. Growing cycles had veered out of sync. Weather patterns changed more rapidly than some species of plant life could adapt.

"Did you read the goals I've set?"

Hermes nodded. She'd always invited his input before today.

"The carbon dioxide levels in Earth's atmosphere need to level off and come down. Weather and Agriculture will help you in any way they can, but they don't have the time or resources to influence mortal behavior. You need to guide the mortals back from extracting and consuming fossil fuels at their present rate."

He pointed to the deadline on his screen. "In two years?"

Veronica arched an eyebrow. "You've already had ten, as I've documented in your review. Earth is half a degree Celsius from the tipping point. If you don't succeed in reducing carbon dioxide levels before that point is reached, it's highly unlikely the mortals will survive another two centuries."

He burned to defend himself, but what was the point? He'd already put gargantuan effort into developing and testing methods for scientifically engineering the reversal of climate change but hadn't reported this to her. Why would he, since every attempt had ended in failure? Now she was directing him to work away from his strengths, to pursue the problem from the behavioral angle. Hermes was a lot of things, but he was neither a lobbyist nor a psychologist.

Veronica's expression half-shifted from stern to welcoming, achieving neither. "See you at the party on Sunday?"

The damnable engagement party. His own effort to smile went sideways.

"Wouldn't miss it."

Hermes stalked to the elevator, telling himself it really wasn't that bad. But it really was.

SUNDAY, JUNE 22, 2025

Persephone

Persephone threaded her way through the packed ballroom of the Odyssey Hotel. Hundreds of voices chattered, their tongues loosened with celebratory champagne. Another family party in the City of Mount Olympus. This one was in honor of Veronica Zeta and her fiancé, Clifford Essex. Absorbed in wondering how Zeus and Hera felt about their daughter marrying a small-g, Persephone tripped over her own feet and sloshed her Mai Tai on an innocent bystander.

"Oops! Sorry."

She reached toward Aunt Hestia, with a cocktail napkin to sponge off the rum and pineapple juice. Hestia took her gently by the wrist. "It's all right, dear. My toga's wash and wear."

On fire with embarrassment, Persephone turned away, her eyes anchored on the wall-to-wall carpeting patterned with waves. She bumped shoulders with someone, hard.

"Sorry!"

"No worries," said her victim, a young man who resembled Poseidon. One of his countless sons, she supposed. All the children of Rhea and Cronus bred like rabbits, except for Aunt Hestia and…

She reached Hades, her husband, without spilling more of her drink. Why hadn't he trimmed his beard like she'd asked him to? He was handsome in a barrel-chested, gruff kind of way but tended to let his grooming go to Tartarus, cared nothing about looking nice for his wife or about romance in general. Theirs was a childless marriage. Children, he said, were too expensive to raise. Persephone had a career of her own that kept her topside nine months of the year. Nanny fees alone, he'd argued, would be crippling.

Hades was talking to Hermes, as he had been when she'd gone to the bar. Hermes didn't look well. His shoulders slumped and there were dark half-moons under his eyes. An attractive young woman stood beside him. She'd been introduced as his executive assistant.

Persephone forced a weak smile. "I'm back."

Hades grunted and continued the conversation, the same

business they'd been discussing when she'd gone to freshen her drink.

"Those bastards are robbing me blind and it's not just the lost revenue, expenses are up, too. Charon's on salary now, says he won't run the ferry for the fares alone, what with international currency fluctuations. Now that he's an employee I have to pay fringe benefits, too. And don't get me started about Cerberus. That dog might have three heads, but he eats like he's got six stomachs!"

Persephone sighed. Ever since she'd arrived in the Underworld, she'd been sneaking treats to the dragon-tailed dog who guarded the gate, short-circuiting Hades' plan to keep him lean and hungry.

Hermes cleared his throat. "I don't suppose you've looked at the security system proposal I dropped off the last time I came by?"

In addition to Hermes' work at Olympus, Inc., he was also the guide to the souls of the recently dead. The souls that came to the Underworld, anyway. Other gods from other pantheons escorted their dead to other places. The contracts, signed between neighboring immortal groups millennia ago, were frequently amended. Hades had recently taken on a new classification of mortal souls: football hooligans. He'd been confident the increased fares would result in a tidy profit but, given the amount of damage the hooligans inflicted even in death, the venture had yet to break even. Hades needed someone to blame. His black eyes narrowed at Hermes.

"Clean out your ears, man! Haven't you been listening? I don't have funds for capital expenditures."

This wasn't true. Persephone knew enough about their finances to suspect her husband was the richest of all the Big-G Gods, from the rights he held to underground minerals and gems alone.

"And I don't have time to invent anything new for you right now," Hermes snapped.

Hermes' executive assistant (her name was Cleo, Persephone remembered) placed a hand on her boss's arm. He shook it off and glared at her. Her deep blue eyes, tilted up at the outside like a cat's, glared back.

"Excuse me," Cleo said and headed toward the bar.

The rumble of conversations around them surged. Someone shouted "Look!" Pan, the God of Shepherds and Flocks, flew near the twenty-foot ceiling. Drunk again, judging from his irregular flight pattern. His wildly curly hair twisted upward like horns and he wore only a loincloth. Persephone tracked the potential barf bomb as if she were watching a fly.

"If he wasn't immortal, I'd kill him," muttered Hermes, who was Pan's father.

"We've got plenty of room," Hades said. His jest fell flat.

"I think I'll try to find Mother," Persephone said, embarrassed by his feeble attempt at humor.

"Why should I be surprised?" Hades bellowed. "Same story every summer. Damn, woman, I'd think you'd have seen enough of Demeter during the spring. Never mind that I made a special trip topside for this wretched party. The hotel is costing me a fortune."

Persephone tapped a conciliatory kiss on her husband's cheek. "Won't be long."

She slurped the dregs of her Mai Tai and shouldered her way through the crowd, her ungainly progress punctuated with "Sorry!" and "Excuse me!" It was hard to imagine the graceful bearing of her youth. Living under Hades' dour dictates in winter and slaving for Mother the rest of the year she'd grown clumsy with servitude.

Demeter, Goddess of the Harvest, was easy to spot in any crowd from the sprigs of wheat that decorated her coiled braids. She was at the champagne fountain, arguing with the server. Demeter's lips formed the words "not from the Champagne region." Persephone decided to rejoin Aunt Hestia's group instead of listening to Mother's criticisms.

Toes crunched under the soles of her sandals.

"Sorry!" Persephone looked down at Zeus. "Sorry, Dad!"

Zeus, the perfect host, smiled and patted her shoulder. "Nice to see you, Persephone. So glad you and Hades could make it to the party." He turned to the tall goddess standing alongside him. "Isn't that right, my love?"

Hera was striking in her signature blood-red toga. Silver hair cascaded down her back. Her smile was frozen, her attention focused on the ceiling.

"The little jerk," Hera hissed as Pan swooped overhead. "How dare he be such an ass at Ronnie's engagement party?"

"Hope for the best, my dear," Zeus said, "hope for the best."

A game started in Persephone's head: who at this gathering would she most like to see drenched in Pan's high-octane vomit?

Ganymede, the eternal cupbearer, approached with a silver tray loaded with champagne flutes. Zeus took two and handed one to Hera. Persephone accepted the other and cashiered her Mai Tai glass. Briana, the groom-elect's mother, plucked one for herself and one for Clifford's father, Ralph. They were both tall and well-muscled. Persephone recalled the couple had taken early retirement from their grueling careers as structurelings.

Ralph also tracked Pan's uneven swoops under the ballroom ceiling. He grinned at Zeus. "Care to make a wager?"

Zeus chuckled but didn't answer.

Persephone nodded goodbye and eased toward Hestia's circle near the bar. The Goddess of Home and Hearth made a space for Persephone and gestured toward a gorgeous woman in a red mini-toga, the famous spokesperson of Marriage and the Media.

"Persephone, dear, I'm sure you've met Candy Smith?"

"Not in person." Persephone timidly extended her hand. She felt like a fading flower beside this full-blown rose, her own corn-silk colored hair pale in comparison to Candy's mane of strawberry blonde. "I'm a fan, though." Starved for relationship advice, Persephone had read all the self-help books published through Marriage and the Media.

Candy Smith smiled and pumped Persephone's hand. A herd of golden bangle bracelets tinkled on Candy's wrist. "Pleased to meet you."

"Candy worked for me long ago, before she married," Aunt Hestia said. "She and her family live in Seattle now. Doesn't that sound nice?"

Persephone nodded and took a mouthful of champagne. She'd never visited Seattle, but everyone on Mount Olympus had heard of the city where Veronica and Clifford first met. And there was something else. Something about a highway and a tunnel...

"This is Candy's husband, Jim." Hestia nodded at a tall, balding man with thick-lensed eyeglasses. A golden-haired toddler was balanced on his hip. "The two of you are cousins, I think."

How not thought Persephone. It was such a tangle of relationships in the Big-G family. There hadn't been many immortals at the start. Brothers and sisters had married out of necessity. Almost everybody here could rightfully call Zeus brother, father or uncle.

"You know the others," Hestia said.

Persephone glanced around the circle. Athena was aloofly beautiful in her golden dress armor. Ares smiled and nodded. She'd worked with him a lot this past decade, since he'd relinquished his God of War responsibilities and taken up agriculture. Short, pudgy Hebe, Goddess of Youthful Beauty, completed the group.

"Whoa!"

The cry came from Ares, who abruptly looked toward the ceiling. Hebe held a cocktail napkin to a wet patch on the front of her pale pink toga. She shook a fist in the air.

"You little monster!" Hebe screamed. Pan flew in lazy circles above the crowd, laughing. "You dropped your champagne on me on purpose, you creep!"

Ares smirked. "You're lucky it was only champagne."

Athena, who was rumored to be chaste, covered her eyes. "I wish he was wearing undergarments." The owl perched on her shoulder hooted softly.

"Not much to see," sniffed Hebe.

"Ma-ma!"

A female toddler yanked on Hebe's toga.

"Not now, Aster, Mama's having a migraine. Let's find Papa and tell him we have to go home, now!"

Mother and daughter left the group.

Athena lowered her hand, eyes cast down. "Is he gone?"

Ares laughed. "A sight more terrifying than battle, sister?"

Athena directed the Department of Armed Forces and was presently engaged in the War Against Hunger. Delivering food and medical supplies to mortals who'd been forced to leave their homes by warring factions was a major part of this effort. The thought of crops she and Mother had blessed going to waste or being sold on the black-market depressed Persephone.

She glanced around the ballroom for a refuge. In a dimly lit corner she spied Heracles. His considerable bulk loomed behind a potted plant. Persephone excused herself and threaded through the crowd in his direction, acutely aware of the poor figure she cut in last millennia's toga amongst the fashionable, festive revelers.

She looked up into the fronds that covered his face. "Hi, Clee. Hiding out?"

"Hi, Seph," he whispered. "Security."

She didn't quite believe Heracles, whose job was protecting the

City of Mount Olympus, would be on duty at a family party but she let it pass. For all his size and strength, he was as shy at these gatherings as she was. They often drifted together on such occasions. She nodded toward Veronica and Clifford who were circulating through their guests.

"They make a handsome couple, don't they?"

Veronica looked like a princess, tall and regal. Thick, dark hair cascaded down her back and her elegant rose-hued toga was edged in gold. Clifford loomed alongside his fiancée. He beamed down at Veronica with obvious tenderness.

Heracles sighed. "Must be nice to choose your own spouse."

Persephone sighed, too. Neither of them had had the option. She'd been abducted by Hades through trickery. Heracles had been ordered to marry Hebe, a known shrew, when Hera made him immortal.

"How's my friend Cerberus?" Heracles asked after a long silence.

A tear caught in Persephone's throat. She missed her dog, the only being who made her life in the Underworld bearable. "Fine, the last time I saw him," she said, trying to smile.

Heracles knew Cerberus from a long-ago visit to the Underworld. He'd come to free the mortal king Theseus, who'd snuck in with a friend who'd fallen in love with Persephone and meant to abduct her. Abduction again. She shuddered. What did her admirers have against getting to know a woman before forcing her into marital duties?

Heracles chuckled. "We almost found him a new home, remember?"

She laughed. "Hell hound rescue. You nearly had him topside when Hades caught up with you."

"Busy day, that. Getting into the Underworld in the first place, tearing Theseus out of the Chair of Forgetfulness. Whatever happened to his friend, anyway?"

She bit her lip. "Still in the Chair but you can't see him anymore. The Forgetfulness sucks them in over time."

The Chair of Forgetfulness was the only truly terrifying object in the Underworld. Hades used it on his worst enemies. Once the Chair was touched, it never let go, its victim's flesh welded to the stone and all memory gone. Zeus must have intervened when

Heracles pulled Theseus free.

"How's the harvest going?" Heracles said.

"Stranger every year," she said, glad for a change of subject. "Mother keeps having to adjust our schedule for climate change. Some of the best growing regions have turned arid, the Monsoon cycles are irregular and, oh, a lot of things."

Heracles nodded. "Here, too. Warmer. More rain. The chariot drivers have switched their horses over to a different grade of hay, some kind of hybrid Hermes invented. Less methane, they say. Haven't particularly noticed, myself. So." His gaze traveled over the ballroom and its inhabitants. "What's your next stop?"

"North America, fruit growing regions. I'm in the middle of it now, in fact." The last place she'd visited was a tiny island in the American state, Oregon. Raspberry harvest had come two weeks earlier than last year. "You?"

He shrugged. "Same old same old. Guard dogging it, just like Cerberus."

"Sorry."

His fate was as miserable as hers. No one in the City of Mount Olympus seemed to remember Heracles had been raised in a noble mortal family and been schooled in all kinds of subjects from languages to engineering. The immortals valued him for his brawn, not his brain.

"Pays the bills," he said.

She'd heard these were considerable, given Hebe's penchant for shopping.

"Heads!"

Heracles threw his arms up like a shield as Pan swooped low enough to touch them.

"Next time, dude!" The inebriated immortal shot away, laughing.

"Thank Zeus I'm not in charge of that imbecile," Heracles muttered at the same time a shrill voice said, "There you are!"

The false fronds were parted by chubby, manicured hands. Hebe's eyes were half-shut, her forehead puckered.

"Get me out of here, you lummox! Can't you see I have a migraine?"

"Papa, come!" piped a child's voice from the region of the knee-high pot.

Heracles, Champion of the Olympians whenever they needed one but otherwise neglected, raised a hand in goodbye. Hebe was already half-way to the door. The child, Aster, led Heracles away by the hem of his toga. He looked as sheepish as a lion on a leash. Alone, Persephone slid behind the potted plant and waited for the party to end.

~ * ~

David Bernstein observed the crowd from his place behind the half-circle bar. In the packed ballroom he could barely see the guests of honor—just Clifford's head and shoulders slowly circling where he and Veronica danced on a low central dais to the drowned-out music of a string quintet.

Another family party. David had attended many of these since he'd arrived in the City of Mount Olympus. Hera had a full-time staff person whose only job was planning this kind of stuff. Family included hundreds of full and partial Big-Gs. Veronica, David's half-sister, had filled him in on some of the history. The rest he'd picked up from gossip and from the course *Immortals 501*, required in his master's program.

There were also the spouses and children of the second-generation immortals, some of them married to small-g gods which, David supposed, enriched the gene pool. He, himself, was half-mortal, the son of some Jewish guy Hera had met two thousand years ago.

"Hey."

His favorite voice whispered in his ear.

"Hi, Cleo."

Beautiful Cleo. No matter how straight he stood she was still half-a-head taller.

"Filling in for Dionysus?"

David tilted his head toward the exit. "He's in the men's room." He gestured at the bottles of premium liquor on the bar. "Can I get you anything?"

"Just some seltzer water." She held out an empty champagne flute. "I'm on duty."

"Hermes?" he said, naming his presumed romantic rival who was also Cleo's boss.

"He's really having a hard time," Cleo said. She looked toward the ceiling. So did David, his eyes following Pan. "I don't think today's antics are helping."

David had heard rumors Hermes was on probation until he halted the progress of climate change. That, or he was having a mid-eternity crisis.

"Bombs away!" Pan buzzed the bar. "Take a good look!" The hem of his loincloth and the frontal feature it was designed to mask cleared the bottles by inches.

"Gheez!" said David.

"Disgusting!" said Cleo.

"I'm glad I'm getting out of here for a while," David said.

"What?"

"It's my first decade break, six months off." He pretended not to notice Cleo's stunned expression. They did stuff together sometimes but gheez, he didn't have to report his every move to her. It wasn't like they were dating. Not that he'd mind, but she'd been clear they were friends, period. Now that she worked for Hermes, the charismatic bad boy of Olympus, Inc., David figured his chances with Cleo were fading.

But would it hurt to test the waters?

"Six months isn't so long," he said, though that was a lie. David had been raised as a mortal. He'd never adjusted to an immortal's sense of time, where a century passed like one mortal year.

"Well, no, but…"

Cleo twisted a section of her hair around a finger. Her lips formed a pout.

"I'm planning a trip," he said. "The Holy Land, for a start."

"I haven't been there in centuries," she said, a wistful note in her voice.

David remembered Aphrodite's advice from when he'd first tried to date Cleo: women like men who sound confident.

"You could come with me." He opened a wine bottle, trying to look nonchalant. She touched his arm. On the inside it jolted him; on the outside, he feigned indifference.

"Oh, David! I'd love to, but I can't right now."

David scanned the crowd and spotted Hermes, who was cornered by Hades. A woman had joined them. Monique, he was pretty sure that was her name, some cousin or other who worked for Aphrodite. Not beautiful like Cleo but attractive in a sexy librarian kind of way. If she'd been standing any closer to Hermes she would have been on his other side. What made that guy irresistible to women?

"Busy at work?" David said, a trace of sarcasm lacing his words.

"You don't know the half of it."

"No one knows what goes on behind closed doors," he said and instantly wished he hadn't.

Cleo turned bright red. "Oh David! You are *so* immature." She slammed her empty glass on the bar and strode away.

He tried to convince himself he didn't care what Cleo did, with or without Hermes. Probably best to go to the Holy Land alone, anyway, since it was more of a quest than a vacation. Much of David's first decade studies had been devoted to recorded mortal history. He had a thorough grounding in the political, economic and religious life of old Jerusalem and the surrounding area. Though he wasn't quite sure how, he was determined to find out something about the mortal man Hera had seduced, the man who was his real father.

Candy Smith stormed up and slapped a palm on the bar. "Red wine. Now!"

"Nice to see you, too, Candy." David uncorked a bottle of Dionysus' Best Table Red. Tending bar was a lot like when he'd been a barista in downtown Seattle, before he'd discovered he was immortal. Candy had been one of his customers, the crazy lady who lived in the skyscraper across the street. She'd calmed down a lot since then, but…

Candy looked around as if someone were sneaking up behind her. Her blonde mane whipped over her shoulders when she looked back at David and grabbed the proffered goblet. "Poseidon's a by-Zeus masher!"

David grimaced. He'd never gotten used to the incestuous nature of the Big-Gs. Poseidon was Candy's father-in-law.

Candy chugged half her wine. "Jim's ready to deck him," she said. "I couldn't frickin' believe it when the old creep grabbed my butt!"

Jim stood a few yards away. He handed his young son, Titus, to Hestia and his eyeglasses to Athena. The revelers near them had backed into a circle. Poseidon stood alone, thick, muscular, and menacing.

"Fight!" somebody shrieked. The ballroom fell silent.

Jim faced Poseidon, shoulders squared and fists at the ready.

"He's gonna get killed!" Candy moaned. She bolted the rest of her wine and hugged herself, her face pinched with anxiety.

A fleshy thud sounded. Jim staggered back but stayed on his feet.

"You show him, Jim!" shouted Candy. "Punch that lecherous son-of-a-bitch!"

Jim reeled forward and aimed a right hook at Poseidon who merely grinned. Until the barf bomb fell.

"Direct hit!" yelled Pan, hovering inches above Poseidon's vomit-soaked head.

Poseidon threw his hands in front of him like a blind man. He staggered to the hors d'oeuvres table and yanked the tablecloth from under a chafing dish. The dish clattered to the floor. Meatballs rolled everywhere. Poseidon made one quick swipe over his head and shoulders and hurled away the soiled linen.

"Come down, you little bastard!" Poseidon screamed, shaking his fists. "Come down so I can tear you apart!"

Candy grabbed Jim and Titus and hustled them out the door, past a returning Dionysus. The God of Wine zipped behind the bar.

"Did I miss anything?"

"Nope," said David. "Just the usual family party."

MONのAY, JUNe 23, 2025

Hermes

Hermes had slept badly. He arrived at work with a tension headache. A vacation request from Cleo was on his desk. He balled up the offending piece of paper and shot it at the wastebasket.

The entire universe was down on him. Hades complaining about Underworld security but not spending a drachma to fix it. Monique barging into their conversation, her words laced with so much sexual innuendo only Hades could have missed it. Pan barf-bombing Poseidon. Apollo, doctor to the Big-Gs, taking Hermes aside to suggest it was time for an intervention. And now Cleo wanted a vacation.

"She's only been working for me three years," he muttered bitterly. Veronica had instituted a new vacation policy when she'd become CEO. Gone were the days when everyone had to work a full century to receive time off.

Hermes rolled back his chair and put his feet up on his desk. Cleo was in the middle of testing his current best-guess solution to climate change and she wanted to leave! It wounded his pride to admit his reliance on her. How could he solve this mess if she wasn't here to help?

Something moved beyond his open office door. Cleo, back from the cafeteria with two cups of coffee.

"Knock, knock." She stood at the threshold, hands full.

He waved her in instead of playing their usual morning game and saying, "Who's there?"

Cleo gave him a faint smile, set one of the mugs on his desk and turned to go.

"Stop. Come back."

She pulled up a chair.

"I thought you wanted to be alone. Cheers." She raised her mug to her lips.

"Cheers."

He sipped the hot brew, mixed with two shots of half-and-half, and looked past her at the glass display case on the opposite wall. It was home to miniature models of mortal inventions he'd inspired. Fulton's steamship. Bell's telephone. A miniature box of Windows software. In the old days he'd been admired. Now Veronica was on his case and Cleo treated him like an equal. Worse yet, they'd both failed to fall in love with him.

Cleo set her mug on his desk. "Did you see my vacation request?"

"You're not happy here?" he snarled.

"Whoa!" Cleo leaned back in her chair. "Feeling confrontational this morning?"

He studied her beautiful, questioning face. What was he to her, just some guy she worked for? He was Hermes, the handsome trickster! He was half Big-G, damn it! But then, so was that twerp Bernstein she chummed around with.

"Forget I said that," he said. "I'm edgy this morning. The party. Too much for me."

Cleo nodded. "It's Pan, isn't it?"

"Don't be ridiculous," he said. "I'm recovering from being in a crowd. You know I hate crowds. I only went to the damn engagement party for Veronica's sake."

Cleo's knowing smile irritated the Tartarus out of him.

"I've got work to do." He grabbed the vacation request from the waste basket, scrawled his signature at the bottom and thrust it in her face. "There. Take your damn vacation."

"Thanks, grouchy," Cleo said, eyes narrowed. "I'll be in the lab monitoring the trial run of Ecosave 153 if you need to yell at me some more."

She slammed the door behind her.

Hermes cradled his head in his hands. What in Tartarus was wrong with him? It took him a moment to realize he was doodling on his blotter—a black hole with paths radiating from it. The first 152 Ecosave models for slowing climate change had failed. Failed! He'd never experienced failure on this scale and it was coming from every direction. Could he at least solve Hades' problem, somehow digitize the delivery of souls to the Underworld with built-in controls to block gate crashers? No. He had to drop all other projects and save the effing Earth.

The black hole on his blotter developed curly hair and a pair of horns. Sending Pan to live with Hades wasn't a real answer, but what other options were there? Olympus Rest for three months and a couple of two-week follow-ups? A stint in the military to help his wayward son develop some discipline?

Hermes smiled for the first time all day. He grabbed his digital tablet and tapped in a message to Ares.

Jim

Jim Smith awoke with a roaring headache. Poseidon (someone Jim would never call Dad) had landed a solid punch and left him with a fist-sized shiner.

For a moment Jim didn't know where he was. He, Candy and Titus had arrived yesterday. They'd barely had time to unpack before Veronica and Clifford's engagement party. The décor of their suite at the Mountain High Plaza was different than the last time they'd stayed there. This prolonged his confusion, but the master bath had the same spatial relationship. Good thing. When bile started rising in his throat he had seconds to make it to the toilet.

Jim prayed mightily to the porcelain god. It had taken a lot of wine to slow his pulse after the scuffle. He wiped his mouth on the back of his hand and berated himself for sinking to the level of a savage to defend his wife's honor.

Candy had left a note on her pillow.

Took Titus to look at the fountain. Don't forget your 10 o'clock with Apollo.

The digital clock on the nightstand read 9:23. Jim groaned and dragged himself into the shower, thankful Apollo's sanitarium was only a ten-minute chariot ride away.

He had to stoop so the warm cascade of droplets could reach his pounding head. No one designed hotel showers for people who were 6' 8". It felt divine to rinse yesterday's grime and today's sour residue from his face. By the time he'd brewed a cup of in-room coffee and put on a fresh shirt and chinos he felt like a new god, ready to face the workday.

The chariot pulled up in front of Olympus Rest at 9:58, according to the display on Jim's cell phone. Today he was giving a private consultation, outside of his duties for Olympus, Inc., and had happily left his corporate-issued digital pad with its numerous apps at the hotel.

The Rest was built of pale green marble. Six columns supported a pediment carved with the Rod of Asclepius. Jim ascended the front steps and entered a glass-domed hall. A young man in a white toga intercepted him and escorted him down the hallway. Soft music issued from an open door. Inside, a handsome man with a good head of shoulder-length hair set the lyre he'd been playing aside and extended his hand to Jim.

"Hail, cousin." Apollo studied Jim's bruised eye socket. "I see Poseidon still packs a wallop."

"I hardly notice it," he said, lying.

"Good thing," said Apollo. "You've got quite a session ahead. I'm curious to hear your thoughts about our patient."

Jim visited the City of Mount Olympus a few times each year to meet with his supervisor, the Director of Immortal Resources, and to lead employee seminars. He also consulted with Zeus, who was a private client. It had been a rough transition for Zeus, from CEO to Provost of Athens U and Athens Tech but he was doing much better now. Jim's third interest in the city was Stella, former Executive Assistant to the CEO at Olympus, Inc. For the past decade she'd lived at the Rest.

"I was surprised by your update," Jim said. "She's progressed so little in ten years."

"I was surprised, too," Apollo said. "Stella's had quite a turnaround. Either that or she's become an extremely good actress. She's stopped ranting. No tirades about Zeus or the rest of us for a month now."

The last time Jim had interviewed Stella she'd torn her hair, spat on him, and called him the sycophantic toady of Zeus. Two sturdy attendants had been needed to return her to her quarters.

"Shall we?" Apollo gestured toward the door.

Jim nodded. The sooner they finished, the sooner he could go back to the hotel and call room service for a raw steak to put on his eye.

They trekked from administration to the resident wing, down a long marble hallway that resonated with muted fear and sorrow. Serious illness was rare among the immortals. Though he was a mental health professional and used to dealing with the exceptions, Jim shivered with empathy for the inmates. But for the grace of Heaven and Earth, it could happen to anyone.

The quietly tasteful commons of Olympus Rest was patronized by a few residents, ensconced in well-upholstered armchairs and couches, working jigsaw puzzles or reading. Two well-muscled attendants stood guard at the door that doubled as entrance and exit.

Jim spotted Stella at a game table. She was seated, the board game *Stratego* set up on the tabletop. It was the first time he'd met with Stella outside a padded interview room. Her copper-colored eyes flashed as he advanced.

Jim sat opposite Stella.

"Hello, Stella."

"I've missed you, counselor," she sneered. "It's been too long since we've matched wits."

Stratego was a favorite diagnostic tool Jim used with his patients. Stella had been provided with instructions in advance. They started with the beginner's version that utilized ten game pieces for each army instead of the full forty. Play commenced in silence.

The barred windows to Jim's back threw a disorienting pattern of light and shadow across the game board. Stella ran a hand over her untidy silver hair, grown long these past ten years, and admonished him for moving one of his playing pieces into a lake.

"That's against the rules, counselor." A smile curdled on her lips.

She kicked his butt. They advanced to the full version. Jim lost half his playing pieces but captured only six of hers. Stella's miners were closing in on his bombs. She was beating him so efficiently he didn't have time to ask the questions he'd designed to determine her mental and emotional state. The way she gleefully proclaimed "Boom!" when his last scout tapped one of her bombs chilled him to the bone. In seconds, she captured Jim's flag.

"Thought you could beat me, didn't you, boy?" A feral gleam lit her eyes.

Crazy like a fox, Jim thought.

"I'm impressed, Stella. You catch on fast."

She reached across the table. Her long thin fingers locked around his wrist. "You gonna tell Pretty Boy to let me out of here?" She nodded toward the two-way mirror, behind which Apollo watched.

"I need to see you again before I can form a recommendation," Jim said. He could feel her will trying to overpower his. "Your progress is impressive, but it might be temporary."

"Want to play again?"

"Some other time." He eased his wrist from her grasp and leaned back in his chair. "Now we're going to talk about you. The last time we met you tore your hair and called me names. Care to tell me what's changed since then?"

"Care to tell me what's changed since then?" she repeated in mocking tones. "Suppose you tell me about that shiner? The grapevine says it's from Poseidon."

"How did you—" Jim silently chastised himself for losing his cool. The City of Mount Olympus was and always had been a hive of gossip. For all he knew, the brawl had made one or more of the newspapers arranged on the table near the common room fireplace.

"That watery blowhard has always been a jerk. *He* didn't need to be ruined by…" Stella hunched over the table and whispered, "…The Power."

The words no sane person would speak. Slowly and methodically Jim placed his game pieces in the storage rack.

"We'll play again next time," he said.

Stella smiled nastily. "Have you developed a taste for losing, counselor?"

"I don't mind losing a game or two, depending on what I learn from it." Jim rose. "My goal is winning the match."

Think that one over, you old bat. Jim felt her eyes drilling into his back as he passed the guards. He tried, and failed, to write it off to his own overly stimulated imagination.

Cleo

At last it was lunch break. Cleo Petra walked at a fierce clip away from Olympus, Inc., corporate headquarters and toward Athens U, turning in at the gate near student housing. The soles of her sandals slapped against the smoothly laid marble walk with a resounding *thwack*. She veered toward the graduate school apartments and jogged up to the third floor. Her knuckles rapped the door of unit 317. No answer. She knocked again.

"Just a minute," said a muffled voice from inside David's

apartment.

He arrived at the door in a bathrobe, bleary eyed, his dark hair curling wildly in every direction. For a split-second Cleo thought *wow*. Something tickled her on the inside.

"Hi," he mumbled. The thick stubble on his face surprised her. He'd been clean-shaven at the engagement party yesterday. "Aren't you supposed to be at work?"

Cleo pushed past him into the main room. She'd been here many times, had cooked dinner for him in the tiny kitchenette. A soft groan rose behind the curtain that masked the sleeping alcove.

"Oh!" She forced a smile. "Didn't know you had company. Sorry to intrude."

As Cleo backed toward the door David lay a hand on her arm.

"H-hey, I can explain," he said, his face crimson.

"No need! None of my business."

Cleo slipped through the door and strolled casually down the hallway. When she got to the stairs, she sprinted for the campus gate, chiding herself for being so naïve. It was supposed to be easy. She'd tell him she had a month of vacation and that she'd love to visit the Holy Land. He'd say yes because he always had before. She'd never imagined David had a life of his own.

Lunch break was over, but she was too upset to return to the office. Cleo walked numbly through downtown Mount Olympus. She paused in front of the Plaza Fountain. Watching the glistening arcs of water had always soothed her, but not today. Hermes was mad at her and David had someone in his bed. The tickly feeling she'd experienced when David had appeared in a state of dishabille returned. She must be the last person in the City of Mount Olympus to realize he wasn't just a lap dog; he was a real catch.

Zeus

Zeus was enjoying a game of chess with someone he'd come to like in spite of himself. In the comfort of the Provost's sitting room, a cozy arrangement of aging armchairs and an unlit fireplace intended for colder seasons, he sat across the checkered board from David Bernstein.

He'd met David fifteen years ago, shortly before learning the boy was the fruit of Hera's only known marital indiscretion. His attitude had evolved from wounded pride to irritation to an almost fatherly regard. After all, the lad was his nephew. No one could deny David Bernstein was a nice kid, though he'd just captured one of Zeus' knights.

"Well played," Zeus said.

David picked up the playing piece, the knight modeled on Hephaestus. "I kind of hate to do this to him."

Zeus repressed a chuckle. Each piece resembled a different Olympian God. It was rumored that the actions carried out on Zeus' chess board had corresponding effects in the real world. This was an overstatement. The game was indeed magical, but few knew its true power.

"You've left your bishop unguarded."

"Shit! Uh, excuse me, sir."

Zeus moved Hermes, his remaining knight, and captured a small replica of Jim Smith. Jim was stopping by later for a long-awaited game of *Stratego*.

"Let's pause for a moment." Zeus leaned back in his armchair, one he particularly liked for its well-worn leather. "I understand you're going to travel during your break."

Bernstein's eyes widened. "Yes, sir."

The lad hadn't shared his plans. Zeus had seen it on the board. That was its magic: the board's owner could see his or her opponent's future.

"Six months isn't much time to see the world."

"It kind of is for me, sir. I guess I still think about time the way mortals do."

"Ah. Your foster parents used a memory-repressing charm on you, as I recall. Perhaps this is an unanticipated side effect. Will you be visiting them in Salt Lake City?"

David shifted his eyes from Zeus to the board.

"If I have time. I'm...I'm going to the Holy Land, first."

Zeus bit the inside of his cheeks and counted to ten. The boy was going to look for Hera's lover, his real father. Natural, of course, the desire to find one's origins. He fought a surge of jealously over someone who'd been dead for millennia.

"Excellent. You can study the remnants of ancient architecture," Zeus said to steer away from the touchy subject. "Traveling alone, are you?"

"It looks that way, sir."

Zeus smiled. The board had revealed there would be more than travel in David's future. It also indicated a passionate encounter, and about time. Young Bernstein had not cut the figure of a campus Romeo during his first decade at Athens U. He'd tagged along with the Petra girl at social gatherings but mostly he'd kept to his studies.

"I'm sure you'll get along splendidly, knowing so much about the ways of mortals."

David looked up, his sullen expression new to Zeus. Something was troubling him. Instinct said it was about more than his pending search for his father. Was the passionate encounter drawing near?

David

Instead of returning to his apartment after Zeus clobbered him at chess, David Bernstein left campus and headed for his favorite bookstore in downtown Mount Olympus. He'd always turned to books when something confused him. Today his brain was in the craziest tangle ever. Besides, the longer he was gone, the better the chance Monique would have left his place.

David strode through the door of World of Books and headed to a remote corner of the store, the self-help section. The shelves held everything from diet books to divorce for dummies. He confined his search to the "relationship" and "sex" sections. None of the spines indicated guidance for what to do after a one-night stand. He finally picked *Breaking Up in Three Easy Steps* by—Hermes. Teeth gritted, David dropped into a chair and thumbed through his rival's guidance.

"Three Easy Steps" were provided for a variety of scenarios: how to break up if he/she is too clingy; what to do if you suddenly find him/her unattractive; how to say sayonara when you've met somebody new.

Unfortunately, there wasn't a chapter for untangling yourself from your cousin who was a thousand years older than you and had probably been even drunker than you'd been. And then there was

Cleo's unexpected visit. He'd had the presence of mind to draw the curtain in front of the bed before he'd opened the door but when Cleo heard Monique groan it had scared him sober.

The whole situation was stupidly ironic. He'd lived like a monk from the time he'd started his studies at Athens U until last night. David had never dreamed Monique would seek him out at the engagement party. All he really knew about her, even now, was that she was Aphrodite's daughter and CFO of Love, Inc. He'd just retired from minding the bar when she stepped up and grabbed his arm.

"David, right?"

"Uh, yeah."

"David, I've been working on preliminary quarterly reports all day." She fingered the short strand of pearls around her neck. "I'd kill for a martini."

He obliged and ordered one for himself, too, glad to have someone to talk to since Cleo had flounced back to Hermes. The party broke up soon after. Dionysus gave David two bottles of his special collection red as thanks for his bartending stint.

It was a beautiful, warm evening. Monique begged to go for a walk. They strolled. Her arm brushed against his. When she tripped a little, he put his arm around her waist and left it there. Somehow, they ended up at David's apartment. Drinking a bottle of the excellent Dionysian wine, then the other, had seemed a good idea. And then...

David broke out in a sweat. Was he remembering right? Monique had said she was a virgin? Or had she said *he* was a virgin? She'd been laughing pretty hard when she'd said it. From the time they'd landed on the bed the details had grown murky.

Disgusted, he shelved the book and headed home. No way was he going to buy a book written by Hermes. The advice was lame, anyway. It boiled down to stop seeing them without giving an explanation, don't return their calls and snub them in public. In short, be a jerk. He could do that on his own.

Hera

Hera, Director of Marriage and the Media, poured herself a

second glass of Chardonnay. Work had once been a source of pride and achievement. Recently it had become as unpleasant as a vacation in Tartarus.

She was home earlier than usual. The penthouse den had been redecorated, the matching Barcaloungers and big-screen home entertainment center consigned to a rummage sale benefitting their granddaughter Aster's pre-school. Hera reclined on a velvet upholstered chaise lounge that was outfitted with heat and massage features. Apollo's new instrumental album played over surround sound. The gentle melodies failed to soothe her intense irritation.

Hera drained half the goblet in a heartbeat. Today was the first day in a decade she'd taken a glass before noon. There was nowhere she could look without finding evidence of Aphrodite's attempts at corporate sabotage.

Damn Aphrodite. The Goddess of Love and Illicit What-Have-You couldn't get it through her thick skull that Love, Inc.'s, market segment was dying a natural death. Today Gilda, Hera's executive assistant, had been invited to lunch by Aphrodite's chief minion, Eros. Doubtless he planned to incite some mischief. Loyal Gilda had declined the invitation and reported the incident to Hera. What would happen if overtures were made to the weaker links in her department?

The rest of the goblet's contents vanished. Hera realized she should share her concerns with Veronica, but Hera and Aphrodite had battled directly for millennia and old habits die hard. Besides, Veronica had no authority over Aphrodite, who held her own commercial empire outside of Olympus, Inc.

The doorbell rang. Footsteps sounded in the marble hallway. Hughes, the butler, on his way to answer the door. Recognizing the hearty voice that greeted Hughes, Hera poured a third goblet for herself, emptied the rest of the Chardonnay into a matching goblet on the low table between the twin chaises and stashed the bottle behind a cushion. Seconds later Zeus passed through the den archway.

"Good evening, my dear! And how was your day?"

"It sucked," she said, but smiled at him nonetheless.

After forty-six hundred years of marriage, Zeus had at last become the husband she'd dreamed of. Courteous, attentive, even faithful. His work as Provost brought out the best in him, melding his intelligence and strength with the gentler side of his nature. No longer her boss, he'd become a confident.

"Ah, how thoughtful." Zeus settled on the chaise opposite her and reached for his goblet. "Not like you to have a glass before dinner, my pet. Tell me what's new."

"Hardly new." She provided the latest installment of Aphrodite's intrigues.

"You can certainly count on old Gilda to guard the gates," Zeus said when she'd finished. "What, exactly, are you afraid Aphrodite is going to do?"

"I'm afraid she's going to sabotage our new book and seminar series, *Deep Marriage*."

"That's the one about making a marriage grow at any phase?"

"Exactly." She reached across the table and patted his hand. "You remember what she did the last time we had a launch, the nasty celebrity break-up she invented about the mortal spokesperson working with Candy? The thought of those dummied up photos on the front of her tabloid makes me want to scream, Zeusy, it really does."

"There, there." He stroked her hand. "Everything came out fine in the end. It will this time, too."

Hera composed herself, reminded herself that marriage was a two-way street. She asked Zeus about his day.

"The usual. A meeting with the bursar to review the end-of-term budget, lunch with both deans. Doctor Renshaw at Athens Tech is working out splendidly. She'll keep old Phineas on his toes at Athens U."

They shared a laugh. Zeus' brow furrowed.

"I met one-on-one with some of the first-decade break students today, young Bernstein included."

Young Bernstein. That's the name they'd settled on for Hera's child who wasn't fathered by Zeus.

"And how was that?" she asked, muting her interest.

"We played a game of chess."

"And?" Zeus never mentioned the magical chess set unless he'd seen something interesting.

"He's going to travel during his break. The Holy Land, he said. He hopes to learn something about his father."

She sipped her wine, thinking. Thelma Bernstein, David's foster mother, was the only one besides herself who knew the identity of David's father. Unflaggingly loyal and conveniently far away in Salt Lake City, Utah, Hera had no fear Thelma would spill the beans. She, herself, had promised to tell David about his father on his two thousand one hundredth birthday. But there was something more, something she alone knew, that would incur Zeus' wrath if discovered.

"I don't know what he thinks he'll find," she said dismissively. "You know what mortal records are. Dust, if anyone bothered to write it down in the first place."

"On that we agree. Something else was worrying him, too." Praise Heaven and Earth Zeus was changing the subject. "Somewhere in the near term the boy is due for an adventure in romance."

"Hah! About time," Hera said. Was this a new trick of Aphrodite's, to get at her through David? The boy was intelligent enough, but Hera doubted his ability to detect the wiles of women. She'd speak with him herself before he left and tease out the truth.

Tuesday, June 24, 2025

Candy

Candy Smith had been reticent to accept Monique's invitation to meet at the Isle of L Coffee House, and not only because she detested sitting on bean bag chairs. Monique worked for the enemy. Monique had said it was purely an exploratory meeting and might benefit Candy's Marriage and the Media work. But how could that be true when Candy's boss and Monique's boss were immortal enemies? Intrigued, Candy said yes.

Monique was waiting. She looked stern and ready to discuss business in her navy-blue wool toga, her dark hair pulled back severely and clipped with a gold barrette at the nape of her neck. If Candy hadn't heard it through the Olympus, Inc., rumor mill, she would never have guessed Monique was Aphrodite's daughter.

"Sorry I'm late." Candy pressed her knees together, braced her thighs and lowered herself onto a turquoise bean bag. "The baby was fussing and...." Candy stopped her recitation of the hectic morning. Why share that Jim had been detained in the bathroom and couldn't help with Titus when Candy was ready to leave?

Monique smiled sympathetically. Candy wondered if she had children of her own.

"Coffee?"

Candy looked toward the barista station. "Double skinny mocha?"

"They make good ones here." Monique signaled the young woman behind the counter.

Candy's red nails (damn, one of them was chipped) drummed the tabletop. "I'm a little nervous about this."

"But it's time, don't you think?" Monique extracted a glossy catalog from her briefcase. "I know Marriage and the Media is a huge success, but don't you think it's time to, well," Monique raised an eyebrow, "spice it up a little?"

Candy's face grew hot. Advance reviews of the forthcoming M & M book, *Deep Marriage*, were good, but she dreaded presenting the companion seminar series. It was all so psychological. The overall tone reminded her of the workshops Jim led at employee retreats. There was no fun in the formula.

Monique slid the catalog toward Candy. The cover image was a head shot of Aphrodite, a finger held to her hot pink lips as if to keep a naughty secret.

"What I'm thinking," Monique said as she flipped to a book-marked page, "is something like this."

The colorful spread touted "Fantasy for Two" gift bags, complete with costumes, character descriptions and suggested scenarios for love play. "Low-carb aphrodisiacs included," she said as Candy studied the page.

The barista delivered their mochas while Candy read the description of the *Arabian Nights* fantasy gift bag, then the one called *Corporate Dream*. The themes reminded her of something. She turned a few more pages. Fifty themes in all...

"Hey!" She looked up at Monique. "The gift bags are modeled on the theme rooms in Aphrodite's mansion!"

Monique smiled. "It's her new product line. When she quit doing personal counseling sessions at the mansion, I wasn't about to let all the theme research go to waste."

Candy caught the point, though her mind was divided between Monique's explanation and the *Pirate Island* gift bag. Jim would look hot in an eye patch. Advance copies of *Deep Marriage* had already gone out, but maybe an appendix could be added before it went to final press?

"It's a lot to think about," Candy said, though she felt like shouting *what a great idea!* She'd pitch the concept to Hera when they met later in the week. But how in Heaven and Earth would she persuade Hera to go for it if Aphrodite would benefit?

Cleo

Cleo Petra soaked in a tub of therapeutic salts mixed with hot water. Tension eased from her neck, shoulders and back. Her face was tightened by a mud mask, her hair slathered with hot oil. The attendant who waited on her wrapped Cleo's slick hair in a heated Turkish towel and withdrew. The door clicked shut. Veronica's voice rose from the adjacent tub.

"Okay. Spill it."

Cleo sighed so hard her mud mask cracked. "It's about David."

"For Dad's sake," Veronica swore. "Don't tell me he's in some kind of trouble?"

"Yes. No. I…not really."

A newly relaxed neck muscle tensed.

"Are you going to make me play twenty questions?" Veronica said.

"Of course not."

The compulsion to confess her change of heart about David had evaporated. What had she been thinking when she'd begged Veronica to take half a wellness day and join her at Spaville? She wasn't ready for this. Now she'd have to improvise.

"I feel like such a loser," Cleo said. "It feels like the world has spun off its axis."

"Because of David?" Veronica said, her tone perplexed.

"Everyone I deal with these days is getting weird on me."

Veronica laughed. "Hermes made sure I knew about your vacation request. I think I'll send him Roderick Waller to sub while you're gone. What do you think?'

"You're joking, right?"

"What? You think he can't handle the job?"

"No. No, Roderick's great. He's my favorite person in the Weather Department." She didn't mention Roderick had provided information for the last few Ecosave trials, since Hermes hadn't mentioned these to Veronica. "He's perfect. It's just that—" Cleo tried to contain her laughter, but it burst from her lips with the restorative effect of a tonic. She choked on another laugh and patted a muddy tear from her face.

"Hermes will have a fit," she said once she could speak again. "He's never had a male executive assistant."

Veronica snorted. "The change will do him good. I've told you before, I think he's on the brink of mid-eternity crisis. Now, let's talk about you. That is, about David."

Tartarus. Veronica had an unerring skill for staying on-topic, which was great when you had nothing to hide, but…everything inside Cleo had gone crazy, all because of David. Who was it she'd heard behind the curtain of his sleeping alcove? The question obsessed her. Who better to confide in than David's sister? Veronica knew him better than anybody in the City of Mount Olympus.

Cleo took a deep breath. "I think…"

She couldn't say it. Instead, she blurted out, "I think I need a leave of absence."

Monique

Monique Raison was through with biting her tongue. For the third time since they'd started their meeting, Aphrodite had tried to change the subject.

"Oh, Mother!"

Monique threw her pen across the conference table in frustration. Aphrodite was terrible at following an agenda and today's meeting was no exception. Love, Inc., revenues were in a worse slump than ever. After a quick glance at the preliminary mid-year financial reports, the Goddess of Love had merely smiled, then started gabbing about her most recent workout with her buff personal trainer. Monique's fingertip slid to the next item on the agenda. She pushed her plain-framed glasses up the bridge of her nose. Mother wasn't going to like her proposal one bit, but it was the last revenue-generating strategy she could think of. Monique sat up extra-tall and squared her shoulders.

"Mother," she said, poised to drop a bombshell. "You need to consider partnering your businesses with the Marriage and the Media group over at Olympus, Inc."

Aphrodite reared back. Her pink-glossed lips parted in a gasp that seemed to suck the air out of the room.

"Viper!" She pointed a hot-pink fingernail at Monique. "All these millennia I've harbored a viper in my bosom!"

Monique watched her mother stomp around the room, kick chairs and glare at the portrait of John D. Rockefeller staring down on the conference table. When Aphrodite had mastered her rage well enough to speak instead of sputter, she wheeled on Monique.

"Ingrate! Who gave you the best education money can buy? Who pulled strings to get you into the Athens U Business Administration PhD program when you said that was what you wanted? What did they teach you at that stupid joint, how to turn traitor to your own mother?"

"It's a twentieth century mortal concept called SWOT analysis," Monique said slowly, as if to a child. "Strengths, Weaknesses, Opportunities and Threats."

Aphrodite shook her fist. "I'll give you threats."

"Mother, please. Sit down and talk to me like a grown-up."

Aphrodite made a face and plopped in the chair opposite Monique.

"Your business interests have been hemorrhaging since Hera's program gained traction with the mortals. In the industrialized countries—"

"Screw them, they're no fun."

"Maybe not, but they're the ones with the money and they've latched onto marital fidelity like it was a cult. You know that's where the threat lies. Your products targeted for immortals are suffering, too. Look at this." She slid a graph across the table. "See that downward sloping line? Hotel Aphrodite used to be booked solid ten months out, but now you can get a room the day you hit Mount Olympus. People like us are copying the mortals for the sheer novelty of it. Hanky-panky is not what the 'in' crowd does these days."

"Fools," Aphrodite grumbled.

"Complain if you want, but complaints won't pay the bills."

"Well, aren't we Little Miss Smug?" Aphrodite's violet eyes narrowed. "Tell me, brain trust, if my business is out of style, how will it help to sidle up to my cow of a mother-in-law and beg her to help me? She'd laugh me out of the City of Mount Olympus."

The lines creasing the corners of Mother's eyes were a sign of worry Monique knew well. Ever since Aphrodite had reconciled with Hephaestus, the Big-G she'd married long before Monique was conceived in an extra-marital affair with a French small-g god, she'd lost her passion for the kinkier departments of her business empire. She'd stopped offering personal counseling services. The fifty rooms decorated to accommodate a panoply of sexual fantasies (the Board Room, in its present mode of decoration, had been one of them) were now home to cobwebs.

"Isn't it possible," Monique said, "that married couples might get a kick out of visiting Rent-A-Room Hot Tubs, or spending the night at one of your no-tell hotels if, I don't know, costumes and made-up identities were part of the package?"

Though she'd never tell Mother, who thought she was some kind of corporate nun, Monique had tried this very thing with an adventurous boyfriend and found it quite stimulating. Aphrodite eyed her suspiciously.

"They could write one of their best-selling books about, oh, I don't know, the playful side of marriage?" Monique coaxed. "Maybe they'd incorporate some of your products into those seminars Candy Smith leads?"

"You make it sound like a twelve-step program." Still, there was a glimmer of interest in Aphrodite's eyes.

"Give it some thought." Monique gathered her reports into her briefcase. "Here's our new mail order catalog." She tossed a glossy booklet like the one she'd given Candy on the conference table.

"If you think I'll go to Hera on my hands and knees—"

"Of course not." She latched the briefcase clasps. "If you're interested, we can talk about how to approach her in a business-like manner. Meanwhile, look through the catalog. I've added a new product line that I think you'll find interesting." Though she'd attributed the gift bag idea to Aphrodite when she'd met with Candy, Mother, in truth, knew nothing about it.

Aphrodite nodded dismissively. Fine by Monique. She'd started to think a little bit too much about the maid's outfit she'd traded back and forth with her boyfriend that memorable weekend. A new outfit waited in a concealed compartment of her briefcase.

WEDNESDAY, JUNE 25, 2025

Athena

Athena, Director of Armed Forces, was annoyed. Ares had interrupted her in the middle of an impact analysis concerning female officers in the mortal military. Whatever he'd started to tell her was lost in a fit of giggling. Athena shifted to adjust the silver snakes belting her toga that chafed her lower ribs. She glanced at her collection of ancient tribal battle masks decorating the wall behind Ares. *Heaven and Earth grant me patience.*

"For Zeus' sake, Ares, spit it out."

Tim, the owl, hooted censoriously from his perch behind her.

Ares sputtered and sniggered. She wondered if he was having a breakdown. For years he'd been on the road, introducing drought resistant crops and agricultural techniques to subsistence farmers in underdeveloped nations. Perhaps the proverbial straw had landed on the camel's back.

At last he wiped his eyes. "I'm sorry. It's a pretty crazy idea, but…" He lost it again.

She scowled. "I can't judge until you tell me."

"Right. Sorry. Did I get to the part where Hermes asked me for a favor?"

"Barely."

Athena had little appreciation for Hermes. The sub-department of Agriculture, which reported directly to her in the War Against Hunger, was stretched to the limit fighting the effects of climate change.

"I've got other things to do besides listen to you snicker, Ares. Either get control of yourself or come back later."

"Okay. Okay." He held up his hands in truce. "It's like this. Hermes is worried about Pan. He thinks time in the military might get him off the grape and straighten him out."

"I'm surprised a bright fellow like Hermes can't remember that I'm the Director of Armed Forces."

"Yeah, I know. He's a sexist asshole. I told him I'd pass his request to you."

She crossed her arms. "Well?"

"At first, I thought no way would Pan make a soldier, but then something occurred to me. You know the problem Elle's having, keeping supply lines open to civilians stuck in war zones?"

Elle (nickname for Ilithyia, Goddess of Childbirth) was assigned to mortal NGO WomanFront Strategies, a humanitarian aid organization. But Elle working with Pan? Pan's drunken antics at the engagement party reinforced Athena's belief that no woman in her right mind would work with him.

"Continue," she said.

"I think Pan can be a big help to us just the way he is."

"Explain."

"You remember how I used to influence their wars?"

Who could forget? As God of War, Ares had nudged mortal warlords, generals, and dictators into unnecessary, bloody conflicts throughout history. It was now known he'd been possessed by The Power, from which he'd been freed a decade ago.

"I remember how you inflamed millions of episodes of loss and misery."

"That's how I think we can use Pan," he said, sobered. "If we give him training and the right backstory, I think we can send him in to raise a little Tartarus. Not the way I used to, but he could distract tyrants from harassing their own people."

Behind her, the owl hooted.

"You think we can trust him?"

"Not completely, but I think it's worth a shot."

"Elle's last report said highwaymen continue to challenge them. Her teams are getting through to most areas, but some of the gangs are tenacious. If we could take down their leaders...if it can work in other regions..."

Athena fell silent. The owl's beak clacked, notice that he was preening.

"Fighting fire with fire, as the mortals say." Athena surfaced from her meditation. "It just might work. I'll talk with Veronica. You talk with Pan and we'll go from there."

"I'm on it." Ares threw her a quick salute. "I'll try him at home."

Pan lived in a cottage surrounded by pastures on the outskirts of the city. At this time of day he was probably sleeping off a hangover.

      Athena pulled her digital pad near and tapped in a quick message to Veronica. It was a long shot, but forward movement in the War Against Hunger was worth the attempt.

FRIDAY, JUNE 27, 2025

David

David had never bonded with Hera in the sense of filial love. But a lifetime of good manners enforced by his foster mother, Thelma Bernstein, compelled him to accept Hera's offer for lunch.

She told him to pick a restaurant. The dining room at the Trident Grotto was lit by illuminated fish tanks. He hoped the restful atmosphere would discourage Hera from raising her voice.

Hera arrived fifteen minutes late and downed the glass of Chardonnay he'd ordered for her in advance.

"Crazy!"

The first word out of her mouth.

David signaled the waiter for more wine. He sipped his own beverage. Hera's eyes narrowed.

"What's that?" she demanded.

"Mortals call it an Arnold Palmer."

"A what?"

"Iced tea mixed with lemonade," he said.

"How can you drink that dreck? Ah, saved," she said as the waiter set a generously filled goblet before her. Hera took a large sip and blotted her lips with a linen napkin, red kisses imprinted on white.

David stifled an irritated sigh. "Good to see you, too."

"Oh dear, where are my manners," Hera said in mock politeness. "Down the by-Zeus drain with all the craziness I had to put up with this morning, that's where. Somehow they've gotten to Candy."

David rolled his eyes. "They" usually referred to Aphrodite, Hera's business rival. He, himself, had once been a pawn in their ongoing battle and was sick to death of hearing about it.

"That daughter of hers, the little accountant, put it into Candy's head that Marriage and the Media should have a component of playfulness. Playfulness!" she spat. "What on earth does playfulness have to do with marriage?"

Anxiety soared at the near mention of Monique. "I'm taking a trip," David said, to change the subject.

"Yes," Hera said icily. "So Zeus said."

Shit. The chess game. Stupid he hadn't thought of that before-hand. David braced himself for confrontation.

"I'm going to find out what I can about my father."

"Why bother?" She took a slice of ciabatta from the basket between them and dropped it on her bread plate. "I'll tell you about him myself when you're twenty-one hundred."

"That might not seem like a long time to you, but it does to me."

"Touché. Telling mother she's getting old, are you?"

"I'm trying to move ahead with my life," he said, his jaw tight. "How would you feel if you didn't know who your father was?"

"Grateful." She downed the rest of her wine. "But if you insist on wasting your first decade break on a wild goose chase, at least let me give you a bon voyage gift."

"No thanks."

Hera raised her hand and swirled her index finger in a circle.

"There," she said, "no one can hear us now, son."

He flinched involuntarily as he always did when she called him that.

"I know you don't love me, David, and I'm not certain I love you, but what kind of a mother would I be if I sent you out into the big, cruel mortal world without a very useful skill? Now, look at me, will you?"

A chill of misgiving shuddered up his spine, but once Hera gave her parting gift a name David listened intently, amazed at his excellent luck.

Aphrodite

The Goddess of Love pitched a throw pillow at her husband.

"Stop laughing this instant, Hef! It's not funny."

Aphrodite pressed the attack by straddling Hephaestus on the sofa and touching her nose to his. "I said, stop laughing!"

The God of Fire, Blacksmiths, etc., vibrated with suppressed laughter—suppressed only because she'd clamped her hand over his mouth. His forge-strong arms easily set her aside and he guffawed with renewed vigor. Disgust with his childish behavior built as she waited for him to stop.

"I hope you're proud of yourself, laughing at your wife," she scolded.

Hephaestus wiped the tears from his cheeks with the back of his hand. "Can't help it," he said, gasping for air. "It cracks me up that you're going to sell sex toys to my mother."

"For Zeus' sake!" Aphrodite sprang from the couch and paced in front of the summer-bare fireplace. "I'm not selling anything to your mother! It's an idea Monique had about regaining market share. She thinks she can get access through Candy what's-her-name—"

"Smith," Hef supplied.

Aphrodite's fabled violet eyes shot ice. "Like I said. You know how boring I find the whole Marriage and the Media campaign. Honestly, Hef, you, of all people should be happy Hera and I might work toward a common goal for once."

"Mom's a bitch," he said amicably. Hera, Hef's mother, had thrown him out of the City of Mount Olympus the day he was born because he wasn't physically perfect, though probably her crappy, incestuous genes had made him that way.

"You're preaching to the chorus," Aphrodite concurred. "I would think you'd support the efforts of your wife, whom you love," here she suspended her pacing and blew him a kiss, "in scoring some moo-la off the old cow."

"No need to call names, Aph."

"What I mean is," she said in saccharine-sweet tones, "I thought you'd be thrilled I'm willing to pitch in to help your dear mother give her department of Mortal Monotony—oops! I mean, monogamy—a dash of excitement."

She grabbed a slick-covered mail order catalog off the coffee table and shook it in his face. "We'll be able to go direct with whatever products Candy is foisting on those short-lived dummies! No more printing costs, that's a twenty percent improvement to the bottom line right there. Monique had the great idea of bundling a few items—naughty nighties, scented gels, those thingies made out of candy—"

"Condoms." Hephaestus sputtered again. "Gheesh!" He took another swipe at his wet eyes. "What would the world think if they knew Aphrodite, the Goddess of Love, can't bring herself to say condom?"

"Argh!" She pitched the catalog at Hef. "It's such a drab word. Why can't it be called something fun sounding, like French Tickler?"

He picked up the catalog and flipped to the index. "Already taken."

Aphrodite flopped into a wing chair, exhausted. She didn't like this room, someone's stupid idea for an English country house fantasy complete with dark wood paneling and framed hunting lithographs. When she was still doing private counseling, she'd worn hot-pink jodhpurs and a form-fitting turtleneck for this theme. It made her neck itch just thinking about it. She was sick of mansion life, but it was part of the game, part of what made her look like the richest woman in the City of Mount Olympus even though her assets were dwindling. The urge to flee grew more appealing with each passing day.

"Honey," she said, shifting gears. She ignored Hef's familiar "now what?" expression and sat alongside him, resting her hand on his thigh. "Aphy wants to forget about silly old business for now. Can we go to Heffy's house to play?"

His place wasn't nearly as grand as hers, but every room was decorated with taste, not like scenery for someone's distorted sexual imaginings.

The muscles in Hef's leg, his good one, tightened.

"Staff's day off," he grunted. "Thought we'd be spending the night here."

"Oooh," she cooed. "Whatever will we do in your big old house, all by ourselves?" She licked her lips, picturing an activity that involved a grass skirt and a prop on page 46 of the catalog.

"Dinner?" he groaned.

She touched a finger to her lips as if deep in thought. "Call for pizza."

He swallowed hard, looked like a fish caught on a hook. Aphrodite smiled sweetly, belying the victorious pounding in her chest. She'd already packed a gift bag, a prototype of what they'd be pitching to the mortals through Marriage and the Media, and was eager, oh so eager, to give it a test run.

MONDAY, JUNE 30, 2025

Cleo

At lunch break Cleo Petra waited outside the benefits manager's office. Immortal Resources was where she'd started at the corporation. It was a new position back then, data entry. The timing had been perfect. She'd graduated from Athens U School of Business Administration shortly after Zeus had implemented one of Veronica's proposals: the transfer of employee records from papyrus to electronic files. Olympus, Inc., bought a vast mainframe computer. It was Cleo's job to prepare and feed punch-cards to the behemoth OIEB, the Olympus, Inc., Electronic Brain.

The manager's door opened. A pale-complexioned girl in a gray pinstripe toga bustled through, a digital pad tucked under her arm. Andeana Aznar, a dark-eyed, dark-haired three- thousand-something, beckoned to Cleo from the doorway. Ms. Aznar took her place behind the desk. Cleo sat opposite. The wall behind Aznar was decorated with framed certificates, mute testimony to all the employee issues she was qualified to address.

Andeana Aznar smiled, her even, white teeth a tribute to the Olympus, Inc., dental plan. "So good to see you, Cleo. I understand you'd like some time away?"

"That's right."

Cleo shifted in her chair. She'd never applied for leave before but had heard through the grapevine not every request was granted. Also, personal questions would be asked to inform the decision.

Ms. Aznar tapped the digital pad resting on her desktop. Her forehead creased.

"Last week you submitted a one-month vacation request, which was approved by your supervisor. Now you're asking to extend that to six months." Her eyes shifted from the screen to Cleo. "Care to tell me what's changed?"

Cleo bit her lower lip. "Nothing really," she fibbed. It would be too embarrassing to tell Andeana Aznar she had suddenly fallen for a guy who'd been just a friend until last Monday. "I guess once I'd been approved for vacation, I realized a month wasn't much time to unwind."

Ms. Aznar nodded, her expression judicial.

"Six months isn't a long time in the larger scheme of things. We're immortal, after all." Aznar flashed a brief smile. "But I'm sure you appreciate how much can change in a fast-paced department in six months, especially with the new climate change project. It is, as you know, our top priority."

Veronica's memo had made the rounds last week. Cleo nodded.

"You realize, while I can guarantee employment when you return, your present position might not be available?"

Cleo curled her fingers into fists. She took a deep breath. "Yes."

"Anything else you'd like to tell me about?" Ms. Aznar pressed.

"No." Cleo knew some women had complained about Hermes sexually harassing them. He'd always been fresh with her, but she'd dismissed it as playfulness.

"Okay. I'll forward this to the Director of IR for consideration." Andeana Aznar stood and extended her hand. They shook. "You'll hear from her soon. Good luck, Cleo."

Cleo left the building. The sun beat down from a cloudless blue sky. She hoped it was a good omen, in spite of her recent lies. At the spa, she'd told Veronica a fib about wanting more time to travel in the mortal world. She didn't reveal her actual desire, to be where David would be. It was possible her leave request might be rejected. If it was approved, how would she work around David's girlfriend?

She came to an abrupt halt. *Did* he have a girlfriend? She'd imagined the worst, but was there another explanation for what she'd heard in his sleeping alcove?

Cleo left the route to her apartment and veered toward Athens U. Either David had a girlfriend, or he didn't. Somehow, she'd find out.

Twenty minutes later she stood at David's apartment door, waiting for a reply to her knock. She'd broken a sweat en route and prayed to Heaven and Earth her eyeliner wasn't melting. It was not her desire to be discovered on David Bernstein's doorstep looking like a raccoon.

No answer. Cleo knocked again. Still no answer. Just because classes were out of session didn't mean he'd be holed up in his studio. She turned away and started down the staircase, nearly running into a stack of hardbound books with legs.

"Whoa!" cried the walking book stack. The legs struggled to regain their balance. Three books toppled from the pile and slid down the concrete steps to the second-floor landing. Cleo scrambled after the runaways.

"Sorry!"

One book was about Galilee, one about Herod Antipas, the third about Jordan.

The legs spoke. "Hi, Cleo."

Her heart pounded in her throat. David!

"Sorry," she said to his eyes and nose, now visible atop the shortened stack. "You want some help?"

It sounded dumb the moment she said it, but he said yeah, sure. She took half the books and followed him to his apartment.

"I wanted to look up a few things before my trip." He fit key to lock and opened the door. "I'm trying to figure out where to look for information about…." He set his stack on the tiny dining table, barely room enough for the two of them the few times she'd made dinner there.

"About?" She plopped her books alongside his.

"Well, you know." He stepped into the kitchenette and opened the refrigerator. "Want a pop or something?"

Her eyes flitted toward the sleeping alcove: curtain open, bed made, no articles of female clothing scattered about.

"Sure. Whatever you're having." She sat in the second-hand armchair he always insisted she take. "Must be exciting, the prospect of learning something about your dad?"

"Yuh," he said, his words muffled as his head was in the refrigerator. "I've got orange juice, cola and one of those power drink things?"

His voice, though it sounded like it always had, made her jittery. "Orange juice, please. When do you plan to leave?"

"Hah! Trying to get rid of me?" David handed her a glass and sat on the only other chair, the straight-backed one that matched his desk. "So, what brings you here? Bored with your vacation already?"

Good, he remembered the message she'd sent him a couple of

days ago. Cleo smoothed the hem of her mini-toga, a peach-colored one David had complimented her on when it was new.

"Hasn't started yet. I put in today for a leave of absence."

"Cool! How long?"

Her face warmed. Would her leave, which coincided with his break, look obvious? But it would be too stupid not to tell him now. In for a drachma, in for a kilo.

"Six months, if it's approved, that is."

"Outstanding!" He clicked his cola bottle against her glass. "What will you do?"

"Oh, you know." Cleo's eyes flitted toward the books on the dining table. "Maybe some travel. My family still has that place in Jordon."

"Hey, I'm probably going to Jordan! Maybe we can get together when you're there? Bet you know stuff that's not in the history books."

"Sure," she said, curbing her voice from sounding too eager. "Home base is Petra."

"Right! I remember the picture in your office of you at the archaeological dig."

David hadn't visited her at Olympus, Inc., since she'd started working for Hermes. It hadn't occurred to her until now. How long had it been since she'd made dinner for him? Time had gone so quickly with the challenge of a new job. Had she missed her chance with David and not realized it?

"They have plenty of room. You can stay there if you want." She took a chance. "You and whoever you're traveling with, that is."

"Hah! I wish. It would be great to have a translator. I tried to talk a guy in my class who speaks a bunch of Arabic languages into coming with me, but he's going to Canada." David snorted. "Fat chance of finding anything about my dad in the Great White North."

Cleo fell back in her chair, astonished. "David, *I* speak Arabic."

"Seriously?" He perched on the edge of his seat.

"Seriously. You more or less have to if you spend much time in Jordon. I might be a little rusty, but—"

His grin was a kilometer wide. "You mean you'd consider traveling with me?"

"Well," she deliberately looked thoughtful, "I should be able to help you some of the time, if I don't have too many family obligations."

Cleo rose and took her juice glass to the kitchenette.

"Better go now, so you can start reading. I'll know in a couple of days if my leave has been approved. We can talk then, okay?"

She barely said goodbye, desperate to get the Tartarus out of there before she exploded with joy. Even if he did have a girlfriend, he'd be traveling alone. She still had a chance!

Hermes

There was no question in Hermes' mind: women were nothing but trouble.

He smoothed the leave of absence form that he'd crumbled into a ball the instant he'd read Cleo's name. The month of vacation he'd authorized wasn't enough for her, now she wanted six months. Six months! What was he, poison? If there hadn't been a note from Veronica attached, urging him to approve this outrage, he would have tossed it without a jot of remorse.

He picked up a pen and set it down again. Why was everything going wrong these days? He was better than any of them, damn it!

Hermes contemplated the tall glass display case, filled with miniature models of technological wonders. He'd stood alongside the great nineteenth century inventors, Fulton, Edison, Cyrus McCormick and dozens more, an invisible whisperer, suggesting refinements that nudged their brainstorms into reality. He'd contributed mightily to the efforts of everyone from the Wright Brothers to Bill Gates, Jr., and associates in the century following. Then climate change showed up on the radar. Now he was the number one failure at Olympus, Inc. Veronica had pushed him into unknown territory, and he was starting from scratch. He was an inventor, not a psychologist. How in Tartarus was he supposed to change mortal behavior?

Eternity looked dismal. Even his confidence as a seducer of women had taken a hard knock and the woman he could have— Hermes shuddered. She'd sunk her claws in before he'd noticed. Her possessiveness drove him crazy. He'd tried his "Three Easy Steps" to get rid of her, but she wouldn't go away. She'd called today. He'd caved when she'd cried and made accusations. He'd agreed to talk it over with her at lunch tomorrow, knowing his will would waver when she started her usual come-on.

He signed the form and dropped it on Cleo's desk. She'd come back late from lunch and had left early but at least she'd be here two more weeks, training her substitute. He'd been angry at first when a male was given the assignment. Sick as Hermes was of dealing with women, he'd come around to feeling relieved.

"Quitting time," he said to himself on his way out the door. A few glasses of red at Club Dionysus would surely make his world a better place.

TUESDAY, JULY 1, 2025

In a Mortal Desert
Elle

In an expanse of rocky desert, a truck rolled to a stop in front of a black and red barricade. Four armed men, dressed in the same color as the sand, scrabbled out from behind strategically placed boulders.

Tartarus.

Elle, at the wheel, tried to keep her temper but she'd run out of soothing mantras. She glared at the men standing in the middle of the primitive road. Their automatic rifles were pointed at the windshield.

"Assholes," she said through gritted teeth.

She slid from behind the wheel and leapt to the ground.

"Howdy, boys."

Their spokesman waved his rifle and ordered her to lie face-down. She pretended she didn't understand what he was saying. When he called her an interfering imperialist bitch the remnants of her sense of humor died.

Elle formed a nasty smile and said in English, "What about humanitarian aid do you camo-wearing morons fail to understand?"

The spokesman leaned forward as if being closer would help him translate her words. "The smiling imperialist bitch has food," he informed his companions. They grinned in unison and stepped toward her.

"Say 'cheese,' boys."

In a fraction of a second she was horizontal and five feet off the ground. Her right leg swung down the row of faces. Her booted foot connected with four sets of decaying teeth. Rifles dropped. The men fell to their knees.

"Now!" Elle shouted.

Six women in traditional dress vaulted over the tailgate. They carried ropes and bandanas. Two of them collected the attackers' weapons. The others bound and gagged their captives.

Elle climbed up to the driver's seat, smoothed her short hair, now soaked with perspiration, under her khaki bill cap, and depressed the radio talk button.

"This is Feast. This is Feast. Over."

"I read you, Feast. This is Fortune. Over."

"Four more for pickup. Do you have my coordinates? Over."

"Roger that. We'll be there before they're too thirsty. Out."

Elle signaled her troops to leave the prisoners and hop on board. The truck, the color of sand except for the unobtrusive WomanFront Strategies logo on the cab doors, continued its trek to a temporary village for the monthly food and medical supplies drop.

The sun was at its apex when they arrived at Beta Village, a code name WomanFront had assigned for internal communications. Her troops had shucked their cowls and kaftans, revealing practical khakis underneath. They lowered the tailgate. A line formed. Bags of rice, crates of dried fruit, boxes of dried milk, baby formula and medical supplies, casks of drinking water and baskets of dried beans were passed down to waiting villagers. Children gathered around the truck, chattering amongst themselves and dancing with excitement.

"They're not as thin as they used to be."

Elle turned to Cantara Ingel, the young nurse practitioner who lived and worked at Beta Village in payment for WomanFront financing her college education. Cantara stood solid and square with her arms crossed. A warm smile belied her stern posture.

"Not so many highwaymen as when we started," Elle said. Word of the female soldiers had traveled among the militants, in spite of the shame attached to being overwhelmed by women. Prisoners were blindfolded and driven to WomanFront encampments, where they were compelled to watch videos and listen to lectures about the interference of warlords in ending preventable disease and hunger. They were then fed a nourishing meal (soup, if Elle had intercepted them), blindfolded again, provided with a three-day supply of food and water and transported to a neutral area from which they could choose to return home or move elsewhere. Still, a determined core, like the ones they'd encountered today, were hanging on.

Cantara tilted her head toward the hospital tent. "I'd like you to meet someone."

Elle removed her dark glasses as she ducked under the canvas door flap. Past the dazzle in her aching eyes, a small figure sat on the examining table, its legs dangling over the side. Her vision cleared. The child, perhaps four years old, was dressed in the tribal outfit of a boy.

"Elle, this is my friend, Abbas," Cantara said in the local dialect.

The boy smiled at the sound of his name.

Elle smiled and nodded. "I am happy to meet you, Abbas."

"Abbas, this is my friend, Elle. She brings us food and medicine."

"I am thankful," said Abbas, bowing where he sat.

"Let's show Elle what you can do."

Cantara lifted the boy to the ground and took his hand. Together they took a few steps, Abbas's legs moving jerkily as if walking were new.

Elle had witnessed this miracle many times since the convoys had become regular. Slowly, the impoverished multitudes were progressing from starvation to better health. She made a silent prayer to Heaven and Earth that Abbas would one day gain the strength and coordination to run and play with the other children.

"Well done, Abbas," said Cantara. "You are as brave as your namesake, the lion. Now," she lifted the boy in her arms, "let's return you to your mother."

Elle followed them. Behind her sunglasses she permitted a tear to fall. Her work was, at last, making a difference. She resisted the tug inside that urged her back to the truck, back to business, and lingered for a moment, looking at the collection of huts and tents that made the village. WomanFront Strategies provided not only food, medicine and shelter, they also supported farming and other industries to help the village achieve self-sufficiency. Most of the adult men in this tribe had been killed by militants or pressed into being soldiers themselves; the women, children and elders had left their traditional home in search of safety. It had taken time to earn their trust, learn their language and recruit young women as WomanFront security guards.

She ambled down what was called the courtyard, an open area bordered by tents and huts. Elle greeted a woman busy at her loom, another teaching her little boy how to prepare rice. An elderly man sat under an impromptu awning made from a plastic poncho. He smoked a clay pipe. When he addressed her as Mother Elle, she smiled.

The truck horn blasted. Halah, Elle's top assistant, signaling for the return trip to camp.

The village had gained strength, but it was still as fragile as a butterfly. A month would pass before she would see these people again, if the WomanFront truck made it past the highwaymen. She prayed to Heaven and Earth to rid her of these desert thugs.

But prayers only did so much. No one had banned Elle from using her supernatural powers in her work and she was too savvy to bring up the subject. With a gesture that appeared to be no more than a parting wave, she laid a spell of protection over the village, shielding it from highwaymen, overlords and anyone who meant the villagers harm.

City of Mount Olympus
Monique

A single-horse chariot stopped in front of Olympus, Inc. Monique stepped down from the rig, paid the driver (gratuity included) and paused, looking up at the marble façade. She didn't like visiting this place, felt daunted by the incredible resources the giant corporation could deploy toward any line of business they chose. It was all for the mortals, of course, all theoretically benevolent and helpful to those short-lived beings. The corporation ran more of the world than any other entity.

She'd replaced her usual navy-blue business toga with a mini toga in hot pink and tangerine, her flat sandals with wedge-soled espadrilles that laced to mid-thigh. Monique was here on personal business. She was meeting her kinky boyfriend for lunch at the employee cafeteria, a setting she perceived as more conducive to a break-up than romance. Hence, the fetching outfit.

Her hips swung just enough to turn the heads of the people she passed. *So what if he dumps me*, she told herself, *I've got plenty of options*. It was a beautiful day and she was a beautiful woman, her luxuriant hair worn loose and swinging seductively as if it had an agenda of its own. Mother hadn't a clue she dressed like this. Sometimes Monique could barely keep from laughing when Aphrodite got all maternal and tried to coax her into wearing something more alluring than navy-blue wool. So much that Mother didn't know.

The cafeteria was on the mezzanine. Monique ascended the left-most of the matching marble and gold staircases and passed through the cafeteria entrance, an archway carved in a grapevine pattern. It wasn't the worst place to eat in the City of Mount Olympus. Linen napkins and upscale tableware were a given, the chefs cooked with premium ingredients and the wine list was tolerable. But at lunchtime, the place was packed. Chattering diners killed the ambiance.

Monique had excellent long vision, a trait from her father, Reynard, the French immortal associated with foxes. She spotted a tanned arm signaling her from the back of the dining room. At least he'd snagged a booth instead of a table. She sauntered through the diners, knowing not a soul in this immortal sea until she recognized David Bernstein at a table near the middle, deep in conversation with Veronica Zeta. Monique sidestepped to avoid them. What had she been thinking, sleeping with an inexperienced twerp? Was it even possible to be drunk enough for that to seem like a good idea? If she hadn't been so pissed at her main squeeze, the martini and wine wouldn't have hit her so hard.

She arrived at the booth and looked down at Hermes. Her lips, polished with the same hot pink as Aphrodite's, formed a well-rehearsed pout. The air between them crackled with sexual hunger. He could try as hard as he wanted; their affair wasn't going to end until it was her idea. She extended a hand and purred, "Darling," leaving him no choice but to take her hand in his.

He smiled, grudgingly. She'd studied males for centuries (Mother would scream if she discovered Monique had been Napoleon's mistress) and she knew how to read them. As much as Hermes paraded his he-man persona in public, the key to keeping him interested was the lure of domination.

"Sit down," he said. "We need to talk."

Her smile broadened. They did need to talk, particularly about his secret penchant for…

The Okanogan, British Columbia, Canada
Persephone

Persephone, cloaked to avoid detection by mortal eyes, fanned herself with the wreath of grape vines she'd plucked from her head. When Demeter had scheduled her in Canada's wine region, she'd never imagined harvest would begin in July. The sugar, acid and tannin levels had reached optimal levels weeks ahead of time. Most of the vineyards were strapped for labor, especially those that insisted their grapes be picked by hand instead of machine.

She waved her hand in benediction over the bourgeoning vineyards, then punched the code for the Department of Weather onto the tiny screen banded to her wrist. This activated a type of software that measured temperature, humidity and several other things, part of a massive data collection for the climate change project. The device made a whirring sound as it took the measurements. A message flashed on the screen.

Measurements exceed two standard deviations. Please reset and try again.

Persephone sighed and did as instructed. Everywhere it had been like this, crops coming in early or, worse yet, dying from prolonged drought like the California vineyards. Growing regions all over the world had shifted away from the equator, toward northern and southern extremes. Demeter had reported a substantial failure in India's rice. Twenty percent of the world's total gone, due to the out-of-kilter monsoon season.

The measurement device whirred, stopped, and repeated the message. She started the process again. After the third iteration *thank you* appeared on the screen. Persephone gazed toward the western mountains. The snowcap was virtually non-existent. How long could the Earth hang on without a massive starvation epidemic? She reached into the side-pocket of her faded summer toga for her lunch of nuts and dried fruit. Even immortals had to eat.

WeDNeSDay, JULy 2, 2025

In a Mortal Desert
Jocelyn Chadwick

Ms. Jocelyn Chadwick bounced through the desert in a no-frills WomanFront Strategies jeep. It was the part of her job she most enjoyed, visiting command units in the War Against Hunger.

Chadwick had maintained contact with Athena Metis, ostensibly CEO of NGO WomanFront Strategies, during her tenure as US Secretary of Defense. When the administration she'd served left office she approached Athena with a proposal: make WomanFront Strategies, a front Athena used for her contacts with mortals, a reality.

"Now is the time," Jocelyn Chadwick had said, citing the upswing in women power brokers around the world. Athena grilled her with strategic and logistical questions. Eventually the two of them mapped out a long-term plan with the goal of world peace through ending hunger. The concept enfolded programs Athena and Ares had already initiated in the most severely underfed parts of the world. Chadwick engaged an attorney to draw up the corporate papers and leased an office space in New York City, close to United Nations headquarters. Athena anonymously donated five million dollars for seed money, assuring Chadwick sufficient charms had been laid on it to deter the authorities from investigating the source.

That was in 2017, eight years ago.

Jocelyn Chadwick was now CEO of the fully incarnated NGO WomanFront Strategies. Her allies and contacts, built over decades of government service, facilitated meetings with national leaders throughout the world. In countries where tribal connections remained stronger than the governments overlaying them the challenges were particularly tough. Negotiating safe passage for food and medicine to those in need was aggravated by the expectation of kickbacks. Elle's security force had been formed when Ares recommended more on-the-ground support.

Chadwick (in the passenger seat with a young woman named Halah at the wheel and two armed security guards perched in the back) grinned. Her teeth rattled as the vehicle bumped down a road that was no more than tire tracks. Seeing this outpost, the one that served Beta Village and three others like it in the surrounding area, had long been on her bucket list. Highwaymen and militants still made attacks here, but it was a risk she was willing to take.

An explosion sounded and the jeep skidded sideways. Chadwick grabbed the roll bar to keep her seat. One of the guards in the back swore and said she thought her arm was broken.

"Blow out," said Halah. She turned off the engine and circled to the back of the jeep, muttering about a spare.

Jocelyn Chadwick stepped out. The sand scuffed the soles of her new desert boots. "Can I help?"

"Yes. Take up a rifle and keep watch while Gertrud sets Chava's arm."

The former Secretary of Defense's stomach soured but she maintained a poker face and did as instructed. Though she'd received training in the use of rifles and other firearms she had a secret abhorrence for guns.

Elle

Elle's WomanFront base was a village of heavy-duty tents. Chadwick wasn't picky, thank Zeus, and didn't object to the cot and sleeping bag she'd been assigned in guest quarters. Elle had suppressed a smirk when the CEO first arrived, resplendent in her upscale city version of desert wear. Chadwick's khaki trousers were pleated and cuffed, tailored to the wearer as was her crisp white blouse. Dark rings had formed under Jocelyn Chadwick's arms courtesy of relentless daytime heat.

After Chadwick had settled in, she returned to Elle's tent, a larger enclosure than the others because it was also a meeting room. She accepted the simple hospitality of sweet tea and dates.

"Halah tells me you had an adventure on the way from the airport," Elle said after preliminaries were exchanged.

"Just a blowout," Chadwick said, shrugging her shoulders as if it happened every day. "I hope—Chava, I think it is? I hope she's feeling better. Her arm must hurt like the Dickens."

"Bed rest and painkillers in the short term and restricted duty for a few weeks. Damn shame, she's one of my best."

Chadwick opened her satchel (another designer special made of high-grade leather with straps that buckled the front flap in place) and fished out a digital pad.

"Have you seen the latest from Olympus, Inc.?" She tapped the screen. "It's a plan to disrupt the remaining warlords from the top down."

Elle shook her head. She'd glanced at the message without much interest, couldn't recall the details. Nothing along that line had worked so far.

"They're sending Ares and someone else, a special agent, to meet with us this evening. It doesn't say when."

"But Ares works the agriculture side," Elle said, puzzled. "This sounds more like diplomacy, more like Athena's job?"

"I would have assumed so," Chadwick said. "There must be extenuating circumstances."

They let the subject drop and addressed business they could resolve—suggestions for changes in inventory levels and content, a recruitment program to attract teachers to the WomanFront sponsored villages, the rotation roster for Elle's staff of fifty. Dinner was served, eaten and cleared away. The sun set. The air grew cold. They waited.

Elle, still at the table and wrapped in her sleeping bag to stay warm, jerked awake. It was a change in the light that startled her. A collection of luminous dots gradually resolved into Ares and—

"Pan?"

No, she must be dreaming.

"Yo, babe! Pan's the man!" He was decked out in a military dress uniform, belonging to no recognizable nation but with lots of braid on the shoulders.

Ares said, "Let me explain, Sis."

Elle held up a hand to stop him. "Wait until I get Chadwick. I don't think I can stand to hear this twice."

When she returned with Jocelyn Chadwick in tow, Ares and Pan had lit a lamp and were sitting at the table. They'd ferreted out the bottle of brandy in Elle's medical supply chest and slopped it into four tin cups.

"I propose a toast." Ares raised his cup. "To Operation Fire Fights Fire."

Elle grimaced. Guys had to give everything they did a name. She swigged her brandy, a distillation known mostly for its medicinal qualities, a bitter cup to ease the pain.

"What on Dad's green earth does Pan have to do with the War Against Hunger?" she growled at Ares.

The God of Shepherds and Flocks butted in. "Pan's the man, like I said. Yo, babes, this dude's gonna party on down with the bad guys!"

The incredulous look Chadwick shot Elle told her this was going to be a very long night.

THURSDAY, JULY 3, 2025

City of Mount Olympus
David

David Bernstein hunched over his skimpy dining table. He looked up from his book and rubbed his eyes. He'd burned through most of the stack he'd brought home Monday, madly skimming page after page in search of his past. The last time he'd talked to his foster mom, Thelma Bernstein, she'd reminded him they'd taken a few family vacations in Palestine and, later, Israel.

"Well of course we took you to Galilee," she'd said. "That's where you were born!"

His memories of these trips were weak, like something he'd seen on TV a long time ago. It was a side-effect of the forgetfulness charm Thelma had renewed on him throughout his life to prevent him from realizing he was not a mortal like everyone else they knew. Weird to think about how many childhood friends he must have made over the centuries, and that all of them were dead.

He put a bookmark in *The Census of Judea* and raided the fridge for an energy drink. It was the second of two books he'd read on the subject but neither author gave the specifics he was looking for. They mostly addressed Roman politics and tax collection. Sometimes people had to register in the city of the house the males descended from, which complicated things. All he had to go on was a male Jewish person who could have fathered a child in about 10 CE. Tens of thousands of men must have fit that description.

David pondered the pile of research books. What was he, crazy? Where did he expect to find two-thousand-year-old census records, intact, in a language he could read? Time was running short. He'd booked a Sunday flight from Athens International to Ben Gurion Airport and had no real plan.

"I guess I'll start with museums," he said to himself. Maybe somewhere there was a drawing or a painted vase in a hermetically sealed glass case that depicted Hera and some guy who looked kind of like him.

He looked around his apartment, glad he didn't have any

plants to entrust to someone while he was gone. Tomorrow he'd pack and get some drachma converted to shekels. Cleo was meeting him for coffee, too, to go over his itinerary and figure out when he might be expected in Petra.

David looked sideways toward the sleeping alcove. A pang of guilt made him queasy. Should he call Monique before he left? He hadn't heard from her since their wild encounter. It still creeped him out that he'd slept with a cousin. Maybe she was upset about it, too? A lifetime of Thelma Bernstein's lectures on being kind to people made him feel like he should call Monique, but…

He forced his thoughts in another direction, overriding the inner voice of Thelma Bernstein, and considered Hera's gift instead. She'd taught him the secret of Biggest of Big-Gs cloaking, effective in hiding from all mortals and deity of even the greatest power. David had practiced in front of the mirror every day. He could now make the transformation in under five seconds. Maybe it was time to try it out on a full-blooded Big-G?

David's stomach rumbled. It was almost time for dinner. He slipped on his sandals and loped down the stairs. At Club Dionysus, maybe he could kill three birds with one stone; eat, say goodbye to his friend, the God of Wine, and spot a powerful relative on whom to test his new powers.

Aphrodite

Thursday night was date night and tonight it was Hef's turn to choose.

Aphrodite had been lukewarm when he named his usual choice, the Club Dionysus. It was lovely—fresh flowers, white table-cloths that touched the floor, a beautifully carved bar—but predictable. He'd booked "the" table. It was the spot where everyone looked when they first entered the restaurant, the very place of their reconciliation ten years ago.

She gazed past the candlelight at her husband. He'd looked so vulnerable in the slave costume from the Mistress and Servant gift bag they'd tried out last night. She had to admit Monique's creations were excellent. The main stumbling block, in Aphrodite's mind, was whether it was really necessary to give Hera a piece of their new retail pie.

Ganymede arrived; a champagne bucket nestled in his arm.

"For Madame's approval." He uncorked the bottle of Soul of Dionysus 1730; a twin of the bottle Hef had ordered a decade ago. She'd grown used to Hef's thoughtful generosity and had nearly reconciled herself to leading a life of perfect contentment. If only there wasn't the eternal obstacle of Hera.

She sipped the wine and pronounced it acceptable, nibbled a few oysters and excused herself to the ladies' room to freshen her lipstick. Hef was wild about glossy lips and she liked to indulge his eccentricities. She passed through the dining room and along the bar, got the job done and was headed back to her table when someone behind her said her name.

Aphrodite turned. No one was there. She resumed her trek, wondering if she was starting to hear things in her advancing eternity.

"My beauty," Hef said upon her return. He rose and held her chair for her, then said abruptly, "Did you hear that?"

She shook her head.

"There! It happened again. Someone said my name."

"Oh! That happened to me too, over there." She pointed toward the bar. "Probably some kind of spell bouncing around. You know how people get when they've had too much to drink."

"Yes!"

They jumped. The voice was in front of their table. The empty space shimmered a few seconds and David Bernstein appeared.

'What the—"

"Sorry, guys," David said, cutting off Hef. "I didn't mean to barge in on your evening, but I wanted to try it out on a Big-G."

"Pretty slick cloaking," Hef said.

"Hera's idea. She thought it would come in handy for my trip."

Aphrodite bristled inwardly when Hef asked David about his travel plans. It was one thing for Hef to be gracious and generous to her, but there was a limit!

"The Holy Land?" Hef said when the kid had run his mouth half a minute. "Odd choice for someone your age. I figured you for something more exciting, like surfing in Australia or doing the club scene in Germany."

"It's more of a quest than a vacation," David said.

Aphrodite's brain clicked. David was going to the Holy Land to find evidence of his father! Hera hadn't even told him the mortal's name, but Hera wasn't the only one who'd visited King Herod's Tiberias palace. Aphrodite had guessed David's origins the instant she'd met him. She'd been holding the information to drop, bomb-like, when the perfect opportunity arrived. Wouldn't it drive the old cow mad if she fed a clue to David to narrow his search?

"If I were you," Aphrodite said in her silkiest tone, "I'd start my quest in Tiberias. It was one of my favorite vacation spots. I saw Hera there once when I was at the hot springs. She looked a little round in the front, if you know what I mean." Hef kicked her under the table but she ignored him. "Someone told me she was chummy with Herod Antipas," she continued. "He was putting the finishing touches on his palace then, if I remember right."

"Wow," said David, eyes wide. "I mean, thanks." He backed away. "Uh, gotta go. Packing and stuff. Sorry for interrupting your evening."

Hef scowled at her but Aphrodite didn't care. Lighting the fuse of David Bernstein's inquiry was well worth a few awkward questions later.

FRIDAY, JULY 4, 2025

Veronica

When Veronica Zeta invited Cleo Petra for a bon voyage lunch her friend selected the College Pub. The cozy underground venue featured exposed brick walls and wooden booths. Tabletops were carved with millennia of undergraduate initials and professions of love. The décor hadn't changed since she, herself, had been at Athens U.

Cleo sat across from her in their wooden cocoon. She fidgeted with a paper napkin. They'd ordered nachos, the house specialty, and a pitcher of iced tea.

Veronica dipped a tortilla chip into the bean and cheese goo. "Excited about your trip?"

"What? Oh, sure. Yes."

Veronica curbed an explosion of *what's wrong with you* from finding her tongue. Cleo had been evasive ever since they'd been seated.

"Sorry," Cleo said. Veronica eased the impatient expression from her own face. "Just nervous, I guess. I haven't been out in the mortal world for more than a century. They say a lot has changed."

It was a side of Cleo she'd never seen, unsure and apologetic. "Nothing to worry about, trust me," Veronica assured. "It's noisier and more crowded than ever, and of course climate change is affecting everything."

The last part came out with a harshness she hadn't intended.

Cleo bit her lip. "It's a terrible time for me to go, isn't it?"

Holy Dad, this was just what she needed on top of her own problems. Clifford had been acting strangely, too. They'd had a routine strategic meeting about the Seattle seawall problem and he'd gotten huffy when she said he should call in Poseidon as a consultant. It was more difficult than she'd imagined, keeping her roles of boss and fiancée separate. Was what she said to him at work going to be taken personally for the rest of eternity?

Veronica reached across the table and patted Cleo's hand. "Just keep your eyes open. Maybe you'll observe something that will help us solve it. You have an excellent replacement in Roderick, right?"

"Right."

"So calm down. Nothing to worry about here. Your parents must be thrilled you're coming for a visit, and you'll get to do some traveling with David."

Cleo turned bright red.

"Cleo." Veronica tightened her grip on Cleo's hand. "Are you nervous about David?"

The story spilled like a wine from a burst cask—Cleo's discovery of a woman in David's bed, the instantaneous realization she, herself, was in love with him, her fear that he didn't love her back. This was Cleo transformed, not the competent, intelligent woman Veronica had befriended decades ago. Heaven and Earth, was Cleo on the verge of a breakdown? She still had a week to go before she left Olympus, Inc.

Veronica nodded sagely as she'd seen Dad do when confronted with alarming revelations. "Interesting."

Cleo pushed aside the nacho platter. Their heads drew close and their voices lowered in speculation. Who'd been sleeping in David's bed?

Hermes

Hermes knew trouble when he saw it. Monique had reserved "the" table at Club Dionysus. He'd downed a bottle of wine to stave off his nerves. She'd kept pace with him. Her outer appearance was mundane—navy-blue business toga, hair pulled back, glasses. Under the floor-length tablecloth one of her feet slid up his inner leg. The contradiction excited the Tartarus out of him.

Monique looked sternly over the top of her glasses. "So, messenger boy," she drawled, "What new thrill can you offer a girl on a Friday night?"

His concealed physical reaction was extreme.

"Define thrill," he said, his voice thick with desire.

"Hmmm." Her eyes lit with tantalizing fire. "Give me one of your secrets, Hermes. You have so many."

"Be careful what you wish for."

Hermes signaled the waiter for the check and a box for Monique's untouched chocolate cheesecake. She'd want it later, after they'd satisfied another appetite.

~ * ~

They arrived at the seventh basement of Olympus, Inc. The guard on duty scanned the bar code on Hermes' ID card and sniffed the air. Stupid, not to pop a breath mint on the way. The guard wouldn't let Monique pass. Hermes reached into a side pocket of his toga and wiggled his fingers. A flat rectangle constituted itself in his hand. He presented the conjured ID card to Monique.

"I found this on my desk," Hermes said to her. "You must have left it there during our planning meeting for the compliance audit."

"Audit?" said the guard. The scowl lines deepened in his brow. "Nobody told me about an audit."

"Let me guess," said Hermes. "You haven't checked your digital pad for messages this week, am I right?"

The guard was part of the Mobius clan that had produced only one great thinker. *That* Mobius, regrettably, had received the recessive mortal longevity gene.

"Too much trouble." Guard Mobius sneered. "Security sends us hard copy if it's important."

"Security doesn't hear about everything," Hermes bluffed. "This is highly classified, Mobius, direct from the CEO herself. Now, let us pass." He raised his hand and swept it in front of the guard's eyes. "Inspector Raison and I need to get on with our business."

The guard's expression glazed over. He stepped aside. Hermes took Monique's arm and escorted her down a long white hallway that terminated in floor-to-ceiling bars. Beyond the bars stood a formidable metal door. Hermes inserted his ID card in a reader box on the wall. A green light flashed. The bars retracted into the ceiling.

"You want a thrill," he said, leading Monique toward the menacing door, "I'll give you a thrill."

Her gasp stirred a primitive excitement he hadn't felt in centuries.

"This is where *It's* kept?" she whispered.

"Nothing a big girl like you can't handle." Hermes' heart beat a feral rhythm. He slid his card into the reader on the metal door. Again, a green light shone. "Come, my pet. We're going to do it in front of The Power."

Monique hesitated but Hermes tugged her over the threshold. The door lowered, sealing them in.

"Nothing to be afraid of." Sexual energy thrummed in his veins. "See?"

A circle of light started as a pinpoint in the ceiling and flared to an inverted cone. A plain black box, four feet square, rested on the cell floor. "I contained It a decade ago and Zeus himself secured It with the Biggest of Big-G charms. Not one leak since then." He glanced at a monitor on the cell wall. The screen displayed six flat lines. "Now, tell me," he said, pulling her against him, "what enticing little outfit have you tucked away in that briefcase of yours?"

SATURDAY, JULY 5, 2025

Clifford

Clifford Essex was the luckiest immortal he knew. He had a beautiful and intelligent fiancée, a challenging dream job and a past without any holes in it since he'd learned the identity of his father.

Today it was hard to feel his good fortune. Today, he was meeting with Poseidon.

The hulking git had called Clifford down to his seldom-used office in the Weather Department. It didn't matter to the Big-G God that Clifford was one of an elite group of Directors who reported directly to Veronica Zeta. The insult stung but he'd play the game of kowtowing to one of the Big Twelve (his private term for the Twelve Olympians). He had no choice. The Seattle project had stalled. It might fail altogether if he didn't bring on someone with marine expertise.

The oversized chairs in Poseidon's office suited Clifford's 6' 9" frame. Poseidon sat behind a large glass desk. Sea creatures and bare-breasted mermaids were etched in waves that rolled down the sides. The God of the Sea was sturdily built. His bare arms sported the biggest biceps Clifford had ever seen. Aside from his impressive height and his icy expression, Poseidon reasonably resembled his younger brother, Zeus.

"Let me see if I've got this straight," Poseidon said, smirking. "You want to recruit me to hold back the sea and keep the mortals from drowning when they drive through a tunnel they never should have built in the first place."

Clifford cleared his throat. "In essence. It wouldn't have to be you, personally, if someone on your staff—"

"Hah! Someone on my *staff*, you say?" Poseidon chuckled at the innuendo. "Sounds good to me."

When Poseidon stopped laughing Clifford continued. "I'm looking for someone who can secure an inadequate seawall while my department tests a new method we've designed to reinforce it."

Poseidon frowned. "Damn the mortals. If they're going to be so stupid, I'd just as soon let 'em drown. Wouldn't be the first time."

"That's not the way we do things now."

"Everything's gone to Tartarus since a skirt's been running this place," Poseidon groused. "That niece of mine ordered me—*me*—to come to the City of Mount Olympus for this by-Zeus meeting. If it wasn't for His Laws, I'd have her begging for mercy."

Clifford deployed a tactic that worked with most bigshots.

"Of course, if you don't think you *can* secure the seawall—"

"Blasphemy!" Poseidon rolled to his feet and raised his arm as if gripping a trident he intended to hurl. "Impudence! For two drachma, I'd—"

"Well, can you or can't you?" The Big Twelve were always poised to go ballistic, but Clifford knew it was a bluff. He hoped so, anyway. He rose. "I'll meet with you or your representative in Seattle next Thursday, then, for an onsite consultation?"

Poseidon held his frozen glare.

"Very good, then, that's settled." Clifford smiled, nodded and prayed to Heaven and Earth Poseidon would help him fix this mess.

Monique

Monique awoke, uncertain of the day, the time, or the location. An inverted cone of light illuminated the center of the space. Her head pounded. Her parched mouth tasted of too much red wine. Awareness trickled back into her consciousness. She was in a detention cell.

"Hermes?" Her voice came out in a croak.

He moaned beyond the light's perimeter. She could see him well enough to recognize the tattered remains of lederhosen, the mate to her disheveled milk maid costume.

Hermes struggled to his feet. He held out a hand to pull her up. "Heaven and Earth," he swore. "What did we do?"

She wanted to laugh but a cold weight in her belly stopped her. Details oozed into her muddy brain. She'd taken the costumes out of her briefcase and said she'd rather not do it on the floor. He'd lifted her onto the big black box. After that, the picture went dark.

Hermes paced across the cell and stared at the monitor. Six flat lines illuminated the screen, the same as when they'd come in last night. He turned to her.

"I don't like it," he said. "There's something about you that makes me do crazy things. Coming here was flat-out dangerous. Do you realize how lucky we are containment wasn't breached?"

Monique's lips curved up as if this confession pleased her, but it didn't. He'd forced her into this cell that held The Power and now he was blaming her.

"Get dressed and get me out of here," she said. Monique peeled off what was left of her costume, wadded it into her briefcase and donned her regular clothes. Her navy-blue toga was creased with wrinkles, the strand of pearls broken but, thank Zeus, the knots had held.

Hermes waited at the metal door. A swipe of his ID card opened the portal. They passed through just in time to miss a wild blip on the monitor.

Veronica

Veronica Zeta was playing big sister. Breakfast with David at a sidewalk cafe. A leafy ash tree shaded their small, round table from the morning sun. It was her last chance to wish him bon voyage.

"So, I think I have enough shekels to see me through the first month," David was saying.

"Uh-huh." She'd missed whatever he'd said before that. It was hard to focus on the conversation, her mind absorbed with who it was Cleo had heard in David's bed. And then there was Clifford. He, too, was leaving next week, bound for Seattle, the seawall and more on-location analysis. The terse digital message he'd sent, announcing his departure time and date, didn't have the usual heart emoticon at the end.

The sound of David's fork scraping his plate called her to the present.

"So, have you ever been to Galilee?" he said.

"A long time ago." Then it struck her. She'd been five or six hundred years old, visiting with Mom who'd been away from Mount Olympus.

"You okay?" David topped off her coffee from the carafe they shared. "You look kind of pale. Don't you want your breakfast?"

Veronica looked down at her untouched blueberry muffin and

fruit cup. "I'll get a to-go box." She reached across the table and took his hand. "David, I remember being there. I soaked in the hot springs. Mom lived in a big, cool house of stone. She gave lots of banquets." She could practically taste the memory. There'd been roasted fowl, fish of every description, endless platters of grapes and olives and cheese, and singing accompanied by a harp. "I was sent back here when she told me she was sick. That must have been when…when you…"

David's eyes bored into hers. "Tell me everything you remember! Wow, I can't believe I didn't think to ask you before now."

She closed her eyes, tried to recall names and faces but besides Hera she could only come up with Thelma and Milton Bernstein. They'd been Mom's servants. At the banquets there'd been lots of other people, but all she could remember of them was their fine, colorful clothing and jewels set in gold.

David slumped back in his chair. "Are you sure you don't remember meeting someone special? A man, some big-shot she treated better than anybody else?"

The look of pain on his face made her wish she did, but all she remembered was the food, the colors and the sound of the singer's sweet voice when Thelma put her to bed.

"David, what are you getting at?"

He heaved an enormous sigh. "I'm kind of wondering if Herod Antipas was my father."

WeDNeSDAY, JULY 9, 2025

Aphrodite

The Goddess of Love hated waiting, especially at elegant but dull Club Dionysus. She drummed her fingers, a muted thud on the white linen tablecloth. Her mother-in-law was late.

Agitated, Aphrodite rolled her thoughts over yesterday's financial report. If revenue kept sliding at its current rate, they'd be out of business by summer's end. The thought of working with Hera after millennia of bitter rivalry was loathsome, but Monique had finally convinced her that making this supreme sacrifice was the only way to save Love, Inc.

Hera arrived at last. She approached the table with a languid gait. Her queenly posture and blood-red toga radiated a shield of dominance. No wonder Hef was so screwed up, with a mother like that. But this was no time to dwell on side-issues, she had to stay on task. Aphrodite was determined not to beg for the opportunity to market her Playtime for Two gift bag line through Marriage and the Media and she had exactly one card to play. She rose to greet her guest.

"Mother-in-law, dear."

"My dear daughter-in-law."

They exchanged icy kisses on the cheek.

Once seated, Aphrodite filled two goblets with Chardonnay. They clinked glasses and drank without a toast.

"Thank you for meeting me today," Aphrodite said, her smile forced. "I trust you've had time to consider my business proposal?"

Hera's cold smile widened. "I've reviewed the subject thoroughly with the *Deep Marriage* team."

A pregnant pause ensued. "And?"

Hera eyes sparkled. "I'm afraid, my dear, novel though your idea is, that our long-term marketing plan would be compromised by incorporating something so—oh dear, how shall I say this? —*tawdry* in our programming."

Hera shook her head pityingly and slugged down more wine. Aphrodite readied her ammunition.

"I am *so* sorry to hear that," she said. "Since our business conversation is over, let's talk about family. I understand your boy, David, is doing some traveling?"

Hera raised an eyebrow. "So he told me. I understand he left on Sunday."

"Yes, on his quest."

Hera refreshed her goblet. "If you say so."

"Fortunately, I was able to offer him guidance."

"Really? How interesting." Hera drank deeply.

Aphrodite leaned forward, her face inches from Hera's. "More interesting than you suppose, dear mother-in-law. You weren't the only visitor in Galilee during the reign of Herod Antipas. Tiberias was a popular vacation spot back then."

Hera set down her goblet. "And?"

Aphrodite warmed to her cat and mouse game. "You know how I love music. I never could have missed the divine young man who sang and played so beautifully at Herod's palace. He looked a lot like David, don't you think?"

"I don't know what you're talking about."

"Oh, I think you do." Aphrodite beamed a radiant smile. "After lunch, why don't you go back to your office and take another look at the joint operating agreement we proposed? I'm sure you'll find the terms favorable, considering how...let's just say, I'd hate for two-thousand-year-old gossip to get out at this late date."

Through a delicious three-course lunch that Hera didn't touch, Aphrodite experienced the pleasure of her rival being, for once, speechless.

ThURSDAY, JULY 10, 2025

Seattle, Washington
Clifford

Poseidon was a hard person to be seen with in public. His shiny turquoise zoot suit, complete with chain and matching fedora, made him conspicuous beyond his impressive height and powerful build. Clifford could sympathize. Mortal modes of dress changed so rapidly it was hard to stay abreast of what looked right without regular reference to their fashion magazines. More than ever, he appreciated his own relatively ageless attire of tweed jacket and trousers.

They'd been walking along the waterfront all morning, discussing the vibrations from the highway tunnel underfoot and the wobbly feeling of the seawall that shielded the tunnel from Elliott Bay. They came to rest on a bench overlooking the water.

"Surely you've dealt with something like this before?" Clifford said.

His companion frowned.

"The short-lives have come up with a real loser. It doesn't take a Big-G to know this whole area is made from fill."

Clifford sighed. The mortal-designed Tunnel Option had been nothing but a headache. The interim fixes by his department had bandaged the project and the adjacent buildings but made the Seattle waterfront look, to his eyes, like an architectural mummy.

A pair of young women in sundresses walked by.

"Yo, foxy mamas," Poseidon said.

They giggled and rushed past.

Poseidon chuckled. "Let 'em drown, that's my advice," he said, returning to the subject at hand. "It's the only way they'll learn."

"Not an option," said Clifford. "How long do you think the seawall will hold?"

"Hard to say." Poseidon tilted back his hat. "There's not much supporting it, no matter what the short-life engineers think. Six months, maybe."

The increased vibration of lunch rush traffic shivered Clifford's bones. Architectural and Computer Services had been wracking their collective brain for years trying to resolve every new complication the tunnel presented. It was a tremendous drain on god power. Veronica had been adamant at their last meeting that a permanent solution was needed ASAP. To Clifford, this goal seemed a moving target. Poseidon was his last hope.

"Are you willing to try a combined effort, like we've discussed? The structurelings and one of your crews? If your lot stood by to stabilize the sea wall, it would give us room to experiment with reinforcement technology."

"Hah!"

But Clifford knew Poseidon didn't have a choice. Ever since Zeus had founded Olympus, Inc., the God of the Sea had held a salaried position in the Department of Weather. Zeus hadn't made Poseidon do anything for his pay. With Veronica at the helm, the God of the Sea would lose his position and considerable income if he didn't perform.

"If you've seen what you need to see, we'll head back to HQ, then?" They'd have to return to their hotel room to cloak unobserved and escape Seattle unseen.

"I'm starving," Poseidon griped.

Clifford eyed the blue and white awning of the nearby Ivar's Fish Stand. Though he relished fish and chips, deep fried food played havoc with his digestion. Veronica had forbidden him to eat here but...

"Let's be quick, then," Clifford said, ignoring the voice of caution. He was still young, still more-or-less single. What Veronica didn't know wouldn't hurt her.

FRIDAY, JULY 11, 2025

The Underworld
Hades

Hades woke from a broken night's sleep. He'd dreamed of loneliness and woe. His sour mood left him ripe for contemplation. He punched the black silk feather pillows into a heap and rested his back against them to think things over.

His life had been one big rip-off. If he hadn't used his helmet of invisibility to sneak up on his father, Cronus, and steal his weapons, Zeus and Poseidon never would have been able to defeat Dad. But when it came to dividing up the world he'd drawn the short straw. Zeus, the perpetual lucky dog, had won the Heavens and Poseidon drew second-best for the Seas. That had left the Underworld. It was a good thing his brothers hadn't considered the mineral wealth below ground; he'd of had to throw them both in the Chair of Forgetfulness to erase their minds of all that glittered. The Chair held its captives forever. The Heavens, the Seas, the Underworld—he could have had it all.

Frustrated by an ancient opportunity missed, Hades lumbered out of bed and paced the polished hematite floor. Hermes' overpriced security system proposal had curled to ashes in the fireplace. Why did everyone think that he, Hades, was made of money? The whole point of stopping the gatecrashers was to collect more coins of passage, not to spend three times the amount in doing so. His palace, where he now agonized, was an opulent display of wealth but the gold that built it was long gone. Staff costs were murder. He'd deferred infrastructure maintenance for centuries, due to increasing operations costs. The fields of Asphodel needed regular reseeding. The reprobates sentenced to Tartarus beat on each other and broke things. The goody-goodies in the Orchards of Elysium were the worst. If Hades had realized how expensive it was to heat and light a vast subterranean cave well enough to grow green lawns and apple trees and provide a blue sky overhead, he would have walked away from it and found something else to be besides a Big-G God.

He stopped in front of a mullioned window that overlooked

the three roads leading to these eternal realms and pondered the latest butcher's bill. That particular payable had been down ten percent for the past few months, primarily due to a decrease in the marrow bones favored by Cerberus. Hades would have considered this good news, but the reason for the variance didn't please him: Persephone's annual nine-month trip topside. Seeing her at the engagement party had left him lonelier than ever. Even his marriage was a rip-off.

A wave of fury overcame him. Hades strode to the bellpull hanging beside his bed and yanked twice. In seconds, his valet arrived from his quarters nearby and bowed in the archway.

"You rang, sir?"

"Anatole," boomed Hades, "I've had enough of these new souls showing their disrespect. We're going to do something about it, you and me."

"Sir?" Anatole, a small-g god of light build, looked quizzically at his master.

"A tour of duty. Pack my helmet of invisibility and whatever you think we need for a reconnaissance mission." If he could solve one problem without paying a by-Zeus fortune, he'd do it. "We're going to flush out the gate-crashers or know the reason why!"

Tuesday, July 15, 2025

In a Mortal Desert
Pan

The God of Shepherds and Flocks tugged at the neck of his uniform jacket. He'd yet to acclimate to the dry misery of the Saharan summer and the high collar had given him a rash.

Three days after he'd arrived at Elle's WomanFront camp (where he'd made no friends cracking jokes about the organization's name), Ares had escorted him to a rendezvous with the warlord of the local rebel movement. They'd cloaked themselves and flown dozens of miles over golden sands, the air so hot it scorched his nostrils. The outlaw camp was a tiny oasis featuring a stone well, four sickly palm trees and a large tent hung with banners. Ares signaled Pan to hide behind a massive rock before they uncloaked and said, "Let me do the talking."

They emerged, fully visible, from their hiding place. Ares shouted in a foreign tongue, "Friend approaching the camp!" according to the button-sized translator in Pan's right ear.

A broad, tall man with a wild beard and fierce eyes stood guard at the tent opening. He held a nasty looking pike in his hands. A sword, flecked with dried blood, rode jauntily in his waist sash.

"State your business," he growled, showing stained teeth.

Ares puffed up his chest. "We have come to see your leader, scum. I am called the Main Man. It is a matter of great importance."

The guard mumbled through the tent opening, "Some dick-head here to see the chief. Calls himself the Main Man."

Within, feet padded away, and, after a brief pause, returned. "Send the dick-head in."

Pan blinked in the dark, cool tent. His footfalls were muted by thick carpet. On a carved wooden throne sat a man of middle age. His build was round, his face hard. Massive hands gripped the armrests.

"Hail, Great Cheese!" Ares bowed low before the warlord. Pan followed his lead.

"Rise, Main Man. It has been a decade or more since we last

met, when I was but a common soldier. You have brought with you a slave?"

Pan felt Ares' elbow in his ribs. He stopped bowing.

"He is not a slave, oh Great One. He is the general of a European army, one sympathetic to your cause."

Great Cheese frowned. "How sympathetic?"

"He brings you the promise of troops and money."

Great Cheese tipped back his head and laughed. "Hah! This I would like to see."

"All in good time, My Lord," Ares said. "I assume the same indoctrination ritual is required for newcomers before business can be discussed?"

Indoctrination ritual? Ares hadn't mentioned this in the briefing. A bead of sweat rolled down Pan's forehead.

"You assume correctly." Great Cheese peered down his nose at Pan as if he were a dung beetle. "We'll see if this European can hold his liquor."

FRIDAY, JULY 18, 2025

City of Mount Olympus
Hera

Hera had left work early on Friday afternoon and was in the penthouse kitchen, hunting for ingredients. It was her standing "date night" with Zeus. She'd given Cook the night off and planned to make Zeus his favorite dish, nachos. Hopefully she'd have the wit to follow the simple recipe. She peered into the cupboards, looking for beans, black olives and—

"Damn!" A bottle of premium olive oil slipped from her hands and shattered on the black marble counter. She had to get hold of herself, stop coloring every thought and movement with fear of Aphrodite's blackmail. Hera took a deep breath and doubled her resolve to create a calm façade but her emotional plaster threatened to crack. The question in her brain would not cease: *how much does she know?*

Aphrodite had hinted around, with references to Herod Antipas, his opulent new palace and days spent at the hot springs spa. Try as she might, Hera could not place her enemy on the scene. Had she been careless not to notice, distracted by her passion for…

Better not to think about the mortal man who was David's father. The resemblance between them was strong. If Aphrodite really had been in Tiberias, as she must have been, and had remembered a certain person's face she could easily connect him with David. That was bad. But if she knew the rest of it…. No, it wasn't possible. Could it be possible? Not even loyal Thelma Bernstein was in on that secret.

Capitulation was a not a word in Hera's vocabulary. Now she reconsidered. Revealing the identity of David's father would open old wounds between herself and Zeus. Hera was certain the damage could be repaired but if the entire story were known…

"Heaven and Earth." She forced the thought from her mind. Zeus would be home in half an hour. She had to clean up the olive oil mess, assemble the ingredients for nachos and make sangria. Hera poured herself a generous glass of Chardonnay, her third since lunch, and set to work. She reviewed a little story in her mind, a story of how she'd decided to let bygones be bygones and work with Aphrodite in a limited way, a project to inject playfulness into the coming *Deep Marriage* campaign. The poor dear's revenues really were suffering and they were family, after all. She'd run it past Zeus after dinner and make the arrangements with Aphrodite next week. If a boost in revenue was enough to keep the bitch from spilling Hera's secret, it was a small price to pay.

SATURDAY, JULY 19, 2025

Tiberias, Israel
David

Though he'd landed in Tel Aviv late on Sunday it had taken David Bernstein until mid-day Saturday to arrive in Tiberias. Guilty feelings persecuted him as he drove his rental car to the ancient city smack in the middle of the Sabbath. In Thelma Bernstein's semi-observant household traveling in vehicles had been forbidden between Friday sunset and Saturday sunset, except during high school basketball season.

David had taken the slow road to Tiberias, meandering up the Mediterranean coast to see the architectural antiquities of Caesarea, Acre and Monfort, delaying the search for his father. Every day he questioned himself. Was it really such a good idea? Did he really want proof he was the son of Herod Antipas? David had queried images of Herod online. Some of them he resembled in one or two points.

The car rolled to a stop in front of a modern sandstone building flanked with palm trees. Tiberias Holiday Flats was written across the awning. He'd reserved a studio apartment for one month, to acclimate to the city and figure out where to look. A young man at the reception desk whose hair was as unruly as his own checked David in and handed him the key to a unit on the third floor. "Overlooking the historic Sea of Galilee," the man said.

The elevator was out of order. David lugged his suitcase up the stairs and entered Unit 303. The apartment was smaller than his place at Athens U. The sofa was a futon that folded down to a bed. He found sheets, pillow and blanket in the closet. The kitchen, tucked into a niche, was a two-burner hot plate stacked on top of a cube refrigerator, a microwave hanging on the wall above and a two-cup coffee maker on the counter. The only sink was in the kitchen. The bathroom, on the other side of an adjacent wall, had only a toilet and a metal shower stall.

David shrugged. He'd stayed in worse places. Not for an entire month, but...

He opened the curtains and looked through a sliding glass door at the blue sea. Tiberias Holiday Flats was dwarfed by towering luxury hotels to either side. They would cast shadows on his balcony when the sun wasn't near its apex, but that was no big deal. He didn't plan to spend much time at home.

David unpacked his suitcase into a two-drawer chest, lightened his backpack of three reference books he probably should have left in Mount Olympus, and set forth in search of food.

Sabbath or no, Tiberias was a tourist town, poised to accommodate the appetites of its visitors. In minutes David purchased a takeout burger and a Coke. He sat against a wall built by the Ottomans in the 18th century, gazed toward the Sea of Galilee, demolished his meal and wondered what in Tartarus he was doing here. Though antiquities abounded, the books he'd read said there wasn't much from his father's era. There were some excavations of the Roman city farther south, including an amphitheater, a gate complex and a bridge, but nothing of Herod's palace. He'd poke around the local museums to see if they had any early 1st century artifacts, maybe unearth a clue that way?

David scanned the beach. Two little boys charged around on the rocky sand, waving their arms and shrieking. A man and woman sat nearby, the mom and dad, he supposed. From what he could remember, Milton Bernstein had been a good father. Maybe that was enough?

The idea came in a flash. Maybe he could send a cell sample to one of those DNA labs that traced your ancestry? How specific were the results and how far back could they go? If he could rule out Herod as a candidate, maybe he wouldn't feel so reluctant to move forward.

David returned to his flat, delighted to find a strong internet connection. He ordered a DNA test kit, express. Who cared if the guy at the front desk rolled his eyes when it showed up? If he could free himself of Herod Antipas, it would be worth the mockery of a hundred guys. If he couldn't—well, he just wasn't going to think about that right now.

END OF MONTH ONE

MONTH TWO

July 20-August 23, 2025

MONDAY, JULY 21, 2025

The Underworld
Hades

The King of the Dead reached under his invisibility helmet and pinched his nostrils together. Of everything detestable about Tartarus, Hades hated the smell most of all. The reek of sweat, urine and spilled ale was so strong in some places it created a fog.

"Anatole," he whispered to his valet turned aide-de-camp.

"Sir?" The small-g god, loaded down with camping gear, trudged alongside him.

"Set down your pack, we need to get our bearings."

Hundreds of years had passed since Hades had made a personal visit to this loathed division of his kingdom. A variety of mortal soul called "football hooligan" had taken up residence in the interval. Minos, the judge on Hades' staff who decided hard cases, had told him these beings ran in packs and advised extreme caution when approaching them.

Master and servant squatted on the cave floor, their backs resting against jagged rock. The air was stifling. Hades peered into the dank gloom and listened intently; not a movement, not a sound. He dared to remove his helmet.

"Map," he said, holding a hand toward his servant.

Anatole opened his pack and extracted a scroll. Hades unrolled the parchment. He squinted to read the place names. They were on the edge of the Great Swamp, as he'd suspected from the sulfurous base note underlying the stench.

"Deploy the sensor," he ordered.

Anatole dug out a small appliance and strapped it to his wrist. The turn of a dial illuminated the gauge. He held out his arm, head bent to monitor the reading.

"No sign of air leaks, sir."

"I thought as much." Hades wrinkled his nose. "Nothing fresh about this place."

Anatole cleared his throat, his annoying way of indicating he had something to say.

"Yes?"

"Sir, our provisions are running low. We need to turn back if we hope to arrive home without fasting."

"Bother."

The trip in had taken two days, much longer than Hades had remembered from his last visit. The expansion projects, he supposed, prompted by increased demand from the mortal population boom. He was weary of walking and ached in every joint from sleeping on the ground.

Hades rose, slipped on his helmet and tucked the map under his arm. "For-*ward*!"

They stepped along, Anatole reporting "no leaks" at regular intervals. Miles passed. At last, a point in the distance glowed red.

"The Pit of Fire, that means we're half-way around," Hades said. He picked up the pace. Anatole panted behind him. As they neared the Pit, the rumble of voices built to a roar. Cries of "Preston North End!" and "Aston Villa!" became distinguishable as heat and light built to a Saharan level.

"Halt!" Hades, forgetting he was invisible, thrust his arm in front of Anatole. The valet's nose crunched into his elbow.

"No leaks," Anatole squeaked.

But danger lurked and there was no time for empathy. "What devils do I see before me?" Hades murmured. Bands of souls surged through the flames, pitching rocks and beating each other with sticks.

"Your team's a bunch of grannies!" hollered a broad-shouldered soul as he pounded another inmate.

"Your ma charges by the hour!" the stricken one yelped, fists flying.

Hades stepped back, accidentally crushing Anatole's foot. The small-g screamed in pain.

The roar of insults stopped. The Pit fell quiet.

"Fresh meat!" cried thousands of flaming souls in unison. They charged toward the King and his valet.

"Run!" Hades grabbed Anatole's arm and sprinted, unable to remember if souls could inflict bodily harm on living beings and unwilling to find out.

WEDNESDAY, JULY 23, 2025

City of Mount Olympus
Hera

Hera presided over the conference table at her Olympus, Inc., office suite. Copies of a joint venture agreement and glossy catalogs hawking Aphrodite's skanky wares littered the tabletop. They'd emptied the coffee carafe. The pitcher of ice water was, as yet, untouched.

She'd scheduled her meeting with Aphrodite, Candy and Monique for morning, to get it over with. Heaven and Earth, she could use a glass of Chardonnay. The three of them were getting on her nerves, including Candy who could hardly wait to endorse the gift bag idea.

"It was like—wow! The whole costume thing sounded fun from the start but I had no idea seeing Jim in an eye patch could make me feel so…but his pirate voice was really great, too, gave me goose bumps and everything." Candy rolled her eyes and tossed her hair over her shoulders. "I think maybe a gift bag of the month club would be a good option for couples in a rut. With sex, I mean."

Hera was sorely tempted to slap the smirk off Aphrodite's face but contained her wrath. The whole point of this joint venture was to placate the blackmailing bitch.

Monique reminded Hera of Veronica at annual budget meetings. She wanted to discuss every trifling line item to the last detail. Bo-ring! Monique was the definition of dowdy in her navy-blue wool and short string of pearls. Her hair would be lovely if she let it down, but she wore it in a bun so tight it made her eyes slant.

Bubbly, Bitchy and Boring. After an hour in their company she would have signed anything to get rid of them. When discussion subsided, Hera promptly authorized the inclusion of a "gift bag for lovers" in every *Deep Marriage* seminar packet. Gilda, her executive assistant, was summoned to make copies of the agreement.

"Tell me, Hera, dear, have you heard from young David?" Aphrodite said while they waited. "I hope the Holy Land turns out to be everything he's looking for."

Hera smiled with her teeth. "So kind of you to point him toward the hot springs at Tiberias, Aphrodite. The poor boy could use some time to unwind, as hard as he's been studying."

"Who knows?" Aphrodite raised a wicked eyebrow. "He might even have a fling or two, virile young man that he is."

"David?" said Candy with a snort. "You've got to be kidding! He's practically a baby. When he was living in Seattle he had no idea how to get a girlfriend. Every time he was interested in someone, she'd treat him like a kid brother."

Monique fell into a violent coughing fit. Hera poured a glass of water and slid it across the conference table.

"You spend far too much time shuffling paper, dear," Hera said. "I'm afraid your mother is working you to death." She smiled sourly at Aphrodite.

Gilda returned with the copies. Hera rose to signal the meeting had ended. Aphrodite and Candy left together, speculating about David's love life. Monique lingered. She held her briefcase and a shiny red shopping bag embossed with the Love, Inc., logo. Hera recalled the girl had slipped it under the conference table when she'd arrived. Monique handed Hera the bag.

"A token of our goodwill," Monique said. "Thanks so much for meeting with us today."

They shook hands and Monique departed. Hera listened until she was sure Gilda had settled at her desk in the reception area. She set the gift bag on the table and peeked inside. Resting on top of she-knew-not-what was a creamy white card printed in gold with *Napoleon and Josephine Special.*

FRIDAY, JULY 25, 2025

Jim

The common room at Olympus Rest appeared as placid as before. Not so Jim's client, who had trounced him four times straight at *Stratego*.

Heaven and Earth, he longed to get back to Seattle! Their three-week visit to Mount Olympus had morphed into five weeks when Hera ordered Candy to take part in some hush-hush negotiations between Marriage and the Media and Love, Inc. Whatever it was (Candy wouldn't say, but hinted she was very excited about the result) had concluded on Wednesday. Their flight home tomorrow was the first one available and he'd pounced on it.

"Well played," he said to Stella as they set up their pieces for game five.

Her eyes narrowed. "Better than you know, counselor."

She'd been throwing out similar hints the entire session. So far he'd let them pass, hoping to prod her into a confession by feigning lack of interest.

"Maybe one day, when you've been released, you'll play in a tournament."

"Sooner than you think," she snarled.

He tapped one of his pieces against what he was pretty sure was a bomb. "General."

"Boom!" Her face lit with cruel pleasure. "You'll never beat me, counselor, at this game or any other."

"I'm sure you're right," he said amicably.

"Imbecile!" Stella swept her arm across the board. Playing pieces tumbled to the floor. The faintest hint of black flickered above her sickly gray aura. "Can't you see It's come back? It's gaining on you fools every day." She cackled and rubbed her hands together. "You'll never guess, none of you, until it's too late. Then you'll see who's in charge."

Jim rose. "I'm going home tomorrow, Stella. I'll miss our little chats."

He left the common room and headed to Apollo's office.

"This time I'm sure of it," Jim confided to his colleague. "There was as a thin black line above her aura when she got menacing. I'm certain there's been a containment breach."

"I'll check again with Hermes." Apollo tapped a short stack of papers on his desk. "All the reports so far have come up negative."

"If I hadn't seen it, I wouldn't believe it myself," Jim said. "Mistakes happen. Things get missed. I recommend round-the-clock surveillance of the—you know what." He hated even to think *The Power*. "Someone should observe Stella 24/7, too."

Apollo started to object but Jim held up a hand to stop him.

"It's true her violent episodes have more or less subsided, but if she does act out and it coincides with even the smallest hint of a breach it would be some kind of evidence."

"I'll do what I can," Apollo said without enthusiasm.

"Keep me posted, even if the results are negative."

They shook hands and parted. Jim elected to walk back to the hotel to clear his mind. Apollo was skeptical in nature, wouldn't believe that something arranged by Hermes and Zeus had gone wrong without tangible proof, but Jim was sold. He prayed to Heaven and Earth someone would figure it out before it was too late.

TUESDAY, JULY 29, 2025

In a Mortal Desert
Pan

In two weeks Pan had stirred up sufficient chaos to depose Great Cheese. As accustomed as he was to his own boisterous and grotesque lifestyle, he still had to suppress a shudder as he walked past the former leader's head, now featured on the end of a pike near the tent opening. Entering cave-like darkness from the searing desert light, he saluted Fat Mac Daddy, his new best friend who now occupied the throne.

"Quite a party last night, Little General," said the current warlord, who was muscular and lean in contrast to his predecessor. His name referred to a specific appendage in which he took great pride.

"Brilliant idea to bring in dancing girls, My Lord." Pan had pulled out his pipes and joined them in their dance, a welcome respite from long nights of swilling, swaggering and boasting.

"You cut quite a carpet, my friend."

Pan bowed in deference to the compliment. "As you cut quite a neck, oh Great One."

Fat Mac Daddy laughed long and loud. He probably wouldn't be amused to know his chief minister, Side of Fries, had already approached Pan to make a deal, pursuant to another execution. The God of Shepherds and Flocks was sick of his assigned playmates and their game of Ruler Roulette. When would they figure out what he, the most dissipated and worthless of Big-G Gods, had realized in a few short days—that leadership was a one-way ticket to eternity? Side of Fries was already planning Fat Mac Daddy's "going away" party. Just this morning he'd recruited Pan to play his pipes at the occasion. No one yet had asked Pan for details about his troops and money.

"So, Little General." Fat Mac Daddy gestured toward Side of Fries, who stood to one side of the throne. "What do you think of my chief minister?"

Pan shifted his gaze to Side of Fries, who winked. "Oh Great One, he is a fine and worthy man made in your own footsteps."

"Hah! Excellent." Fat Mac Daddy laughed until tears streamed down his weathered cheeks. "Excellent!"

Suddenly Pan wondered if his companions knew exactly what fate awaited them. If so, they seemed to take great joy in their game. He hated this mission, could hardly wait for it to be over, but Elle's reports were good. Supply trucks were completing their routes with little obstruction. Partying every night in the Great Cheese cum Fat Mac Daddy camp left the raiders too tired to terrorize during the day.

"With your permission, My Lord," Pan said. "I must retire to review the progress of my troops. They will soon be at the border, waiting for my signal."

Fat Mac Daddy waved his hand in dismissal. In truth, Pan was going to make himself invisible, lie down behind a rock and take a nap. He had to pace himself. After this assignment he had five more camps to engage in his specialized form of single-to-many combat. The methods Ares had coached him in were succeeding but how long could he endure this duty?

Pan turned his thoughts to streamlining the process. The mortals had a story about a boy who was beset by a group of tigers. One stole his shoes, another his coat and the last his umbrella. Their jealousy of each other had finished them off in one neat batch. Pan powered up his digital pad and tapped in a message to Ares, subject line "Tigers into Butter."

Thursday, July 31, 2025

Tiberias, Israel
David

David Bernstein awoke with a throbbing head. He'd been in Tiberias for almost two weeks with zero progress in his quest. To numb his frustration, last night he'd visited a karaoke club and downed way too much of the local red wine.

He dragged himself to the kitchenette and drank a glass of water, then another. The dry, sharp taste in his mouth eased. He ran more water into the coffee carafe. The bitter aroma of French Roast put his stomach on edge, but he soldiered on and toasted a bagel on the hot plate.

When breakfast was ready David opened the curtains and the sliding glass door. The balcony was shaded. The sun, its escaped rays obnoxiously white, was behind one of the neighboring monstrous hotels. He ducked back in for his sunglasses and moved the dining table (as he called the TV tray) and the folding chair to the balcony, figuring fresh air would improve his appetite.

As David munched and sipped, his optimism returned. It could be worse. Although he'd so far learned nothing about his father, he had to admit he was having a pretty good time. Every day the weather had been ideal, warm without being hot which had something to do with the city being 200 feet below sea level. Yesterday he'd taken a break from scouring the ruins of the Roman 1st Century CE south gate and poring over various antiquity collections. He'd rented a bike and pedaled from Tiberias to a nearby kibbutz. The kibbutzniks had a dairy operation, both cows and goats. He'd come away with a week's supply of butter, cheese and whole milk for his coffee. If only he hadn't stayed so late at the karaoke club, the wine going down so easily. David grimaced. Had he really stood up in front of a bunch of strangers and given an out-of-sync rendition of "My Way"? His foster dad, a huge Sinatra fan, would have gotten a kick out of that.

Thinking about Milton Bernstein shifted David's thoughts to the DNA test. The kit had arrived, and he'd sent away his cell sample but the results wouldn't be available for six to eight weeks, long past his stay in Tiberias. He'd be visiting Cleo and her family in Jordan starting August 25, but wasn't sure how long he'd be staying there or where he'd go afterwards. The Tiberias Holiday Flats manager, for a moderate consideration, had agreed to hold his mail until the end of September. He'd either have to come back for it or have it forwarded to wherever he ended up.

David lingered over a second cup of coffee and enjoyed the view of the Sea of Galilee. It was a breezy morning. The lake's surface rippled with waves and wind surfers. Maybe he'd take today off, too, and go to the beach. He'd take his journal, go over his notes and get an idea of how to further his quest. David rinsed out his coffee cup and readied his backpack for the day. Serious breakfast was required.

He ordered the special—four pancakes, four eggs, hash browns and a monster glass of orange juice—at a Mom-and-Pop restaurant nearby. The waitress, a middle-aged woman with lots of hair held back in a ponytail, looked at him funny as she scribbled on her pad. When she returned with his meal she asked where he was from.

"So you're an American," she said, a quizzical light in her eyes. "Didn't I hear you sing at the Retread Club last night?"

He admitted he had.

The woman rested a hand on his shoulder. "Not that you have much of a voice, but you reminded me of a fella who used to be on the television back when I was a kid. I mean, you kinda look like him, with the nose and the hair and all. Man, could that guy sing! His name was…it's right on the tip of my tongue, it was…it started with a 'C' I'm pretty sure."

David's stomach rumbled but his polite upbringing nudged him to ask her what kind of music ("Like the thing you did, like Sinatra"), was the singer from Israel ("I'm pretty sure, yes"). A bell over the front door rang. Three customers walked in.

"Enjoy your breakfast, kid," the waitress said, and hurried off.

David dug into his pancakes. On his way to the beach he'd stop and get a post card to send to the Bernsteins. Milton would get a kick out of the karaoke story. Heck, he might even remember an Israeli singer forty years back who made hits with Sinatra standards.

TUESDAY, AUGUST 5, 2025

The Underworld
Hades

Master and servant waded through acres of waving grass and ghostly flowers. Hades took long strides. Multiple treatments from the palace masseuse had eased the aches and pains he'd acquired in Tartarus. Anatole trotted behind in spite of the whacking bruise on his right thigh, sustained from a rock pitched by a football hooligan.

The inhabitants of Asphodel were souls Hades could admire—the pale shadows of fallen heroes and heroines. Faded figures dotted the meadow. They lunged and parried with transparent weapons, restless in the confines of eternity.

A tall, strong shade with drawn sword approached them. He bowed and said in a shout as faint as a whisper, "Hail, King!"

"Ah, Orion," said Hades. "How goes the hunting?"

He shook his shaggy head. "Not so well, your majesty. The deer seem to have migrated. Are the apples ripe in the Orchard of Elysium?"

Hades affirmed they were. They always were. It was like that in Elysium.

"I thought as much," said Orion. He sheathed his sword and wandered off.

Hades turned to Anatole. "Any interesting readings?"

The valet consulted the sensor strapped to his wrist. "None, sir."

The pale grass swayed in weak wind. Hades' eyes drooped as they moved forward. They passed through a section favored by heroes who'd been strategists as well as warriors. These shades were scattered about at game tables, engaged in ghostly games of chess. Hades' head lolled. He longed to sleep.

"Time for a rest, Anatole."

He sank to his knees. Small hands tugged on his arm.

"You mustn't go to sleep, sir. The atmosphere is noxious and you refused to take your preventive stimulant before we left."

"That stuff's for babies," Hades murmured, every muscle

relaxed. "Brute," he said when Anatole pulled, poked and prodded him back to his feet.

"I recommend retreat, sir. When I set the gauge to extrapolate," he said, nodding at the device strapped to his arm, "it indicates 99.99% probability of Asphodel being leak free."

They turned back toward the palace. Soon Hades' head cleared.

"99.99%, you say?"

"Yes, sir."

"Pretty good odds," he said, though skeptical. "Call it a day, then, Anatole?"

"Yes, sir."

Though glad to leave the torpor of Asphodel, Hades was reluctant to return to his large, lonely palace.

"What day is it, Anatole?"

"The fifth, sir."

"Of what?"

"August, sir."

The news left him mournful. Even if harvest was early this year it would be at least two months before Persephone came back from helping her mother. Persephone didn't talk much, didn't eat much and was anything but jolly, but he missed her, by Zeus!

The palace loomed sad and vacant on the horizon. Every trace of lightness left his step

"Anatole."

"Yes, sir?"

"I wish to invite the Furies to dinner tomorrow."

A pause ensued. "Yes, sir."

Tisiphone, Alecto and Megaera could be charitably described as vile crones, but they were excellent at their work: hearing complaints about nasty, living mortals and hounding them relentlessly in punishment for their crimes. The old girls had an endless supply of war stories. An evening amidst their shrieks and cackles would beat the Tartarus out of eating alone.

City of Mount Olympus
Heracles

Heracles sat uncomfortably in a chair across from Hermes. He hated being summoned by any of the Twelve Olympian big shots for any reason; also, the office furniture in Digital Devices and Robotics was sized for regular-sized immortals. Heracles was definitely an Extra-Extra Large.

He shouldn't complain, though. Irritated as Heracles was, Hermes, who'd called the meeting, looked downright shabby. Dark circles sagged under his eyes, suggesting severe lack of sleep. Stubble covered his lower jaw and his shaggy hair looked unwashed. Heracles, meticulous about his own grooming, noticed these things.

"Thanks for meeting me on such short notice," Hermes said. *Like I had a choice*, thought Heracles.

"I hate to admit it, but I need help," the God of Thieves and the world's foremost inventor continued. "Work overload, confidential project. I can't go into the details. It's not about that, anyway."

Hermes ran a hand through his lank locks and sighed.

"And?" prompted Heracles. Hermes hadn't mentioned the security employees he'd drafted for the mystery project. Heracles was already putting in extra hours, covering for them.

"It's the guide work," Hermes said, an apologetic grimace on his face. "I can't keep up with the souls who need to be conducted to the River Styx with these new demands."

Word of Hermes' failed efforts to curb climate change had circulated company-wide. How not, with Weather involved, a notorious department for gossip? They said Veronica had read Hermes the riot act at his last evaluation and had set a strict time limit to achieve results. Now, apparently, something else had been heaped on top of this demand.

"Heracles, you're the only one topside, besides me, who knows anything practical about the Underworld. Don't argue," Hermes said, holding up a hand when Heracles started to respond. "You got to the other side of the River Styx and back when you were a mortal. A mortal, for Zeus' sake! And now that you're part of the family, well…"

Another crappy assignment for the ex-mortal, like he should be grateful. But perhaps there was a silver lining.

"Any transfer of powers?" Heracles asked.

"Temporarily, of course," Hermes said. The fingers of one hand started tapping the desktop. "I'll need to teach you the summoning call to gather the souls we have under contract. European mortals, mostly, except for the ones Odin and Hel pick up in Norway. Four to six hours, twice a week, usually gets the job done."

Great. Hebe was already on him for working late. Heracles contemplated the tirade that would greet this new assignment—tears, outrage, a vase pitched at his head.

"I summon them, and then what?"

"Piece of baklava. They can't resist following you after you summon them. Stand outside the entrance to the Underworld. You know where that is, right? The summoning call gathers the souls of the newly dead in minutes. Send back the ones who don't have their fare for crossing and lead the rest to the banks of the Styx. Wait for Charon, put 'em on board when he arrives. That's it."

"Sounds simple enough," Heracles said, though he felt an eyebrow rising.

"It is, I swear by Heaven and Earth."

"Overtime premium?"

"Heracles, I'm asking you for a favor."

Heracles held out for a weekly bonus to cover an overdue payment on Hebe's maxed out Bank of Olympus Platinum card.

"Bleeding me dry," Hermes groused. They shook on it and Hermes taught him the summoning call. Heracles turned to go.

"By the way," Hermes said, "it might take a while to clear the backlog. Haven't had time to do the call for a couple of weeks, you understand."

Heracles chastised himself for not driving a harder bargain. Then he realized there might be a hidden benefit. Maybe if he bribed Charon, the ferryman would take him over and back to see Cerberus, the three-headed dog who guarded the gates. The poor hound must get lonely when Persephone worked the harvest. Maybe he could sneak him a marrow bone or three, without notice? He could hear the dog's serpent tail thumping the ground with pleasure even now.

WEDNESDAY, AUGUST 6, 2025

The Underworld
Hades

At a round table covered with cloth-of-gold and set for four, Hades entertained his guests. It was a family event if one attended to genealogical details. The Furies—Thisiphone, Alecto and Magaera—were, technically, his aunts. They'd been created from the spilled blood of Hades' grandfather, Uranus, who was honored in immortal religion as the Father of the Sky.

The three had dressed for dinner which Hades viewed with relief. At work, they appeared naked. Now in their eight thousands, the trio's physical features had migrated south.

"Pass the ribs," said Tisiphone, the eldest sister. Her voice, low and growling, suited her bared canine teeth.

Magaera wrapped her arms around the serving plate. "Not until you say the magic word!" she hissed.

Tisiphone wrinkled her nose. "Pleeease."

"Please *what?*" snapped short-tempered Alecto. "You know I hate it when you use incomplete sentences."

Tisiphone's beady eyes skewered Alecto. "Pleeease pass the ribs."

Magaera, who was hoarding all the serving dishes though her own plate was full, reluctantly passed the entrée.

"You're looking well tonight, aunts," Hades said in an effort to break the tension.

"What do you mean by *that?*" said Alecto. She fiddled with her hair, a writhing coil of snakes. Alecto wore her snakes up. Tisiphone left hers free, spilling down her back. Magaera was somewhere in between and had dyed her serpents blue.

Magaera preened. "Shut up, Alecto, he was talking to me."

Hades rang the bejeweled bell alongside his plate. In seconds, Anatole arrived.

"Yes, sir?"

Hades nodded toward the Furies, engaged in an argument as to who was the most beautiful.

"More wine."

"Very good, sir."

"Aunt Tisiphone," Hades cut in. "Tell me again about the time you avenged the murder of Aurelius Pennymaker."

The story was one they loved to tell, from the days when they were young and agile and could seduce their victims before chasing them down and beating them to death with metal-tipped scourges.

"Sweet!" Tisiphone set down the bone she'd been gnawing and licked the barbeque sauce from her lips. "It was the worst of all crimes, the murder of Pennymaker." The other two murmured in agreement. "Not murder alone, but patricide!"

"The very worst crime of all," said Magaera.

"The very worst crime except for matricide!" Alecto corrected.

Tisiphone glared at her sisters. "Who's telling this story?"

Magaera pouted. Alecto muttered "bitch" under her breath.

Anatole arrived with the wine. Hades signaled to him to fill all goblets to the brim. He drank deeply from his own.

"As I was saying before I was so *rudely* interrupted," Tisiphone continued, "Pennymaker was killed by his own son!"

"His own son!" said the other two in chorus.

Aunt Tis raised her goblet. "Nothing worse than a child killing a parent!"

Alecto and Mageara raised their goblets in reply. "Nothing worse!"

They all drank. Something nagged at the back of Hades' mind, a sense of déjà vu.

"What devil would kill his own father?" Tisiphone queried.

"What devil indeed?" sang her chorus.

What devil indeed? thought Hades. But then he remembered. If he could slink away without being noticed…

"As wicked as Zeus when he killed his own father, our brother Cronus!" shrieked Tisiphone. "Zeus and his brothers did old Cronus in!"

Three pairs of eyes bored into Hades. Three crowning glories of snakes hissed.

"I can explain!" Hades cried, but it was too late. Alecto had loaded her hands with dinner rolls and Magaera held the coleslaw spoon like a catapult.

"Food fight!" screamed Tisiphone.

A sparerib smacked Hades in the temple. Sauce dripped down his cheek like blood. Coleslaw splatted square in his face.

"We can't kill you," Magaera said, "but we can make one Tartarus of a mess!"

"I didn't kill him!" Hades protested. "I just made myself invisible and took his sword."

He ducked. A fusillade of dinner rolls rained on the tabletop.

Shrieks of glee echoed around the dining room. It would be hours before they wore down, slinging food, shredding the tapestries, breaking furniture and relieving themselves in the strangest locations imaginable. He prayed to his late, lamented grandfather, Heaven, and his grandmother Earth, promising them anything if they made the Furies forget about him as long as he stayed very, very quiet. If Persephone had been here, he never would have made this mistake.

FRIDAY, AUGUST 8, 2025

City of Mount Olympus
Monique

Monique Raison sat at the desk in her private office, a small place downtown where she could focus without distractions. She'd let go her personal assistant, couldn't justify the expense given the Love, Inc., revenue decline. Now, after days of working out the details of pricing, quantities and delivery with Hera's Marriage and the Media staff, Ms. Raison dared to look at the future with optimism. She'd negotiated a deal she was proud of: selling gift bag components at a thirty percent mark-up over cost and leaving the assembly process to them. They would start with four theme options and expand the product line in six months, based on mortal response.

She looked up at the wall chronometer, the big hand nearly at XII and the little hand nudging V. Five PM on Friday. Tomorrow would be her first day off in weeks. She thought of Hermes. He hadn't called or messaged her since their night in the security vault with…

Monique pushed the memory away. He was an ass, but she'd give it one more try. She picked up her digital pad and scrolled to his address. Her provocative message was almost finished when a muscle spasm pierced her lower back.

"Heaven and Earth!" She stood up and stretched. Served her right for barricading herself at the desk, day after day. She hadn't exercised in ages. Her back was a collection of knots and her midsection had started to bulge.

The spasm eased. Monique deleted the message to Hermes and scrolled to the address for her health club. Hopefully one of the masseuses would have an opening tomorrow. She'd pick up some take-out on the way home and spend the evening soaking in her Jacuzzi with a bottle of wine for company.

MONDAY, AUGUST 11, 2025

Clifford

Clifford shifted on Veronica's sofa. His eyes itched. His rival, Veronica's beloved cat Bill Gates, Jr., stared at him from a chair across the living room.

"Here you are." Veronica swept in from the kitchen with two glasses of wine. She handed one to Clifford and doubled back to scratch the feline behind the ears. "Mama's good little kitty boy," she crooned, a phrase Clifford had heard so often he'd lost the impulse to gag.

"Wow, what a day." She lit on the sofa next to Clifford and patted his knee. "So glad you're back."

He'd just returned from Seattle. The seawall readings his field assistant had monitored from their offshore unit (a luxury power boat that cruised the waterfront) hadn't varied since his last visit. It seemed good news on the surface, but, according to Poseidon, the seawall could give without a moment's notice. And as to the question of sinkholes…

"Clifford, where do you want to go for dinner?" Veronica's voice carried a trace of irritation. "Didn't you hear me the first time?"

"Warp speed lag," he said. She bought the excuse. Anyone who'd flown at an accelerated rate from Seattle to the City of Mount Olympus understood the immense physical and mental exertion required. He was glad she'd granted him the power to do that, of course, to get back to her as soon as possible. But his thoughts lagged behind him as a side-effect.

Clifford sneezed. The cat's purr rumbled across the room.

"Poor thing." Veronica patted Clifford's knee again. "You should make an appointment with Apollo."

Another appointment with Apollo. He'd tried pills, he'd tried nose rinses, he'd tried injections, but nothing known to medical science had eased his allergic reaction to cats. Clifford hoped against hope Veronica would find another home for Bill Gates, Jr., before the wedding, an event mere decades in the future.

They sipped their wine. Clifford fought the need to talk about work. They'd agreed they'd never do this after they left Olympus, Inc., for the day. How long did he have to solve the seawall problem? How many unsuspecting mortals would be sent to a watery grave, their vehicles serving as caskets, when the seawall breached and took the Seattle waterfront with it?

"Earth to Clifford!" Veronica waved a hand in front of his face. "Are you in a trance? I just asked if Club Dionysus is okay."

The calculating feline meowed, knowing he'd be the beneficiary of a kitty bag of scraps.

"Yes. Of course."

They set their wineglasses on the coffee table and rose. Bill Gates, Jr., slinked toward them as sinuously as a butterball covered with orange fur could. The cat rubbed his head on Veronica's shins.

"Mommy won't be long, sweetie." Veronica gathered him into her arms and tapped a kiss on his flat, imperious nose. When she set him down, he trotted off to what she called the kitty habitat, a filthy room outfitted with cat posts, toys, food and a rank-smelling litter box. Would Clifford's allergies ease if the kitty habitat was thoroughly cleaned every few months? He only had another thirty years to pose this idea to Veronica.

They left the condo. Outdoors, his symptoms immediately lightened.

"David messaged me today," Veronica said. "He said to say hello to you. He's given up on finding anything about his father in Tiberias."

Clifford could sympathize. He, himself, hadn't known the identity of his own father for most of his life. He'd been trying not to think about Ralph, though Poseidon had pointed out an experienced old-school structureling might have some useful insights to solving the seawall dilemma. No one knew the Seattle waterfront better than Ralph, whose molecules had been dispersed in the Alaskan Way Viaduct for a half-century plus. But Dad was retired now, and Clifford's mom was ecstatic to be reunited with her old love. The seawall was a troubling and potentially dangerous problem. Clifford's gut (for lack of a better way to describe visceral intuition) told him something in Seattle was very wrong. He didn't want Ralph to be part of it.

WEDNESDAY, AUGUST 13, 2025

Hermes

Hermes monitored two small screens on his desktop. One, which he watched from the corner of his eye, was the live feed from the cell that housed The Power. The other ran in fast forward, a file of yesterday's twenty-four hours. He'd been doing this drill for weeks. It had yielded nothing. Not a blip, not a hiccup, nothing reported by the dozen security employees who spelled each other, watching the monitor in real time. They hadn't been told what the six lines represented, only that anything besides a flat reading must be reported immediately to Hermes or his on-shift designee.

When yesterday's file was finished, he allowed himself to blink. He should have seen something by now, an aberration indicating a lapse in the strength of the charms laid on the specially forged metal casket. Not that Zeus' charms would have failed; Hermes had begun to doubt the charm he, himself, had laid.

He'd started work at six AM. It was now ten. He called for Roderick Waller, the temp covering for Cleo. Roderick Waller, rising Olympus, Inc., star whose mother was the Continental Manager of Africa. The handsome, dark-skinned youth appeared in the doorway.

"Yes, sir?"

"Have you had time to review yesterday's file, Waller?"

"Yes, sir. Nothing, sir."

"Okay." Hermes slumped back in his chair, bleary-eyed. "I need to get out of here for a few minutes, get myself some coffee. Want anything?"

"No, sir. Thank you, sir."

The kid was too polite to be believed. Hermes missed the way he and Cleo had bantered, would have welcomed someone to talk to who treated him like an equal instead of a big shot.

"Back soon."

Hermes took the stairs instead of the elevator, his strategy for staying fit when he was tied to his desk. He tried to ignore the guilt that had hammered away at him ever since Apollo, who had authority in matters of public health on Mount Olympus, had insisted he monitor The Power around the clock. If there was a leak, it was Hermes' own damn fault. If something had gone wrong as early as July fourth, he and Monique might be infected. He should have returned her calls before Apollo had ordered him to tell no one about the possible breach.

Coffee breakers milled around the mezzanine—clerks, assistants, and middle managers. If Cleo were here, she'd be among them, queuing up for two coffees to go. He'd never asked her to do this, she just did it. When she came back, he'd start saying thank you.

Hermes got in line behind three clerks from the Department of Weather who chattered about drought projections. He lowered his eyes, shamed by his inability to curb climate change and thought of Pan, deployed in the War Against Hunger. What had he been thinking when he'd marched his wayward son into Ares' office and pressured him to enlist? The mortals couldn't kill Pan, but what if he came back physically injured or mentally ill?

The trio in front of him had advanced to the cashier and paid for their coffees.

"Two large coffees," he said to the cashier. He selected two large paper cups from the service table beyond the register. He couldn't talk to Monique or Cleo or Pan, couldn't tell any of them how sorry he was for being an ass, but he could make Roderick Waller's day a little brighter with an unanticipated cup of coffee.

Tuesday, August 19, 2025

Masada, Israel
David

It had taken David Bernstein a while to realize there was one benefit if he was Herod Antipas's son. He would also be the grandson of Herod the Great. As terrible a tyrant as the Roman client King of Judea had been (just thinking about the Slaughter of the Innocents made David's flesh crawl), he had also been an avid builder and was responsible for raising many impressive structures.

After a month in the Tiberias Holiday Flats, David treated himself to a luxury hotel within ten miles of one of Herod's strongholds, now called Masada National Park. Every day he boarded the first tour bus to the fortress ruins and caught the last bus back. Each time he ascended the path to the hilltop a somber mood settled over him. He was familiar with the story of the Zealots and their last stand against the Romans in 73 CE, ending with the mass suicide of over 900 men, women and children. Herod's structures had been built about 100 years before that. In spite of his distaste for the builder, David couldn't help but admire Herod's elegant palace-villa, built on three terraces on the northern cliff-side. There were the remains of a larger, official palace, too, and a well-preserved Roman-style bathhouse. Storerooms and cisterns, built to provide for the inhabitants if the fort fell under siege, were grim reminders of the violent clashes between the Jews and Romans. To the east, the fortress overlooked the Dead Sea.

Magnificent as the ruins were, they weren't what kept David coming back. Today, his third visit, he was drawn by intuition; something significant was going to happen to him at Masada.

He wandered through the remains of structures grown familiar, searching for something unexpected. Many times he backtracked to the official palace where the feeling was strongest. Nothing he looked at answered the pulse beating inside him. When he visited the Masada Museum at the base of the mountain, he was moved by the artifacts from the Zealots' occupation but it wasn't enough. No matter who his father was, there was little chance he'd lived to 73 CE.

Even if he had, it was unlikely someone of advanced age would have taken up with the Jewish rebels. Maybe Masada was just an intriguing dead end.

Back at the hotel he inquired at the desk about the best way to travel to Petra. He was surprised to learn he couldn't take an Israeli rental car into Jordan. It was recommended he hire an Israeli driver with his or her own car for the trip. The desk clerk handed him a list of names and telephone numbers. He thanked the clerk and stuck the list in his pants pocket.

David flopped on the bed in his well-appointed room, empty and discouraged. Why had Masada called to him if it had nothing to give?

His stomach rumbled. He got up, changed the sweat-stained shirt he'd worn on his excursion, attempted to tame his springy hair. Bereft of his usual sense of adventure, he opted for the hotel restaurant and ordered beef stew off a menu that catered to Americans. It was just past five. A handful of diners, all of them middle-aged or older, were scattered around the dining room. In a distant corner a singer accompanied himself on guitar, mostly mid-twentieth century swing tunes. It felt like a preview of living in the old folks' home.

His stew arrived and he ordered a glass of wine. Eating, sipping, and thinking, David marveled at how he'd taken on a task with no likely solution. The room began to fill. An older couple, in their seventies he guessed, were seated at the table next to him. They smiled. He smiled. They picked up their menus. The man looked at him a couple of times, like he was trying to remember something. The couple fell into their own conversation when their drinks arrived. David overheard bits and pieces about the wife's spa day.

"I swear, Lou, I don't know what they put in that mud pack, but my pores are tingling, absolutely tingling."

"That's it, listen!" said the man Lou. The two fell quiet, straining to hear the singer. "It's 'All of Me' can you hear it? Old Blue Eyes. That's why the kid looks familiar." He nodded toward David. "He's a dead ringer for that guy who did all the Sinatra covers. You remember? Oh shoot, what's his name? Had it right on the tip of my tongue."

The woman laid a hand on the man's arm and leaned toward David. "You'll have to pardon my husband's enthusiasm, young man. Lou," she said, swatting Lou's shoulder, "how can you be so rude? You're right, though, he does look like…what was that guy's name anyway? I haven't thought about him in years!"

She asked David if he knew, since he must have heard this before.

"Sorry, no."

David pushed aside his empty dish and finished his wine, didn't linger as the waitress would bill his room for the meal. This whole trip was a bust. The only thing he'd learned in six and a half weeks was that he looked like some Sinatra-singing has-been. What good was that?

END OF MONTH TWO

MONTH THREE
August 25-September 21, 2025

MONDAY, AUGUST 25, 2025

Petra, Jordan
Cleo

Cleo Petra paced the packed sand in front of The Treasury. David's message had indicated he'd arrive two hours ago, but she hadn't spotted him among the tourists who spent more time taking selfies with the camels than appreciating the majestic tomb carved in the hills. David was late. It wouldn't improve Mother's mood. Already she was unhappy that Cleo's guest was Jewish.

"It's just another Religion of the Millennium Club," Titania Petra had fumed. "They say they're ancient? I'll give them ancient! No better than those, what-do-you-call-them? The ones in Utah with all the imagination."

Cleo looked up to her mother, literally. The top of her head was at the same level as Titania's nose, which cast a large shadow. Peter Petra was relatively short compared to his wife, as was David to Cleo.

The realization jarred her. Did this explain her newfound attraction to David? Cleo glanced at Dad, who sat on a folding chair nearby, and dismissed the thought. Peter Petra was as bald as a discus and sported a mead gut. Whereas David was...

"I can't wait with you any longer, Pumpkin." Dad folded his chair, a gaudy-colored mortal-made contraption of aluminum and plastic webbing. Mother despised it, but Dad kept a herd of them at their vacation home. "Your mother will be in a rage if I don't take her an update."

"Thanks, Dad." Cleo hugged him and planted a kiss on his forehead. "I don't know what's keeping David."

"His camel must have run out of gas," Dad joked. He patted Cleo's shoulder. "Don't worry, I'm sure your fella has a good explanation."

"He's not my fella, Dad. We're just friends."

"Why sure you are." Dad winked. "I'll give your mother your respects."

Cleo's visit had gone fairly well so far, if you didn't count

Mother's insistence she be a fourth at Mahjong when one of her friends couldn't make the weekly game. What was the point of being in Petra if you spent hours indoors fiddling with tiles? She looked up the incredible height of the stone-carved Treasury, its rosy pediments and ornamentation well-preserved in spite of the local idiots who'd fired bullets into it looking for legendary treasure. Tourists from everywhere flocked to Petra, one of the New Seven Wonders of the World according to the mortal agency UNESCO.

"Hey, hi!"

She spun around. "David!"

His hair sprang in every direction and his grin stretched from ear to ear. Without thought, Cleo wrapped him in a hug. After a thrilling moment of entanglement, David stepped back.

"Wow." He looked as dizzy as she felt. "Sorry I'm late. My lameness with Arabic kind of screwed things up. The driver thought I wanted to go to some sacred cave. Cool, though, walking down the passage to get here." He pointed back to the towering walls of rock that formed the rose-hued sandstone gorge.

"The Siq," she said, studying him. By Zeus, David looked good. Lean, tan, shaving gone by the wayside. Cleo struggled to collect her wits. "Welcome to Petra. Look." She pointed. "The Treasury, in person."

His tilted back his head. "Wow!"

A crazy impulse to mess up his hair beyond its natural chaotic state seized her. Cleo wished for the millionth time she had the nerve to confess her feelings. She longed to pounce on him, an urge that had escalated in the weeks they'd been apart.

"Come on." She tugged his elbow. "Mother doesn't like to be kept waiting."

A new kind of nervousness rose in Cleo. She'd neglected to tell David the Petra summer home was a mansion, carved into a charm-protected region behind The Treasury. Hopefully he'd enjoy the little bit of magic required to pass through the portal, hidden from mortal eyes. And hopefully he'd have a sense of humor when he learned they were a kind of royalty. Secrecy about her origins had been Dad's one condition for letting Cleo move to the City of Mount Olympus and earn her own keep.

~ * ~

"Wow!" said David, for about the hundredth time since he'd arrived in Petra. They stood in a vast entry hall, impressive enough for a palace.

They'd slipped through from the mortal world using a magical portal, something he'd grown accustomed to in his new immortal life. The tip of his nose throbbed, fiery and tender; a well-documented consequence some travelers suffered when passing from one world to the other.

"That burn looks painful," Cleo said. "Let me find something for it. Won't be a minute."

She darted through a side archway he hadn't noticed. Alone in the hall, David noted the central staircase flanked by two rows of statuary, the sunbeams that illuminated it falling through skylights. Torches in wall brackets were unlit, must provide light when darkness fell. He looked closer. "Wow." The room, the staircase and the statues were all carved out of the same rock, everything joined in one piece. "Wow."

"Here I am." Cleo entered from a different archway than the one she'd disappeared through, a green, dripping spike in her hand. "What do you think? About this place, I mean."

"It must have taken centuries to do the carving," he said, "especially when you consider the tools available at the time."

"Oh, you'd be surprised," she said lightly. "Hold still and I'll treat your nose."

A coat of vegetable goo cooled the burn on contact.

"Thanks. So...."

He wanted to ask how her family could afford this place but couldn't think of words that wouldn't sound vulgar.

"So?" She glanced at the staircase and back at him. "What do you think?"

"Uh, it's quite a place."

"Yeah." She shrugged her shoulders, like she was apologizing for something. "Come on, I'll introduce you to my parents."

Side by side, sandal soles slapping the stairs, they ascended. A long corridor stretched before them with half a dozen archways on either side.

"Guest rooms," Cleo said. She stopped at the first archway. "You can put your things in here."

The room was four times the size of his apartment at Athens

U and had an archway in one corner.

"Private bath. Mother insisted on indoor plumbing, praise Zeus." Cleo walked toward the massive bed; a powerful and pleasing sensation jolted through his body. She gestured at a wide embroidered sash hanging next to the carved bed frame. "If you need something, here's the bell."

Servants? Well, duh. Who could run a place like this without servants? David set his backpack and suitcase on the bed, his head swimming. Cleo had never hinted she was anything but a hardworking and ambitious small-g. He'd known for years she was much more than a pretty face, but.... He sagged against a bedpost.

"David? Are you okay?"

She grabbed his shoulders, steadying him.

"Uh, fine, yeah. Not acclimated to being indoors after all the sun, I guess."

"We're running really late, but maybe you'd better rest for a while, before you meet my folks?" Cleo eased him onto the bed. Her face was flushed, probably from all the fussing she'd had to do since he'd arrived.

"I don't want to be any trouble." He sat up so abruptly his nose almost bumped hers.

Eye to eye, they were suspended in silence. Cleo buried her fingers in his hair. Overwhelmed, David wrapped his arms around her and pulled her into the deepest kiss of his life. She fell right in.

Centuries seemed to pass before they broke apart. David was as stunned as if he'd been hit over the head with a two-by-four, and Cleo looked...wow....

"I, uh, I'll let my parents know you're here. As soon as you're ready, come to the end of the hall and turn right." She looked him up and down, her smile loopy. "Mother will appreciate it if you wear a toga to dinner."

Cleo scurried away, leaving him to ponder what had happened. Was their kiss real, was this place even real? He staggered to the bathroom and splashed water on his face. Most of his trip was scheduled for the mortal world so he'd only brought one toga. He fished the wrinkled linen garment from the bottom of his suitcase and pulled the bell cord in the fervent hope a valet could press it into a condition that would satisfy Mrs. Petra.

~ * ~

David touched a fingertip to the staunched nick on his chin. He'd cut himself shaving, then been chastised by the valet who'd come for his toga ("Not of the best quality," the man had sniffed when he'd taken it away for pressing). When the valet returned with the toga, not only pressed but scented with rose water, he provided David with terse directions to the great room. Presentable and on edge, David began his journey down the long hallway. A heaviness descended on him. He felt as tense as Dorothy Gale walking the hallway toward her first meeting with the Wizard of Oz.

Mr. Petra, a stout man with a warm smile, greeted him at the great room archway. He gripped David's hand and pumped it a couple of times. "David, my boy! Cleo's told us so much about you."

"Nice to meet you, sir."

"None of this 'sir' business, David, just call me Peter." Mr. Petra lowered his voice to a whisper. "Don't let Titania worry you," he said, nodding his head to the right. "She's a real softie, once you get to know her."

David looked to the side. Across the room stood Cleo and a steely-eyed matron who did not appear soft in any way. Mrs. Petra's shoulders were square, her back ramrod straight, her impressive nose sited down as if it were attached to a rifle. Peter Petra chuckled and propelled David forward with a palm between his shoulder blades.

Cleo, dressed in a formal evening toga, smiled apologetically.

"Mother, this is my friend, David Bernstein. David, this is Titania Petra."

David stood under the hard gaze of Cleo's mother. A cold hand with long fingers enveloped his.

"Charmed, I'm sure," she said, though she didn't look it.

"Nice to meet you, Mrs. Petra," he said with barely a shiver. Was it possible Cleo would one day resemble this maternal monolith? "Thank you for having me as your guest."

Mr. Petra clamped a hand on David's shoulder. "It's the least we can do for a friend of Cleo's. Care for a drink before dinner?"

Peter Petra's face beamed with goodwill. Titania's scowl deepened. David looked to Cleo for the answer to this riddle.

"Let us fix the drinks, Dad." Cleo took David's elbow and escorted him to a mirrored wet bar tucked into an alcove.

"Sorry," she said. She took a cocktail shaker from the mini fridge under the bar, poured in a double shot of vodka and two drops of vermouth. "They have mixed messages down to an art. You can fix Mother's glass, it's in the fridge. She likes two olives, on a toothpick."

It never ceased to amaze David how adaptable immortals were to contemporary mortal customs. Almost everyone he'd met since moving to the City of Mount Olympus knew what twenty-first century mortals ate and drank and many made a hobby of adopting the current trends. Dionysus had explained it to him once: *It helps to pass the time.*

"What does your Dad take?"

"Scotch and soda, light on the soda."

David reached for a square whiskey glass on the shelf behind the bar. "Ice?"

"Neat, thanks. Fill it to the top."

"You?"

"Oh!" She stopped shaking the martini. By Zeus, he'd kiss her a good one if parental eyes weren't on them. "I could use a little something, I guess," she stammered.

"Wine?" he suggested, pulling the nearest bottle from a tall, well-stocked rack. "Oh, but maybe not this one," he said after recognizing the label. It was the highest priced bottle on the Club Dionysus wine list, the stuff people who didn't like champagne ordered for special occasions.

"You don't like it?" Cleo said. "It's from the family vineyard. Dad's been working on this varietal for millennia. It's really very good. We even have a few collectors who buy a case now and then."

Reassured he wasn't plundering something rare, David poured them each a glass and set it on the tray with the other drinks. Cleo whisked up the tray and headed back to Mr. and Mrs. Petra, now seated opposite each other on matching sofas that framed an unlit fireplace. David tried not to stare at Cleo's swishing hips. Today he'd learned a staggering amount of new information, things he'd never suspected. Cleo was not only beautiful, extremely intelligent and hard-working, she was also rich, the kind of girl who lived in a mansion, dressed for dinner and drank the best wine on Earth as casually as if it were bulk-market swill. Who, exactly, was Cleo Petra? Why had she consumed him with her kiss? When would he get another?

~ * ~

Cleo eyed her dinner companions, looking for evidence her parents and David were capable of getting along for eternity. Dad asked David about his travels. They were comparing notes on the Herodium, the last site David had visited before coming to Petra.

"Amazing place," Dad said. "Leave it to Herod the Great to build a hill, hollow it out and build a city in it. Do you think it's true he's buried there?"

David said there was evidence both ways. Dad shifted the conversation to his recollections of the first time he, himself, had visited the full-scale model of the completely intact Parthenon at Athens U.

"Not very manly to admit this," Dad said, winking at Cleo, "but when I saw the statue of Athena towering above me, I wept."

"Honestly, Peter." Mother glared at Dad as if he were something presented on a slide under a microscope, but Dad just smiled.

David's table manners were good, though the plethora of forks flanking his plate had him watching her for clues. Mother had insisted on a seven-course meal. Cook and her assistant (with the help of every modern kitchen appliance in existence) had slaved all day, from quail eggs to pomegranate ganache. The waiters in attendance seemed to distract David. His head and shoulders turned as if he felt the impulse to help them. Mother's eyes tracked his fidgets with disapproval.

Dinner ended at last. Dad thanked Mother for the meal and led the way to the sofas for after dinner drinks. He poured brandy, distilled from the best of the family wine, for each of them and gestured for David to sit beside him.

"David, my boy, you may be wondering about the Petra family history."

David darted a glance at Cleo. "Sir?"

Cleo set her brandy snifter on an end table and gripped the edge of the sofa she shared with Mother.

"My wife is obviously of very good family," Dad raised his glass to Mother, "but we Petras were humble people until a little incident near the Sea of Kinneret. What's the new name for it?"

"Galilee," Cleo said. Her fingernails dug deeper into the cushion.

David's expression brightened. "I've been there."

"The Petras weren't up to much in those days." Dad grinned. "Hunting, gathering, fishing like the rest of the mortals. My dear mother, may she rest in peace, was busy on the lakeshore, cleaning the fish her brothers had caught, and, well…" he laughed "…a pretty young girl working near a body of water in those days. I'm sure you can guess what happened."

Cleo closed her eyes to avoid the confused look David shot her.

"Sir?"

David had said more than once that immortal morals were hard for him to accept. The promiscuity of gods Big and small upset him, as did the fact everyone seemed to be related.

"Poseidon," Dad said, his smile wide. "He's my father. Our tribal priest said immortality rarely resulted in the child of a mortal and immortal union, but I was an exception. And, being the son of one of the Twelve Great Olympians, this lovely lady," Dad waved a hand in Mother's direction, "agreed to be my wife. What do you say to that?"

Fearing the worst, Cleo opened her eyes. David had sunk deep into the sofa, his jaw slack.

"That's right, my boy, you and I are cousins!"

TueSOAy, AUGUST 26, 2025

David

David excused himself from last night's conversation shortly after he learned Peter Petra was his cousin. Dazed, he walked the long hall to his room. No matter how he looked at it, Cleo was his first cousin at one remove, just like Monique.

He ruminated over his one-night stand with Aphrodite's daughter. Was it really the cousin thing that bothered him, or was it that he'd slept with her without knowing or caring much about her? It was different with Cleo. It had to be different with Cleo. His dreams that night pirated a scene from the Spencer Tracey movie *Dr. Jekyll and Mr. Hyde*, the part where Tracey drives a coach and the two horses' heads change to Ingrid Bergman and Lana Turner, only it was Cleo and Monique.

Now it was morning. He had to face all three Petras. David showered and dressed with reluctance. It was bad enough Cleo hadn't told him about her family. She knew how he felt about incest. Why hadn't she mentioned they were related? He tried to sort out feelings of anger and betrayal that jostled alongside yesterday's incredible kiss. Since the moment he'd met her he'd wanted to be more than friends, but this cousin thing, it was—

Someone knocked at the archway.

"Breakfast is served, Mr. Bernstein," said a male voice. In this place, it was probably a footman or something.

"Coming."

The walk down the hall gave him time to replay his insecurities. Nothing irrevocable had happened between him and Cleo. Would he love her more—or less—once he forgave her for keeping her secret?

He passed into the great room. Cleo, her back to him, served herself from the dining area sideboard. His heart thudded.

Mr. and Mrs. Petra were seated at the dining table. "Sorry I'm late."

"You got away from us before I went over the house rules," Peter Petra said. "They must have worn you out in Israel, you were so eager to get to bed."

These last words came as Cleo turned around. Her eyes were downcast.

Great. Now what do I do?

David approached the sideboard and loaded a plate with bacon, eggs, toast and hash browns, wondering if the Petras always ate like this or if Cleo had arranged the breakfast menu especially for him.

"Orange juice?" Mrs. Petra passed him a crystal pitcher filled with the stuff.

"Thanks."

"Did you sleep well?" Peter said.

David glanced at Cleo, who studied her untouched plate.

"Yes, thank you, sir."

"So, Cleo," Peter said, "what are you kids up to today, checking out the ruins?"

"If David wants to," she said, looking at her dad.

"Of course he wants to." Peter winked at David. "It's all you've talked about this past week, how much he'll enjoy seeing the place."

"Cook has been fussing over a picnic lunch for the two of you," Mrs. Petra added, her expression arch. "It isn't often she gets the chance to concoct mortal favorites."

Mr. Petra scraped up the last of his eggs. "Good stuff, this. Cleo tells us mortal cuisine is all the rage in Big-G City."

"Sir?"

"That's what Dad calls the City of Mount Olympus," Cleo said, speaking at last.

"Haven't been there in millennia, myself." Peter Petra pushed away his empty plate. "Cleo tells me Poseidon still works at Olympus, Inc. He doesn't know about her, of course. Being his granddaughter, I mean." Cleo looked at David with an expression he couldn't read. "We insisted she not tell anyone about her family connections. That was our one condition when she told us she wanted to go to college and work in Mount Olympus. We wanted her to rise on her own merits."

David let out a breath and Cleo smiled. She'd probably wanted to tell him but wouldn't break her promise to her parents.

He dug into his bacon and eggs, thinking. The fact of Cleo's secret was one thing, but the content of it was another. They were cousins. How long, if ever, would it take for him to accept the Olympian customs surrounding intimate relationships? Would he ever feel less like a mortal and more like a god?

~ * ~

It was definitely shorts weather. Cleo wiped her sweating palms on her khakis as she trudged in the lead past a four-tiered structure of sandstone tombs called the Street of Facades. Everything she'd shown David so far was a tomb, including the misnamed Treasury where he'd lingered to admire the exterior. "Wow!" he'd said, interlaced with remarks about the Egyptian influence in the architecture. She'd visited the Treasury hundreds of times. Today, what impressed her most was that it offered shade.

"Come on." She headed north of the site. Her sneakers were so hot it felt as if they were melting. "Stop rubbernecking the tombs, we're almost there." Her words came out bitchy, but she didn't care, it was so hot. The predicted high of 35 Celsius had surely been surpassed.

When the Theatre came into view, David said, "Wow!" He wandered toward the tiers of semi-circular seating, but she grabbed his arm and pulled him into the shade of an entrance portal.

"You can admire the auditorium from here," she said, sitting on a large, cool piece of fallen stone. "I'm starving."

They shrugged off their packs and pulled out the flat boxes Cook had filled for them.

"Wow! Cold pizza. My favorite."

Was there anything David experienced that didn't make him say Wow? She lifted a slice of pizza from her box lunch, noting the rest of the contents: grapes from the family vineyard, chocolate chip cookies and commercially bottled tea.

"I can't get over the rose color of the stone," David said between bites. "It's a lot like some places I've seen in Utah. They're not so big on tombs there, though."

Cleo sipped her tea, her spirits rehydrating. "I'd like to see Utah some time."

"Hah!"

"No, I mean it," she said. "I've never been to America."

David stopped chewing. "None of it?"

"No. Mother thinks the only things worth seeing are in the Eastern Hemisphere."

"Your mom's from a really important family, isn't she?"

Cleo waved a hand to dismiss the subject. "She's some kind of royalty. We don't talk about it much."

"So," he said, looking thoughtful, "you're some kind of royalty, too?"

"Sure. I guess."

This time, he didn't say Wow, just picked up a cookie.

"Your dad, though, he's my first cousin," he said and took a bite.

"Yes."

David's brow furrowed as he chewed.

"The way I figure it," he said, "that makes us first cousins at one remove."

She put her grapes back in the box, appetite gone. "Yes."

He said, "Why didn't you tell me?" at the same time she said, "I wanted to tell you!"

"Is it really such a big deal?" she snapped. "Your uncle is my grandfather. That wouldn't even be taboo for most mortals."

Cleo clapped her hands over her mouth, but the words had already escaped.

"Wow." They sat in silence, looking at each other. Gradually, his lips rumpled into a cautious smile. "Trade you my grapes for your cookie?"

And how could he not smile, Cleo mused. She'd as good as admitted she was in love with him.

~ * ~

David continued to follow Cleo, though he was tempted to walk beside her and take her hand. He grinned so hard it hurt. Cleo had romantic feelings for him! The cousin thing continued to bug him, though.

They stopped and stood side by side, admiring another Hellenistic-style burial place. "One thing's for sure, they built these tombs to last."

"Hard not to, since they're carved in the cliffs," Cleo said.

David studied her out of the corner of his eye. She hadn't smiled or said much since they'd left the Theatre.

"Did you know any of the people buried here?" he said, to keep her talking.

"Not really. There was a big earthquake when I was little. They didn't use the tombs much after that. My parents knew some of them, of course."

Peter Petra is my cousin. He couldn't get it out of his mind, but logic was clearing an inroad to David's mortal morals. Cleo wasn't a child he was taking advantage of. She was a few centuries older than him and a lot more sophisticated. Maybe if he—

The scuffle of feet edging toward them broke his thoughts. Before he realized what was happening, they were attacked. Cleo was on the ground underneath one of them. Someone behind David wrenched off his pack.

"Help!"

Cleo's cry echoed off the cliffs.

David, free for a second, glanced around. Except for their attackers, they were alone. The man on top of Cleo tore open her blouse. Two other men lurched toward him.

Adrenaline coursed through David's limbs. He started swinging, couldn't remember anything Milton Bernstein had taught him about how to fight. One of the men, who was missing his front teeth, landed a solid punch in David's gut. He doubled over and dropped to his knees. Cleo's screams rang in his ears, but he was helpless to save her. His eyes were tearing with pain when he remembered and spoke the words Hera had taught him. Invisible under Biggest of Big-G cloaking, he staggered behind Cleo's attacker who was hunched over her and kicked him in the nuts.

"Aiiiiieeeeee!" The man fell over on his side. His companions, who had drawn close to the scene, backed away, talking heatedly in a language David didn't understand. Cleo lay on the ground, trembling. He knelt beside her and whispered in her ear.

"You okay?"

She flinched, her eyes darting toward him.

"Cleo, it's me, David. Stay still. I'll get rid of them."

The man who'd attacked Cleo had struggled to his feet. The three thugs were arguing with each other. One of David's attackers gestured at Cleo, his intentions plain. Now David remembered what Milton Bernstein had taught him. He forked the other two jerks and landed his fist on their noses when they doubled over.

He returned to Cleo and grabbed her hand. "Get up, quick, and no matter what happens, don't let go."

David strained to get airborne. They flew slowly, about ten feet above the ground, Cleo visible and wobbling alongside him. Their attackers looked up at Cleo in flight, shrieked and disappeared into the tombs.

"Do you know how to fly?"

"A little," she said, sniffling.

He coached her on how to distribute her weight for optimal buoyancy and they rose a few feet higher. Fortunately, Cleo went unobserved by the other tourists as these had taken refuge from the searing afternoon sun. In little time they'd retraced their route. No one was in the gorge of the Siq, the passageway he'd come down yesterday. David landed between the rosy stone cliffs and spoke the words to uncloak.

"Oh, David!"

Cleo threw her arms around him, sagged against him and cried. He held her close and rubbed her back.

"You saved me from…" she said between ragged sobs.

"Is everything okay?"

"Just a few bruises, I think, nothing worse." Cleo shuddered. "They said they were going to kill us, David. For whatever was in our packs."

He wiped away her tears with his fingertips. "You know they can't kill us."

"No, but they could maim us or disfigure us, or—"

"Try not to think about it."

They walked in silence, past the Treasury and around to the Petra mansion's hidden entrance. This time passing from the mortal to immortal world didn't singe his nose. Cleo was still trembling. Sand caked her hair. She held her blouse closed with one hand. He escorted her down the long hallway to the family rooms and turned back toward his distant guest room.

"Will you come in with me, to my room?" She blinked back a tear. "Please? I know it's silly, but I don't want to be alone right now."

Her suite was decorated with Turkish carpets, carved rosewood furniture, silk hangings and a curtained, generously proportioned bed. A dining area and a den were visible through two arches.

"Sit wherever you want." She disappeared behind a door, to the bathroom he supposed.

David sank into a carved chair as tall as a throne. The soft tapestry-covered cushions cradled his back. Every muscle ached. As adrenaline ebbed away a flow of confidence replaced it. He'd saved Cleo. He was no longer her goofy half-mortal pet. For once, he'd acted like a god instead of just a guy.

~ * ~

Cleo changed her tourist clothes for a summer toga. She brushed her hair until her scalp felt tender, though a few tenacious grains of sand remained. Her heart still pounded from near-rape and proposed murder, but she was now calm enough to put on a good face. David reluctantly agreed to keep the story from her parents.

He'd gone to his own room to change for dinner. Mother would certainly notice David had only one toga with him but Cleo could care less. She'd loved him before the rescue; now she adored him.

David was sitting with Mother and Dad in the cocktail area when she arrived. He looked at her with concern, but she dismissed it with a smile.

"Your dad was telling me he used to work for the Romans as a census-taker."

"More of a hobby," Dad said with a shrug. "You were too little to remember, Cleo. It was during the reign of Herod and sons. That family was Tartarus on wheels for building things."

David laughed but Cleo detected an underlying seriousness in his eyes. She stepped behind the bar and poured herself a glass of wine.

"I feel like I looked at every artifact in Israel, sir." David said. "I saw the Dead Sea Scrolls and some other records but there wasn't anything described as a census."

"Hah!" Dad drained his cocktail and signaled Cleo to make him another. "They took them to Rome. Didn't trust the local governors to calculate the taxes. Took a shipment to Rome myself, once."

"That's very interesting, sir."

"Don't get him started on his travel stories, young man," Mother said. "He'll keep you up all night."

"Here, Dad." Cleo handed Dad his drink and sat beside David, close but not as close as she wanted. Something had shifted between them this afternoon, a sense of protectiveness he'd shown when he'd hugged her and stood on his toes to kiss her forehead before he'd gone back to his room.

"Where in Rome, sir?"

"Some administrator's office or other," Dad said. "I imagine they've been destroyed by now, or at least archived somewhere."

"Did you count everybody in every household?" said David.

"Certainly did! Slaves, of course, were recorded by age and sex only. Typical mortal protocol. But we wrote up the men, the free ones that is, in detail. Name, age, occupation," he said, counting off categories on his fingers. "Wealth, religion, other things, too."

David was quiet after that. Mother changed the subject to Veronica and Clifford's engagement.

"They'll have the standard engagement period, I trust?"

"Thirty years," Cleo said.

Mother sniffed. "That's on the short side. Has she asked you to be her maid of honor?"

Cleo glanced at David. "Mother, please!"

"You are her closest confident, I'm sure, after your time as her assistant. Certainly, if she knew about your family connections, she'd—"

"Mother!"

"I don't think it would matter to Veronica, Mrs. Petra," David said, saving her. "Her big deal is recognizing people for their own merit."

"And how would you…oh, yes." Mother turned a gimlet eye on David. "I'd forgotten. You're her brother."

Mother warmed considerably to David that evening, laughing at his stories and offering him seconds of every dish. When after-dinner drinks had concluded she insisted David take a bottle of brandy back to his room for his later enjoyment. Cleo said a firm good night for both of them and escorted David down the hall.

"Wow," he said, once they were out of her parents' hearing. "Your mom is really into rank, isn't she?"

Cleo sighed. "I suppose she can't help it with her upbringing, but honestly, it's embarrassing sometimes. I hope you won't hold it against her."

"Not likely," he said, raising the bottle of brandy. They stopped in front of her door. "Can I come in for a minute? There's something I want to ask you."

A thrill rushed through her. Heaven and Earth, was he going to talk about love?

"Sure." She led him to the den and motioned him to sit on the sofa. David took two glasses from the low table in front of him. He poured two brandies and handed one to her.

"I don't know how long your parents plan to have me. They're great and everything, but when you think it's okay for me to leave, would you like come to Rome?"

WeDNeSDAY, SePTeMBeR 3, 2025

The Underworld
Hades

"Anatole?"

Hades hadn't heard Anatole's footfalls for a while. He looked around. Toward the palace from where they'd set out, his valet had stopped, his head bent over the leak monitoring device. Hades retraced his steps.

"Problem?"

"Yes, sir." Anatole shook the detector and held it to his ear. "It won't boot up, sir. I fear we shall have to conduct our reconnaissance manually."

Hades glanced at the light gray sky above and the pale blue glow ahead. "Nice day for it anyway. Let's get a move on."

The King of the Underworld had saved his least favorite location for last. Mortals, of course, longed to spend eternity in Elysium with its rolling green lawns and bounteous orchards but the neighborhood depressed Hades. It was too much like the upper world; too light, too bright, too cheerful.

The path between the palace and Elysium was short, an hour's journey. Anatole hadn't even packed a lunch. All too soon, birdsong filled Hades' ears. They sang every minute of every day, the souls of departed birds, because there was no sun to go down. Unrelieved blue sky overtook the gray. The fragrance of apples, ready for picking, perfumed the air.

Hades spotted the Macedonian nun, name of Teresa, sitting on the grass with her back against a tree. She spoke to a group of newcomers seated on the soft, green turf. Her soul glistened in its robes of white trimmed with blue. Everybody in Elysium loved her. It was like that here.

Yawning at the tedium of so much goodness, Hades nodded in response to her enthusiastic wave and moved on. He surveyed all that lay around him for signs of a breach.

"Sky clear, grass green, apples ripe," he said to Anatole, who walked alongside him taking notes on a pad. "Population…" Hades turned in a circle, making a rough count in his mind "…thin but average." Sometimes souls from Elysium were reincarnated and the number of occupants fell.

"Shall we visit the arborist, sir?"

"Good thinking, Anatole." The arborist managed Elysium and supervised the lawn care workers. She was observant and kept meticulous records. If anyone had noticed a breach, it would be her.

The arborist's shed, a small house agleam with windows, was in the middle of the orchard. Hades rapped on the door. It was answered by a lovely being, not a soul but a Big-G Goddess of another tribe.

"Hello, Freya."

"Hades." She smiled and shook his hand.

Freya, a northern Goddess much like Aphrodite but without the bite, had come to Elysium centuries ago. She'd grown bored with her duties in Folkvangr, the Norse field of the afterlife. The dull task of choosing half of those who'd fallen in battle and leaving the other half for Odin's kingdom, Valhalla, had been easily delegated. Freya had exchanged her regal trappings for overalls and never looked back.

She stepped out and closed the shed door behind her. "It's good to see you. What brings you to Elysium?"

"Security issues," he whispered.

Her silvery laugh made the leaves rustle. "Walk with me and I'll show you some hybrids I'm experimenting with. You can tell me about your issues on the way."

They walked side-by-side, Anatole bringing up the rear, through rows upon rows of fruit-burdened apple, plum and cherry trees. Freya listened without comment as Hades rehashed his worries about gatecrashers and lost revenue. When he was finished they walked on in silence.

"This is the hybrid I especially wanted you to see." Freya paused beside a tree with bright red, perfectly round fruit. "It's cherry, crossed with apple." Freya plucked one of the fruits. She extracted a small knife from her bib pocket, sliced the orb in half, removed the pit and handed the halves to Hades and Anatole. Hades took a bite. A juicy, sweet yet tart sensation burst in his mouth.

"The best characteristics of both and they make excellent pies.

I'll send a bushel to the castle for you."

He thanked her and asked if she'd noticed anything unusual, security-wise, in her sector.

"I've been stalling for time to think," she said, matter-of-factly. "Every year I do a budget analysis, comparing the average number of souls in Elysium to the amount of fruit consumed. The mortals now eat more than they used to, so I've ignored a small but steady upward variance in consumption per soul."

"Or possibly unauthorized souls are hiding out in here, eating the fruit?"

"It's possible." Freya's brow furrowed. "We're on the honor system here. We don't check IDs or anything like that. I'll ask Teresa about it, if you don't mind. She's our volunteer who handles intake."

The damn cheerful nun. Hades frowned. "Whatever you think is best. If you uncover anything, let me know."

With that, he and Anatole walked the perimeter, looking for holes, cracks or tunnels. Nothing. Hades' stomach rumbled. "I think we've done all we can here, Anatole."

They trod over green lawn, headed back toward the castle. "Sir?"

Anatole stood like a dog at point, his gaze fixed on the center of the blue dome.

"Yes?"

"There, sir." He pointed. "A faded patch."

"Heaven and Earth," Hades swore. A spot of white blemished the pale blue. One more item for the deferred maintenance list.

Friday, September 5, 2025

City of Mount Olympus
Monique

Monique sat across from Aphrodite in the Love, Inc., board room. She pointed at a graph on the table between them. Her finger traced a steep upward line.

"The change has been dramatic, even in three weeks," she said, beaming. "Marriage and the Media is buying gift bag components as quickly as we can make them. If this trend continues, I can see us expanding costume production. The other items can be outsourced, but we want the costumes to be as well-made as possible, not like the cheap, itchy stuff you find in mortal erotica stores that falls apart the first time it's worn."

Aphrodite smirked. "Since when have you been an expert?"

"Market research," Monique fibbed. She'd mastered lying to Mother ages ago.

"My little pencil-head," Aphrodite said affectionately. "Who in Heaven and Earth would believe you were my daughter?"

"Real estate is at a premium, of course," said Monique, steering her mother back to the subject at hand. "There's a lot of unused space in the mansion now. What do you think about converting some of the old counseling rooms into production space?"

Aphrodite frowned. "Not very glamorous to have small-g worker bees coming in and out of the place."

"Your property backs on a street," Monique said. "We can put in a rear entrance. Think about it, anyway."

Aphrodite removed her pink rhinestone readers and slumped in her chair.

"Mother?"

"Honestly, Monique, I'm five thousand years old. I'm not sure how hard I want to work on this."

Were the dark circles under Mother's eyes new or had she, unbelievably, forgotten to use concealer?

"Are you feeling all right?"

"Never better. Just tired of it all."

"But Mother, you've finally done it! You've finally got Hera working with you instead of against you!"

"I know." The Goddess of Love pouted. "Where's the fun in that?"

Aphrodite was spared a lecture on petulance only because Monique experienced a sudden wave of nausea.

"See you next week." Monique tucked papers into her briefcase, loped down the grand staircase and strode out of the mansion. Given Aphrodite's lukewarm attitude toward success, no wonder Monique felt like she was going to vomit.

Tuesday, September 9, 2025

Rome, Italy
David

Morning, their first full day in Rome, and David could kill for a coffee. He spotted Cleo, waving vigorously from a table in the middle of the bustling hotel dining room. Her cheeks were flushed. A list was in her hand.

"I know you'll love all the sights, even if we have to wait in line for some of them," she said, without saying good morning.

David dropped onto the chair across from her. In spite of Cleo's enthusiasm, the trip wasn't going well. Not the way he'd hoped, anyway.

"The Colosseum is a must-see," she blathered. "Don't you know someone who worked there as a structureling?"

David's stomach grumbled. "Ralph, Clifford's dad."

Cleo's mother had insisted they book separate rooms, a plan they'd privately agreed wouldn't make any difference once they escaped Petra. That agreement had changed. Last night was supposed to be their first night together. They checked into their separate rooms and he'd ordered champagne sent to his. Cleo arrived. They drank, talked, teased. If she hadn't lured him into revealing who it was she'd heard in his sleeping alcove that morning in June…. She'd stormed off before they even got started.

"There's the Sistine Chapel," her finger moved down the list, "and St. Peter's Basilica—"

"Speaking of Peter," David said, taking Cleo's hand so she'd look at him, "we can't forget our appointment with your dad's friend who knows about the census archives."

The expression in her eyes hardened. She pulled her hand away. "Of course we'll see Uncle Massimo. Tomorrow." She returned to the list. "We definitely have to see the Spanish Steps and Trevi Fountain."

David flagged down a waiter. "Do we have to do it all today?"

"Just coffee for me," Cleo said to the waiter.

David said, "I want the biggest breakfast you serve, whatever it is."

"He wants coffee, too."

True, but the way she cut in irritated him. What were they, an old married couple who finished each other's sentences? They hadn't even slept together and she was getting bossy.

Breakfast arrived on a platter—fresh fruit, an assortment of cheeses, hard sausage and a loaf of bread. Cleo picked off his plate, which also bugged him. If she wanted something to eat she should have ordered it.

Cleo proved a relentless tour guide. The Colosseum, the Roman Forum, the Pantheon all swept by in an architectural blur. Each site was packed with tourists. Dozens of languages filled David's ears, adding to his disorientation. It was late afternoon when they approached Trevi Fountain.

"Oh, look, it's—"

David grabbed Cleo's hand and tugged her to the nearest sidewalk café. "It'll still be here in half an hour," he groused, hot, tired and starving.

"Well," she said when they found a table, "you're no fun."

"We're immortal, we don't have to see it all in one day!"

He felt bad when she pouted, bad enough to order champagne. After he'd devoured a plate of Spaghetti Grande, he apologized.

"Whatever," she said.

The food and wine gradually worked its magic. They took a leisurely stroll in front of the fountain and compared the statue of Ocean to Poseidon.

"Of course the Romans had to rename him," said Cleo. "They never could resist fixing things that weren't broken. That's what Dad says, anyway."

"Still, it's a pretty amazing installation." David lingered at the pool's edge, admiring the animation in the carved winged horses that burst from the sea.

Cleo held out a coin in the palm of her hand. "Want to?"

"Huh?"

She smiled. "It's a superstition. If you turn around and throw a coin over your left shoulder with your right hand, it means you'll return to Rome one day."

"Sure. Okay." He rummaged a coin out of his jeans pocket,

closed his eyes and listened for the coin to hit the water, along with his wish that they'd find evidence about his father when they met with Cleo's Uncle Massimo.

~ * ~

When Cleo and David returned to their hotel, the concierge handed Cleo an envelope. It contained a note from Uncle Massimo and two tickets for a tour of some crypts.

"More sightseeing?" David groaned.

She scanned the note. "He says it's his way of getting us in the right frame of mind."

"The right frame of mind for what?"

"Oh brother." She took David's hand and guided him into the hotel bar. "You need an attitude adjustment." He'd been a pill all day. Cleo ordered a bottle of wine and Antipasto Grande. She'd always known David had an appetite, but lately she'd come to think of him as a bottomless pit.

WeöNesöay, SepTeMBeR 10, 2025

Cleo

En route to the crypts the next morning, Cleo ducked into a pasticceria and bought David a bag of pastries, in case of emergency.

"Very funny," he said, but he polished them off while they waited for their tour bus.

Soon an extra-long van with 'Bump in the Night' written on the side in gothic lettering pulled up to the curb. The front doors opened with a hiss. The driver grinned. "Crypts?"

The driver stopped for pick-ups at half a dozen locations. He announced sites of interest over the intercom and regularly mentioned his wife and six children. Each of the twenty or so tourists tipped him when they arrived at their destination, a side entrance to the church of Santa Maria della Concezione dei Cappuccini.

They waited several minutes outside a black iron gate. Cleo had assumed Uncle Massimo would meet them here, but no one matching his description (very tall and of her father's generation) appeared. David struck up a conversation with a couple who looked about forty in mortal years. They were Americans, from a state called Kansas. The woman of the couple squeezed the man's arm and squealed, "I just can't believe we're on this tour. Doesn't it just give you the creeps?"

The thought intrigued her. Mortals would, of course, have personal feelings about death, burial and remains. To Cleo, a crypt was just another interesting antiquity.

At last the well-oiled gate opened without a squeak. The guide, a twentyish mortal woman, dressed in jeans and a polo shirt with the company logo printed on the breast, came forth. She clapped her hands to get their attention.

"Welcome to Bump in the Night Travels and our English-speaking tour of the world's finest crypts."

Her sharp, nasal accent was American, probably New York according to David though he said he'd never been there.

"Our tour runs one hour and fifteen minutes. Photographs are prohibited."

The guide shepherded them through the side door and led them down a dimly lit staircase. She explained the friars had arrived at the church in 1631, with 300 cartloads of deceased friars from their old monastery. Space was at a premium, so over the years the longest buried were exhumed to make room for the newly deceased. The new bodies spent about thirty years decomposing before they were exhumed. The skeletal remains were then used to decorate five of the six rooms in the crypt. The guide pointed her flashlight at a placard in five languages that read: *What you are now, we once were; what we are now, you shall be.* The smell of decay was palpable.

"Wow," David said as they passed down the dank corridor. Its vast side openings looked on to rooms decorated with human bones. One crypt highlighted skulls, another pelvises, a third leg and thigh bones, formed into macabre images and tableaux. A few complete skeletons in friars' robes punctuated the designs. In the Crypt of the Three Skeletons the center skeleton, the guide explained, was enclosed in an oval as a symbol of life and rebirth. It held a scythe in one hand and the scales of justice in the other, each formed of bones. The skeleton was so small it must have belonged to a child. Cleo felt a pang of sadness. A mortal of any age could die of course, but, with children, it was strangely moving.

"Wow," David said when they ascended from the crypt to the gift store. "I've gotta buy some postcards." Cleo said she'd meet him outside.

The sky had lifted from gray to pale blue. The streets bustled with small automobiles. Exhaust clogged the air, so different than when she'd visited Rome centuries ago. She tried to pick Uncle Massimo out of the sidewalk crowds, wondering what he had planned for them if he considered a tour of the Capuchin Crypts a fitting prequel. When she spotted a tall figure in friar's robes identical to the ones she'd seen on the tour she smiled and waved.

"Massimo! Over here!"

A grin beamed under his hood. Massimo, five thousand-ish and handsomely aged, extended a hand. It covered hers like an oven mitt.

"Cleo. What a woman you've become! So like your mother in her youth. And how is your father?"

The words flew rapidly in Italian and set her brain to vigorous translation. Dad was well, she replied, and sent his greetings.

"And where is your friend, the boy who is looking for his father?"

"David's in there." She tilted her head toward the gift shop, trying to remember the Italian word for postcard. "We loved the tour, Massimo. Thank you so much for sending the tickets."

"Yes." He laughed. "It was my way of preparing you for what's to come."

His robe of brown homespun looked hot. The last time she'd seen him he'd been working as a tax collector for an Italian prince.

"Dad didn't tell me you were a friar."

"Only for a few hundred years," he said with a shrug. "It was my best option for staying close to the records. That's what I—oh, is this the young man?"

David stood beside her, a small paper bag in his hand.

"Massimo, this is my friend, David Bernstein." She switched languages to introduce David to Uncle Massimo.

"Glad to meet you, sir." David looked at Cleo hopefully. She translated.

"Forgive me," said Massimo in slightly accented English. "We only speak Italian in the monastery, but my English is, I think, still passable. And now," he said with a smile, "for another tour!"

Massimo led them to the back of the church. A short metal door was set in the wall.

"Here," he said, "I keep the records your father and I made for the Romans when we were young."

"The census records?" David said, his voice tight.

"From the Herodian Era and a ways beyond," Massimo said. "I've shown them only to immortal scholars before today. Yours is a rare case, the search for your mortal father as I understand it?"

"Yes, sir."

Massimo took a key from his pocket and unlocked the door. He entered first, bent nearly double to accommodate his height, followed by Cleo and David. Massimo clicked on a flashlight and closed the door. He led them down a flight of broad stone stairs and switched on an overhead light at the bottom. It was another crypt, without lavish decoration. Robed skeletons reclined on earthen bunks cut into the walls. In an open space in the middle was an ancient-looking stone table flanked with a half-dozen folding chairs.

"The research room," Massimo said. He gestured to a wooden slat door on the back wall. "Archives this way."

Beyond the wooden door was a room the size of a hotel ballroom, filled with a maze of shelves. The air was drier than in the crypt. The hum of a motor suggested some sort of climate control system had been installed.

"*All* of these are from the Herodian Era?" David said.

"Well." Massimo spread his palms as if apologizing. "I've added a few things here and there. It's become a hobby as well as a vocation. What you want is near the back. Do you know where your father resided?"

"Tiberias, I'm pretty sure."

"Good. That will narrow our search. It was a new city the first few years of CE."

"That's where my mother was staying," David said.

"And she is?"

"Hera."

"Ah, that makes you of noble birth. I remember the villa she occupied. A place fit for a queen. Not far from the mineral baths."

"Herod had a palace there, didn't he? Herod Antipas?" David said. He looked pale. Hungry, Cleo supposed.

"Hah! In those days, he had palaces everywhere. Yes, quite a nice one and every kind of servant you could imagine. One just to fix his hair, another for massage. Guests coming and going all the time, banquets and entertainments most nights he was in residence. Music, dancing, everything you could imagine."

"And Hera?"

"Certainly she entertained, though not on his scale. Not so many servants. For big occasions she could have borrowed some from him or the other wealthy residents. Quite a resort was Tiberias," Massimo said, his voice wistful. He clapped his hands, breaking the spell. "But now for the census records!"

He led them to a floor-to-ceiling shelf, loaded with scrolls.

"Let me see." Massimo pointed at the top shelf and worked his way down. "Here we are, Tiberias census 10 to 30 CE." He handed each of them a scroll and took one for himself. "Parchment, made from animal skins. The Romans favored it over papyrus. More durable than papyrus but care is still due. Back to the research room?"

They unrolled 10 CE across the stone table. Massimo stood between Cleo and David and bent over the scroll. Cleo recognized the text as Latin, all in capital letters.

"Hmmm. Not much here, barely worth the trouble to collect taxes. Roll this one up, please, David. Cleo, hand me the next one."

The 20 CE scroll was longer and more densely written than the first.

"Ah. Now I see some population. Herod was definitely there. I don't remember if he was at the palace yet. There are enough household members to staff a pretty big place."

"What about Hera?" David leaned over the scroll. "I'm not that hot at Latin but this listing says something about Greece, doesn't it?"

"Indeed. The abode of a lady of considerable wealth, leased from Herod himself. Her age is listed as thirty."

"It must not be her, then. She was forty-six hundred when I was born."

"Not so hasty, young man." Massimo laughed and clamped a hand on David's shoulder. "It might be that you don't understand women? They have a tendency to lie about their age. This woman is Hester of Greece, an alias, perhaps?"

Cleo scanned the document, looking for women listed as head of household. "I think you're right, Uncle Massimo. The other two, here and here," she said, pointing, "only have one or two servants and their own children."

"Okay," David said. "We'll assume she lied about her age. Who else is in the household?"

"A husband and wife, twenty-four and twenty-two years of age, servants, with an infant boy, less than two years. Husband's name is Myles, wife Thelma——"

"Bernstein?"

Cleo darted to David's side and put and arm around his shoulders. She could feel him holding his breath.

"No last name given and no name for the boy."

"It has to be them, David's foster parents," Cleo said. "Myles probably changed his name to Milton at some point to modernize it."

"Hmmm." Massimo crossed his arms and tilted his head to one side. "The husband is the shorter of the two?"

David was trembling. "Yes."

"Then I do remember them. She was quite protective of the baby."

Massimo began rolling up the 20 CE scroll.

David lay his hand on Massimo's. "But wait! You were there?"

"Of course." Massimo looked surprised. "Did I forget to mention it?"

"Then—" David's voice cracked with emotion. "Then you must have seen Herod?"

"Certainly I did."

"Do I look anything like him?"

David's words shot out so fast they were almost unintelligible.

Massimo looked quizzically at David for several seconds, then threw his head back and laughed. "Is that what you think? Oh, my dear young man, you look nothing like him, nothing at all. The nose, the eyes, the shape of your head. All wrong."

"But who else was there?" David pushed Massimo's hand from the scroll and hovered over the section listing the Greek woman's household. "Anyone who could be my father?"

The three of them read together, Massimo reading out loud.

"Gardener, male, seventy-nine years of age. Horse master, eunuch. The rest are women."

Cleo tried to remember what the world was like when she was three centuries old. There was something missing from the household…

"Did she have guards? I think we had some then."

"A good point, but no, not listed at her household. Perhaps Herod provided them for her. He sometimes did for people of rank. As a beautiful woman, she would only have had to make the request. Soldiers, extra servants, whatever she wanted."

When they reexamined Herod's household census the listing yielded a dozen potential fathers, aged fourteen to fifty. David wrote their names, ages and occupations on the backs of the postcards he'd purchased at the bookstore. His expression was hard to read.

"It's a start," Cleo said to encourage him.

Massimo rolled up the 20 CE scroll and spread 30 CE on the table.

"One more look for the house of Hester of Greece. Ah, yes, here she is. The married couple are no longer listed, nor is their child. One more thought. We'll look at Herod's household again." Massimo held out a hand to David. "May I see your postcards, please?"

Of the original twelve possible fathers, only five were counted in 30 CE.

"If we apply logic, perhaps we can cull your list down to seven. Do you think it likely your father might have gone with you and the married couple?"

"I don't know," David said. "He might have."

"If so, that would narrow it down to two guards, a cook, a flute player and three personal servants. Think, for a moment. Is there anything else we need to consider before returning the scrolls to the archives?"

"No. Thanks," David said. He looked as if he might cry.

"Won't be a minute." Massimo disappeared with the scrolls. When he returned, the three of them left the crypt.

"Thank you very much, sir." David shook Uncle Massimo's hand. "I'm not sure where to look next, but…"

"It's been quite a day for you, David. Perhaps," Massimo said, looking at Cleo, "this young lady will dream up an entertainment to take your mind off your quest?" He hugged Cleo. "Take care of him," he said in Italian, "and give my best regards to your father."

Massimo walked away. His brown hood disappeared in the crowd.

Cleo took David's hand. "Hungry?"

"Yeah. I guess so." His voice was faint.

"Honest to Zeus, traveling with you is an experience in extremes." She tugged him into a walk. "Let's go someplace where we can sit down and feed you."

They found a restaurant tucked into a tiny building nearby. David wolfed a huge plate of spaghetti with sausages. Cleo picked at a spicy eggplant dish. They split a carafe of red wine. Relaxed, Cleo said, "Did you really think Herod was your father?"

"Herod Antipas," David amended. "Yeah, I kind of did. Who else in Tiberias was as good a match for Hera? I'm glad he's not, though." He leaned back in his chair, hands resting on his stomach. "It would be okay to have a guard or a servant for a father, I guess. Seeing all the bones in the crypt today, though, it kind of brought it home. Whoever he is, he's been dead a long time."

He looked so sad. She scrambled for a change of subject.

"Ever seen the Borgia Apartments?"

He smiled a little. "Only in pictures. Remember the paper I did on them?"

She laughed. "I proof-read it for you before you turned it in. We're not that far from the Vatican Museums, if you can stand one more tourist attraction."

It was one PM when they paid their fee and stood near the entrance, studying a map.

"Fifty-four galleries," Cleo said. "Lots to see before six."

David pointed to a couple of spots. "The Borgia Apartments first, I want to see the frescoes. Maybe the Sistine Chapel after that?"

They managed to squeeze in a visit to the sculpture museums, too. They laughed so hard at the heroic representations of the Greek gods they knew personally they almost got thrown out.

"Wow." David wiped the tears from his eyes. The guard who'd scolded them deepened his scowl. They started laughing again.

"Never mind," said Cleo, waving at the guard. "We're leaving."

The evening was warm, the air alive with voices and traffic. They strolled, uncertain as to the location of their hotel but not at all concerned. Passing through St. Peter's Square, David pointed out architectural components of interest. "Designed by Bernini," he said in a reverent tone. "It's amazing what mortals have achieved."

They crossed the river and continued on foot to take in the local scene. David bought gelato from a street vendor.

"Hungry again?" Cleo said, accepting her cone.

"The next place that looks good for dinner, we're stopping."

Peach gelato melted in her mouth as they walked. Within minutes, David steered her inside a place with big front windows. The restaurant was modern in decor, all black and white and stainless steel. A waiter showed them to a padded booth near the front.

"There's a stage," Cleo said, looking at the back wall. "Maybe they'll have music later."

David turned around and looked over the back of the booth. "Not much equipment, just one mic and some speakers. Probably just karaoke."

"What's that? It sounds Japanese."

"It's kind of weird," he said. "They play recorded music but without the lyrics and someone gets up and sings along." He turned around again. "Yep, they have a monitor. Most people don't know the lyrics very well so they need prompting."

"Can anyone get up and sing?" she asked, intrigued.

"Sure, in most places anyway. It helps if you have a drink first."

A large dinner and plenty of wine evaporated.

David nudged a list of specials toward her. "You up for dessert?"

"Probably should," she said, thinking to offset the wine. They ordered cake with a ricotta filling, one piece for Cleo and two for David, plus espresso. Dessert had just arrived when an electronic squeal announced the sound system coming to life. One of the waiters ascended the stage. He spoke quickly over the microphone and pointed to a boy who hovered over a machine nearby. A sweeping instrumental arrangement of "That's Amore" filled the room, the waiter lending his pleasant, unpolished tenor to the mix.

"So that's karaoke," she said.

David rolled his eyes.

"Hey, he did a good job!"

"He was awful!"

"I suppose you could do a lot better?"

"If I felt like it."

He looked so smug she could hardly stand him.

"Feel like it, then. I dare you!"

David scowled, tossed his napkin on the table and strode to the stage. He said something to the boy running the sound machine. The boy nodded. An instrumental track swelled. David picked up the mic and started singing. He'd barely finished the first phrase when an old woman at a table up front shouted, "Frankie! Frankie's come to life again!"

It was all so strange. David shed his slightly apologetic stance and strolled across the stage as if he owned it, singing about doing it his way. When he finished, everyone applauded. Some rose to their feet.

"Bravo!" shouted the old woman. David paused to kiss her cheek on his way back to their booth.

"Satisfied?" he said, grinning.

Cleo was so surprised she didn't know what to say and she

didn't have to, since five people had followed David to their booth.

"Magnificent!" said a man with an English accent. He and David shook hands. "Better than Sinatra, like that fellow from the Mediterranean who recorded the same songs fifty years ago."

"Thanks," said David.

"He looks like him, too, wouldn't you say?" asked a woman who seemed to be the English man's wife.

"Like him but not quite. The coloring is all wrong," said one of the others. "What was that man's name, anyway? Didn't it start with a K? I'm sure it started with a K."

The waiter arrived with their bill, which the English couple insisted on paying. A young woman got up to sing a song David said was from an American musical. The room settled down, presenting them an opportunity to leave.

"You were wonderful," Cleo admitted once they were outside. "I had no idea you could sing like that."

David shrugged. "Milton Bernstein is a huge Sinatra fan. I guess I absorbed it from listening with him."

"That thing about the other singer, what's that all about?"

"Hah! Third time I've heard it on this trip. No one can ever remember his name."

It seemed so obvious that of course he must have thought of it already. She asked anyway if the singer, whoever he was, might be a distant relative on his father's side.

"It's tempting to think so," he said, "but I don't really see how. I doubt it's possible for a strong physical resemblance to pass down through a hundred generations."

Cleo made a resolution. Somewhere, somehow, she was going to put David in touch with this singer.

mondaY, september 15, 2025

Seattle, Washington
Clifford

Clifford Essex looked landward from the deck of the *Ms. Zeta*. His eyes rested on the Space Needle. Contemplating his old haunt, the space-age tourist tower he'd worked in as an old-style structureling, made him yearn for the simplicity of his past existence. In retrospect, it seemed better to be trapped in sky-high steel with his molecules disbursed, dreaming of the day he'd resume his humanoid form and pursue digital architectural support to its limits. Now, after fifteen years of physical and intellectual freedom, he'd run up against a problem he simply could not solve. He and his assistant, Heinrich, had experimented with new variables in the seawall equations all morning, without success. It made him feel like dog droppings.

He descended to the saloon, the nautical word he preferred over the lubberly term *main cabin*. "Heinrich, let's dock this tub."

The tall German immortal swiveled his chair to face Clifford. "Sir?"

"We're getting nowhere and I'm fresh out of ideas. I need you to return to Olympus, Inc. The autumnal equinox is next week. Structureling seasonal reports will be coming in. I need you to review them for me and adjust staffing as you see fit. I'll stay here and monitor the seawall."

Heinrich rubbed his thumb and forefinger along his chin. "Will Ms. Zeta approve, sir?"

"I have autonomy to make this level of decision," Clifford said with heat. Ever since the engagement had been announced, Heinrich had treated him as if he and Veronica were joined at the hip. "If you don't want to fly on your own, I'll book you a seat on the corporate account."

Heinrich, who was not trained or authorized to fly at warp speed, opted for the latter. He docked the boat, packed his duffel and marched uphill to the light rail station for the next train to Seattle-Tacoma International Airport.

Clifford kicked off his deck shoes and collapsed on the long sofa in the saloon, built especially to accommodate his six-foot-nine frame. Gulls cried without, begging french-fries from the fish and chips bar on the wharf. He could feel the vibration of lunch-rush traffic humming through the tunnel, that vulnerable highway disaster the mortals had insisted on building. If the drivers speeding through to appointments and errands had any notion how much effort was necessary to ensure the stability of the seawall, they'd likely have a group heart attack.

Heavy footsteps sounded on the deck. Clifford sat up and slipped on his shoes.

"Poseidon." He rose and extended his hand.

"Ahoy, skipper!" the God of the Sea bellowed, followed by a snicker. The last time Poseidon had been in Seattle he'd adopted the nautical terms mortals used, his way of mocking Clifford's use of *saloon*. Today's zoot suit was iridescent blue.

Clifford regarded the Big-G, perplexed. He hadn't sent for him. "What brings you to this fair city?"

"Thought I'd take a dive and check things out, unless you've solved the problem. Want to make sure I didn't miss anything."

On his last visit Poseidon had made a thorough study of the seawall for tell-tale cracks or any visible signs of weakening. He'd come up blank, but agreed with Clifford that the structure wasn't stable, said he felt a steady tremor deep down in the Earth's crust.

Clifford piloted the boat near the seawall and stood off as Poseidon, now in a sparkling turquoise wet suit, sat backward on the cockpit railing and flipped over the side. Half an hour passed, then another quarter. A shimmering turquoise head popped above the surface.

"No change," Poseidon said as he climbed the ladder aft. "No cracks, same vibration."

They exchanged a sober glance, neither of them bothering to add, "But it's only a matter of time."

Clifford steered *Ms. Zeta* to the dock. Mooring lines secured, he liberated two beers from the galley. They clinked their bottles together in salute and drank.

"Can't figure it out," Poseidon said on his way to the galley for two more. "There's seismic activity of some kind but like nothing I've ever felt."

"Perhaps an earthquake or a volcano?" That would be a jolly

mess.

Poseidon raised an eyebrow. "It doesn't feel like an explosion building up, more like…" he thought long enough to drain his second beer "…something stretching."

"Like a balloon being inflated?" Clifford suggested.

Poseidon shook his head. "Like nothing I've ever felt before." He forced a belch, a behavior Clifford found off-putting. "That seawall is driving me crazy." Poseidon lurched to his feet. "Whaddya say we go for a few drinks, get our minds off it for a while?"

They adjourned to a nearby oyster bar for martinis and calamari, watched the sports channel on the big screen television and talked about Poseidon's romantic adventures. Recently, he'd started treating Clifford like a colleague instead of an annoyance. Though the intellectual small-g wasn't keen to hear about Poseidon's legendary sexual caprices, he nodded tolerantly. He'd come to realize being a Big-G wasn't as easy as it looked. So much was expected of them and they all had their demons, even Veronica.

City of Mount Olympus
Hermes

Hermes looked away from the security monitors and rubbed his eyes. Another month of monitoring The Power had passed with nothing to show for it. He felt like a caged animal, chained to a pointless and unending task.

"Waller!" he bellowed through the open office door. In seconds his assistant appeared.

"Sir?"

"I've had enough of this security monitoring, Waller. I want it out of my department. Immediately. Send the people security loaned us back and tell them to take their monitors," he gestured violently toward the two on his desk, "with them."

"But Apollo's directive, sir—"

"His directive can go straight to Tartarus. Do what I say and report back when you're finished. That is all."

Hermes unclenched his jaws. He barely snarled when an apologetic security minion arrived to unhook the damnable monitors and cart them away. His desk cleared of the nuisance, he grabbed his digital pad and started tapping in whatever came to mind about climate change. Sea temperatures rising. Coral reefs dying. Drought cycles lengthening. Crops dwindling. Poseidon and Ares were both on his ass to turn things around, and the weekly reports Veronica now required showed no positive progress. The forecast models Waller had devised projected a dead Earth in two centuries if the mortals continued with business as usual. If the end of the mortals really did mean the end of the gods, Hermes wouldn't live to see his five-thousandth birthday.

He sensed a presence in the doorway.

"Waller. Sit down. We need to brainstorm."

Roderick Waller listened without comment while Hermes talked through the items on his list. "Anything to add?" he said when he'd finished.

"It's an excellent list sir, but I do have two suggestions."

"Don't keep me in suspense, Waller, spit it out. And dispense with the sirs."

Waller looked pained at the last request but continued. "So far you've tried to solve the problem by manipulating nature. The Ecosave tests have focused on scientific methods of cooling the oceans, blocking UV rays and so on. I believe," Waller said, his eyes brightening, "that the most effective plan is to alter mortal behavior."

Same opinion as Veronica's but so far he'd resisted. "All right, Waller, let's have the details."

"At Athens University I made a special study in mortal economics and political science. It was decades ago, but I believe my conclusion is still relevant, that the gods need to cultivate influence over mortal political and economic leaders for the overall good. In this instance, leaders in the extractive industries would be a crucial population to approach."

Hermes stifled a groan. Talking heads. He uniformly despised them, preferred the company of mortal inventors and adventurers to the power brokers.

"I'm supposed to become a diplomat?" he sneered.

"Not you, directly. But I believe the Director of Armed Forces has some connections along those lines."

Athena. He'd rather eat rocks than ask that superior-acting spinster for help.

"You said two suggestions. What's the other one?"

"An immortal-led lifestyle program, like Marriage and the Media. Something to inspire the rank-and-file mortals to dramatically lower consumption of fossil fuels, grow more trees, that sort of thing. The media component is, I believe, the key. As I understand it, they have a passion for seeing themselves onscreen."

Public relations was outside his expertise but Hermes grudgingly admitted the idea might have teeth. "But it will take years to build," he added.

"Fifteen years ago, when Hera's program started, perhaps." Waller smiled. "Mortal social media is a hobby of mine. What we need is an attractive platform and a message that will go viral."

Hermes shrugged. What could it hurt? He authorized Waller to work up a proposal.

"Right away, sir! Thank you, sir."

Waller zipped through the door and started clicking away on the desktop computer in the outer office. Doubtless it felt good to pursue a project that drew on his strengths.

Not so for Hermes. He tapped his digital pad with reluctance, requesting a meeting with Athena.

TUESDAY, SEPTEMBER 16, 2025

Hera

Hera, stuck in meetings all day, had at last returned home to the Penthouse. Time to unwind with Zeus and enjoy a few goblets of Chardonnay. Just as she was settling on a chaise the doorbell rang. She hoisted herself up, grumbling about Hughes's once-monthly meeting at his fraternal lodge, and opened the door to—

"Veronica?"

Her daughter, red-faced, trembled with rage on the threshold.

"Mother, he didn't come back! He sent his assistant to review the seasonal reports and stayed in Seattle!"

"And hello to you, too." Hera set her lips in a maternal smile and escorted Veronica to the den. Even as a child she'd sometimes erred on the side of tyranny. "Come, sit. I'm sure there's a reasonable explanation."

Veronica plopped down on the chaise Zeus favored. "The seasonal structureling reports are coming in and Clifford delegated Heinrich to do the review. He's never done anything like this before." She crossed her arms and pouted.

"Now, Ronnie, you know he's within his rights as a director." Hera opened the bottle of Chardonnay on the low table between them, made two generous pours and handed one to Veronica. "Here, drink this."

Veronica set the goblet down. "We have tickets for the symphony this week, Mother, and he knows it!"

"Then he must think it's critical for him, personally, to monitor the situation in Seattle," Hera said, trying to remember exactly what that meant. Something about a seawall or a tunnel or whatever.

"He's probably doing the town with his new buddy, Poseidon," Veronica muttered. "They're thick as thieves these days."

Hera sipped, thinking. "Poseidon's part of the project, isn't he?"

"Yes," Veronica ceded. "But they don't have to be so chummy."

Hera pointed to Veronica's goblet. "Drink." Ronnie took a

grudging sip. "Veronica Zeta, I believe you're jealous."

She sprang from her seat. "Jealous! Of Poseidon? Oh Mother, don't make me laugh!"

"Then what are you worried about? Sit down, drink your wine and be sensible, Ronnie."

There was a long silence. "Now that we're engaged, I don't think Clifford loves me as much." Veronica collapsed on the chaise. Tears flowed.

Hormones, thought Hera. They could make you do funny things. Like bear the child of a mortal. Like...no, she wouldn't let the words enter her mind. Aphrodite knew who David's father was. She might one day tell the secret to Zeus. His anger would pass. But the other thing—no, she wouldn't think about it. No one knew, and no one was going to know.

She found Ronnie a handkerchief and listened to her sorrows. By the time Zeus arrived Veronica was red-eyed but sane. Cook set an extra plate and the three of them dined together as in the old days. The Goddess of Marriage well knew her daughter's troubles would pass. Heaven and Earth be praised if she could manage the same for herself.

ThURSDAY, SePTeMBeR 18, 2025

Aphrodite

Construction noises vibrated the entire mansion. The rip of saws and pounding of hammers invaded Aphrodite's sanctum, her boudoir. She'd tried to take an interest in the deconstruction of half the old counseling rooms, twenty-five in all. Witnessing the veneer of fantasy being stripped away for theme after theme was too much to bear. Every room, even the ones that had been abandoned for centuries, held memories of different people, different romantic puzzles to solve, memories of a younger self. She'd left the project, feigning boredom, and had a good cry in front of her heart-shaped mirror. Her hand trembled as she tried to repair her mascara. A fresh smudge appeared under her eye.

"Tartarus!" Aphrodite threw the mascara wand across the room and opened a vanity drawer. She hadn't used the Highland Room for at least fifty years; the bottle of Scotch she'd rescued from the plaid playroom should be well-aged by now. She didn't bother with a glass. The first swig burned a little, but the liquor was smooth with a hint of smoke. The second gulp went down easy.

"Why?" she asked her mirror after her third mouthful. The mirror was not magic and did not answer. Aphrodite nodded, acknowledging this new phase for Love, Inc., a fairytale gone sour. She didn't care anymore if Zeus learned the identity of David's father. What good would it do, now that she and Hera were allies? According to Monique, Love, Inc., was poised to be a bigger success than ever. But what was the use of prosperity and wealth when she couldn't gloat about being one-up on her life-long rival? The reality of them rising together smacked of boredom. She hadn't complained to Hef about his mother for weeks, hadn't needled him to take sides and put her first, and he was always up for a new gift bag, curse the invention. Monique's idea was brilliant, however the little prude had managed it. Probably she'd read a couple of hot romance novels and figured it out with a computer program.

The whine of a drill echoed down the corridor. Thank Zeus the mansion was going to be divided so the costume-making worker bees would stay on their own side of the wall. She'd ordered the best soundproofing available to kill the noise of sewing machines humming, presses steaming, robotic arms cutting the fabric. The mere thought of all that activity made her weary. She was five thousand years old, tired of a lifetime of work.

A fresh wave of anxiety rose. She had no hobbies. If she quit working, what would she do with herself? With Candy Smith fronting Marriage and the Media, she wouldn't even be the spokesperson for her own products.

The Scotch bottle had somehow become half-empty. Lunch was two hours in the future. Plenty of time for a nap. That's what aging, obsolete immortals did, wasn't it, take naps? Aphrodite retired to a well-padded chaise lounge to rest her red, smudged eyes. Failure, she now realized, was exciting. Success was nothing but a trap.

MONDAY, SEPTEMBER 22, 2025

Tiberias, Israel
Cleo

Cleo and David lingered in Rome for ten days. They made a side-trip to Pisa and lunched with a middle-aged structureling named Bob. Bob was responsible for the Leaning Tower. He'd retrained from the molecule disbursement method to computerized reinforcement.

"I have a life! For over ten years, I have a life!" Bob said after his second glass of wine. "Holy Zeus, how did we stand it all those centuries, spread so thin and bearing all that weight? And I was one of the lucky ones. The mortals finally started stabilizing me and even fixed some of the tilt." Bob rubbed his left leg, which was noticeably shorter than his right.

Talk about work made Cleo wonder how things were with Hermes. She'd messaged him a couple of times with touristy selfies attached but he hadn't replied. Hopefully, her temporary replacement was working well, but not too well. She wasn't sure what she'd do if her old job wasn't waiting for her when she got back.

They left Italy for Israel and arrived at Tiberias on the autumnal equinox. David stopped at a plain-looking vacation apartment building to pick up something. It was a business-sized envelope with a fancy logo for a return address. He shoved it in the pocket of his khakis. Without a word they were back on the street.

"Aren't you going to open it?"

"Later." He led her to a wine bar and ordered them a bottle of red.

Curiosity ate at Cleo as she sipped, but she wasn't going to ask. She hadn't felt as close to David since she'd learned it was that creepy Monique person he'd slept with, the one who was always bothering Hermes at family parties. Also, he'd griped at her for stopping at every used record store in Rome in search of albums by the Frank Sinatra sing-alike. No one had his recordings and there was nothing about him on the Internet. Every mortal who'd ever sung a note seemed to have a YouTube posting, except Sinatra types who looked like David Bernstein.

David opened the mysterious envelope after his second glass of red. She watched him intently. Was it a love letter from Monique? The thought irritated her.

Finally he said, "Huh."

"What is it?"

He squinted, looked as if he were puzzling something out. "What kind of mortal in 10 or 20 CE would be of both Syrian and Latin ancestry?"

"Could be anyone," she said. "There was a lot of trade back and forth then. The Romans had control of Syria and lots of other places. Merchants and soldiers met up with local women all the time."

David looked back at the letter. "Holy Zeus!" He pointed to a paragraph near the bottom. "They want additional samples to figure out my matrilineal line. They think it might be a missing link! Boy, am I glad they don't have my permanent address."

"Who?"

He explained about sending a DNA sample to a mortal lab for analysis. "Heaven and Earth, I might end up dissected if they find me!"

"Give me that." She yanked the letter from his hand and scanned the paragraph. "All it says is they'd be happy to send one of their associates to interview you and collect the sample."

"You don't get it about mortals. When they say associates, they mean hit men."

"Don't be an idiot. Relax." She poured him another glass of wine.

He conceded to eating dinner but refused to show her the Tiberias night life: "Someone might be looking for me already."

They took backstreets to their hotel. He'd reserved his own room but insisted on staying in hers.

"They'll look in my room first, so we'll have some warning. You take the first watch."

David sat on the edge of the bed and tapped furiously on his digital pad.

"What are you doing?" she said, exasperated.

"Getting us plane tickets to Salt Lake City. That's where the Bernsteins stowed me so I'd be safe." He looked up from his pad.

"Our bus connection leaves here at six AM."

She wanted to shout "Yes, Sir!" and salute but it seemed a bad time for sarcasm. "Great," she said instead. "I can't wait to meet your foster parents."

END OF MONTH THREE

MONTH FOUR
September 22-October 19, 2025

WEDNESDAY, SEPTEMBER 24, 2025

Salt Lake City, Utah
David

Seatbelts fastened, backpacks stowed under the seats in front of them, their plane descended to Salt Lake City. Cleo stared out the tiny window at the lake below.

"I never imagined there'd be so much salt. Can you taste it in the air?"

"Not that I've noticed," said David.

"Is it really true the men here have dozens of wives?"

"Cleo!" For a smart person she was having a tough time grasping what he'd told her about the Mormons. Most of them, anyway. "Just try not to refer to them as upstarts like your mother does."

She turned from the window and glared at him. "I'll thank you to leave my mother out of this, David Bernstein!"

It had been a grueling trip, two days in airports and nearby hotels. The earliest flight he could arrange was a pieced-together mess. Right now he was too jet-lagged to worry about DNA-hungry ghouls hunting him down and chopping him into pieces for analysis. This line of thought had been crazy, he realized, but here they were. Too late to reconsider.

He and Cleo didn't speak to each other as they shouldered their packs and followed the signs from their arrival gate to the luggage collection point. A wiry middle-aged woman with frizzy red hair stood near the New York to SLC carousel. When she spotted David, she crossed her hands over her heart.

David took Cleo's elbow and steered her toward Thelma Bernstein. "Try to smile."

In seconds he was wrapped in his foster mother's arms. "David! Sweetheart!" A life-long hugger, she squeezed the air out of him.

"Thelma," he said once he'd been released. Her given name felt strange in his mouth though he'd been calling her that for fifteen years, ever since he'd found out he wasn't really her son. "This is my friend, Cleo Petra."

Thelma took Cleo's hands. "So pretty!" she said. "Welcome to Utah. So nice you could make the trip with David."

Cleo blushed. "Thank you, Mrs. Bernstein."

"Please, call me Thelma. Now, tell me about your trip."

To David's annoyance, the two of them chatted like old friends. He turned toward the luggage carousel, waited for it to hum to life and spit up their bags.

Thelma and Cleo were still talking when the Bernsteins' ancient Subaru pulled into the home driveway. Nothing had changed in the ten years he'd been away. Same rose bushes in front of the modest rambler, same cement garden gnome lurking by a decorative wishing well. Thelma ushered them through the front door.

"Milton's out back, setting up the barbeque. David, please show Cleo to the guest room."

It hadn't occurred to him before that the Bernsteins had always had a guest room but never had any guests. "It's not a palace," David said, pointing Cleo through an open door half-way down the hall. The room was furnished with a second-hand dresser Thelma had antiqued, the double-bed's headboard painted to match. Her sewing table was covered with a piece of tapestry. He'd seen something like it while touring museums in Israel. What other clues had he missed, living with them through the centuries?

"I'm sure I'll be comfortable," Cleo said, not looking at him. She hoisted her suitcase onto the bed. "The bathroom is?"

"Down the hall, first door to the right."

David stepped across the hall to his own room. He closed the door, dropped his suitcase and backpack. It was just as he'd left it—a Utah Jazz pennant tacked up alongside a Deron Williams poster; a framed photo of himself shaking hands with the high school principal as he received his diploma; a two-shelf bookcase filled with Hardy Boys mysteries, Tolkien's Ring Trilogy and a Hebrew and English Bible. David flopped on his bed and stared at the ceiling. Thelma assumed he and Cleo were a couple. He wasn't so sure. He closed his eyes.

A familiar triple knock sounded on his door.

"David?" The door opened and Thelma stuck her head in. "Honey, are you sleeping? You've been in there for more than an hour. Milton's ready to put on the steaks."

"Be right there," he mumbled. He took a clean shirt from the closet. It fit too tight for comfort.

Milton Bernstein hadn't changed, from his balding head to his "Kiss the Cook" barbeque apron. "David!" Milton crushed him in a bear-hug. "Great to see you, kid. Thanks for bringing this lovely young lady with you. We've been having quite a chat. Turns out we like the same kind of music. Get yourself a drink." He pointed to an ice chest. "I'll put the steaks on. Never knew you to be less than starving."

Prime slabs of beef sizzled on Milton's prized propane barbeque. The aroma of well-seasoned meat assailed David's nostrils. Cleo sat in one of four matching patio chairs at a table with an umbrella sticking up through the middle. She sipped a bottled wine cooler. Her travel clothes had been exchanged for a sundress that flattered every curve. She smiled at him like she knew something that he didn't. David rummaged a beer from the melting party ice and joined her.

"So, you and Milton are pals," he said, unable to resist smiling back.

Her smile broadened to a grin. "I know his name!"

"Yeah, it's Milton," he said, confused.

She laughed. "No, I mean the Sinatra singer. His name is Ari Cantor!"

"Hey, I think I have some of his albums out in the garage. Vinyl, or maybe 78s," Milton said. "I'll go look after dinner."

Thelma set a round dish on the table, a pot of honey in the midst of sliced apples.

"Can I help you, Thelma?" Cleo said, rising.

"No, dear, thank you. Just one thing more for now." She returned with a cutting board, a loaf of braided bread on top.

"We've celebrated Rosh Hashanah so many times with David," she said to Cleo. "It's hard to give up some of the customs, now that he knows he's immortal."

"Wow." David slumped back in his chair. Had he even once observed the holidays during his years at Athens U?

"What beautiful bread," said Cleo.

"It's called challah."

"So." Cleo paused, her expression thoughtful. "Is there a point in immortals observing mortal celebrations?"

"Sure." Thelma smiled. "If we hadn't been ordered to raise David in the Jewish faith we would have missed out on a lot. Today, for example, is the second day of the Jewish New Year, part of a ten-day period of reflection and self-examination." She shrugged. "What could it hurt?"

David's mind swam. In the past three months all kinds of things had broken loose in his life. What he wouldn't give for ten days alone to sort it out and let it settle.

"One of the things about Rosh Hashanah is to make some noise." Thelma's eyes sparkled. "If we were in a synagogue the rabbi would blow on the shofar, a ram's horn, to welcome the New Year. I guess we'll turn up the volume on some Ari Cantor records instead, if Milton can find them in that rat's nest he calls a garage." She wrinkled her nose at her husband.

David dipped a slice of apple in honey, a food symbolic of wishes for sweetness in the New Year. The treat he'd loved as a kid was too sticky, too sweet and a lousy pairing with beer.

After dinner, David helped Milton unearth the promised Ari Cantor albums. They took the vinyl and left the 78s. "They won't play anymore," Milton said. "A real shame. He sang a lot of great tunes in those early years. Heck of a career that guy had, fifty or sixty years, anyway. It was Thelma who heard him first and started buying these. Remember when we lived in L.A., back in the forties?"

Thanks to the gaps caused by the forgetfulness charm the Bernsteins had renewed on David from time to time, he didn't.

"Great stuff, though. You remember me playing it when you were in high school, I bet. Can't believe I haven't listened to 'em since you left home, but what's fifteen or sixteen years in the big scheme of things, right? Cheers." He clinked his beer bottle against David's.

Cleo and Thelma were laughing when they joined them in the den.

"Yes, I can believe he did that," said Thelma.

Talking about me. Like Cleo thought she owned him or something. Three months ago he would have been grateful for this kind of attention. Now it felt like she was taking over his life.

"Ladies, we have music!" Milton waved two albums in the air.

"Oooh! Let me see." Cleo stood alongside Milton to study the covers. Her face fell. "No pictures of him, just landscapes."

"The fashion of the time," Milton said. "Supposed to reinforce a romantic theme." He moved to the turntable. "Don't look so disappointed, young lady, you're gonna love this."

Cleo sat by Thelma on the sofa, leaving room for David, but he sat on the fireplace hearth instead. The four of them listened to "Young at Heart." Milton closed his eyes and swayed to the music. "Pure ambrosia," he said when the song ended.

"It's lovely, Mr. Bernstein," Cleo said. "All those violins in the background."

Milton shook his head. "They don't make 'em that way anymore."

"I wish you had a picture of Ari Cantor. Some people say David looks like him."

Milton perked up. "Now that you mention it—"

"Not so much," Thelma cut in. "I mean, it's hard to say. Ari Cantor was in his forties when he really became known. In two or three millennia I'll give my opinion."

David was on his feet before he had time to think. "What's the use of talking about some old crooner like he's something to me? Heaven and Earth, he's gotta be dead by now!"

He slammed his beer bottle on the hearth and stormed out. Cleo and Thelma made protesting noises behind him, but he ignored them. This whole quest thing had been a stupid idea from the start. What would some distant relative, born two millennia later than he, himself, have to tell him about his father? Absolutely nothing, that's what, but Cleo was making it into something to rival Alex Hailey's *Roots*. He strode down the street of the Salt Lake City suburb, feeling more lost than when he'd started.

FRIDAY, SEPTEMBER 26, 2025

City of Mount Olympus
Monique

One month could have been a fluke. Two months might have been a couple of flukes. But three months? Three months was trouble.

On her way home from going over preliminary third quarter results with Aphrodite, Monique wrapped her hair in a scarf, donned a pair of dark glasses and slipped into a pharmacy. The test kit cost twice what she expected but she didn't haggle. Now was no time to draw attention to herself. The salesclerk, a dumpy woman in a cotton-candy pink toga, slipped Monique's purchase into a brown paper bag.

She kept her head down and her strides long on an alternate route home. Stupid to be so secretive when virtually everybody in the City of Mount Olympus was a love child. The home pregnancy test would tell her for sure. Motherhood was not a line item on Monique's schedule of life. She was an educated, capable woman, damn it, she didn't have to rely on seductive charms like Mother. Mother wouldn't take it well if Monique was pregnant—Aphrodite violently hated the "g" word, though she had grandchildren squirrelled away all around the globe.

Few people were on the street in her New Mycenae neighborhood. Monique slipped unobserved into her condo tower. Her unit was sleek and efficient, a single bedroom with luxury bath (complete with hot tub and fireplace). Not a place to raise a kid. Monique entered the marble-appointed bathroom, read the instructions on the test kit and performed the required steps. She counted down on the second-hand of her wrist chronometer, breath suspended as if doing so could hold back the result.

In two minutes the unwanted news arrived.

"Tartarus!"

Monique disposed of the incriminating evidence and liberated a bottle of Chateau Apollo red from the temperature-controlled vault off her kitchen. The label warned of the dangers of consuming alcohol during pregnancy. This baby would have to deal with it. She opened the bottle to let the wine breathe and started to pace. Why, why, why had this happened at all? She'd been so careful in her affairs, had always taken precautions to prevent this outcome. Except, maybe, that night at David's. The details of her romp with Hermes in the detention cell were a bit fuzzy as well.

She poured a glass of Chateau Apollo and sipped, vaguely noticing the bouquet had yet to reach its peak. The second glass had more character, but then, didn't it always? She resumed contemplating the damnable test results. Another type of test could solve part of the mystery.

"DNA," she said to the bottle and poured a third glass. It wouldn't take much, just a strand of hair or a fingernail paring. Monique set her wineglass on the kitchen counter and passed through her bedroom to the walk-in closet. She pawed through half-a-dozen hangers, praying to Heaven and Earth the togas she'd worn hadn't been sent out for cleaning in the interim. Just one strand of uncontrollably curly black hair and one of shaggy greying blonde would suffice.

Minutes passed. Several samples from Hermes surfaced, but for David—well, it had only been one time. Monique, eyes crossed from strain, slumped to the closet floor. David was gone, wouldn't return to the City of Mount Olympus until the New Year. By then she'd be huge and her interest in him would be obvious. She had to get a genetic sample from him, but how and where?

She rested her hands on her thickening middle. Would she keep the baby? Would she give it up for adoption? Was it a boy or a girl? With the new population restrictions, it was the only baby she'd be allowed. A tear slipped down her cheek. Whoever it was, she'd do her best. This mess wasn't the baby's fault.

Monique roused herself from her closet refuge. She poured her third glass back into the bottle and presented the partial fifth to her surprised next-door neighbor. At home she returned to pacing. Who would be there to help when the baby arrived? Hermes was well acquainted with her sexual appetite. He'd insist on a paternity test. Could she track David down in the mortal world? She could make up some story about checking Aphrodite's business holdings around the globe. Somewhere there was an answer, but time was tight. Her togas were feeling that way, too.

Hermes

Hermes was grateful his meeting with Athena had been delayed for eleven days. He'd never liked her, all superior attitude and virginity and thinking she knew more than everyone else. Her former assignment as Provost of Athens U and Athens Tech had been perfect; Veronica's decision to appoint the Goddess of War and Wisdom to Director of Armed Forces had filled him with disgust.

Today, he was at her mercy. She'd summoned him to her ninth-floor office instead of visiting his department on the fourth. Athena sat behind her desk. From the perch behind her, the damnable owl stared at Hermes with vast yellow eyes. The wall full of battle masks behind him reinforced the sense he was watched from all sides.

He'd finished his pitch for diplomatic support in the fight against climate change. She'd listened without interrupting him and had yet to reply. The sober, contemplative expression on her face irritated him. At last she spoke.

"Your assistant, Waller, has already launched the social media campaign?"

"Yes. It went live on Monday."

Her silver eyes pierced him. "And the results so far?"

"Over a million hits." He knew he was being stupid to resent the early success of Waller's plan but the feeling was beyond his control. "Not much response in China yet, problems with the censorship filters, but we're on it."

Athena appeared to whirl this information in her head, eyes moving in a way that reminded him of a mid-20th century mainframe computer performing a calculation.

"Has the campaign affected fossil fuel producers?"

"We have anecdotal evidence the mortals are cutting back on their consumption but the drop in demand hasn't raised many hackles."

"No drop in prices?"

"Not enough to indicate a trend."

Again, Athena's face took on a calculating expression.

"It may take time to nudge the industry," she said. "Until then, I don't think diplomatic intervention will be effective, but here's what I can do."

Hermes hadn't realized Athena had a number of operatives deployed to gather information in the mortal world. She proposed to assign agents to investigate the biggest players in the fossil fuel industry and compile dossiers on what she referred to as persuasive leverage.

He grinned. "Blackmail?"

"Regrettable, but given the short timeframe I believe it's the best choice."

They agreed to meet again, once sufficient information had been obtained. Athena extended her hand. They shook. He thanked her for her time. As Hermes waited for the descending elevator, he wondered what else he'd missed about the person who was Athena.

SATURDAY, SEPTEMBER 27, 2025

Monique

Though it was hot enough this morning to turn on the air conditioning, Monique was bundled up in a chenille bathrobe. The chill wouldn't abate, seemed to come from inside her. After a restless night with little sleep her worries had multiplied. Could a paternity test be performed before the baby was born? How could she raise a child and manage her career? What would Mother's reaction be?

She made a pot of coffee, then poured it down the drain when she remembered pregnant women weren't supposed to have caffeine. Desperate, she called Apollo's clinic and was surprised to get the doctor, not his message service.

"It's easier for my working patients to come in on the weekend," he explained. Yes, he could see her today, had an opening at 1 PM if that suited her.

Monique studied her swelling middle in the mirror before dressing. The baby seemed to have visibly grown overnight. "Reality check," she said to her sideways reflection. Probably she'd been too upset last night to register the size of the baby bump. Her breasts were rounder, too. She reached for the toga she'd worn yesterday and tugged it down over her new dimensions, the fit snug but bearable.

After an unZeusly slow morning she arrived at Apollo's clinic, not the one at Olympus Rest (that was for crazy people) but his general practitioner digs in her own fashionable New Mycenae neighborhood. A bell chimed when she entered. The waiting room was empty. A door beyond the unattended reception desk swung open when the clock above it chimed one and there stood Apollo, serene as always and handsome beyond all reason.

"Just back from lunch," he said. "I hope you haven't waited long. Our waiting room magazines are as old as Methuselah."

Apollo led her to an examining room and pointed her toward a chair. He seated himself on a stool with wheels, picked up a digital device from the counter and tapped the screen a few times, scrolling down a page or two.

"What brings you in today?"

She named her condition.

"Ah." The empathy in his eyes set her at ease. "First time?"

"Yes."

"How do you feel about that?"

Monique stared at him. The question was one she hadn't anticipated.

"Nervous," she said at last.

"I see." He patted her hand. "Let's get a height and weight on you and go from there."

Monique stepped on to the scale. Her weight hadn't varied for centuries but she'd gained twelve pounds since her last visit. During the physical exam, Apollo estimated the pregnancy was well into the second trimester.

"But that's impossible!" Monique lay her hands on her belly that had suddenly grown cold. "My last cycle ended on the summer solstice."

Apollo raised his eyebrows, looking thoughtful.

"It's not common for immortals, but you might be carrying more than one."

"Twins?" Monique felt faint. This could not possibly be her life.

"We can find out next week when the lab technician is back." He handed her his card. "We're closed on Monday, but I want you to call first thing on Tuesday and make an appointment for an ultrasound."

Overwhelmed, Monique didn't have the presence of mind to ask about a paternity test. Armed with a sheet of prenatal care instructions she stumbled out into a beautiful autumn afternoon, her only desire to cuddle back into her bathrobe and have a cup of herbal tea.

Salt Lake City, Utah
Cleo

Cleo Petra sat on the guest room bed, legs crossed in the lotus position, back braced against the headboard, eyes fixed on her digital tablet. It was an obsession, the search for Ari Cantor. She'd followed screens and screens of links to esoteric pages that offered any hope at all—Sinatra, mid-twentieth century concerts in LA, Jewish recording artists. Nothing about the singer had surfaced.

Ding!

She sighed, irritated. An appeal to sign up for some environmental website had popped up for the third time this session. It had been happening for days, some organization called Green Something-or-Other that promised to make every subscriber a star. The ad blocker she'd applied couldn't stop it. Whoever was doing this—

Ding!

Here it was again! A different picture was behind the text but like all the others it depicted mortals using what they called public transportation. Municipal busses, light rail trains and the like. *Save the Earth and Share!* was their motto.

Cleo quit fighting and hit the "Join" button. The screen changed, requesting an upload of selfies that promoted public transportation, carpooling, walking and commuting by bicycle. She tapped the box labeled "Thanks, not now" and went back to querying for Ari Cantor.

WeDNeSDAY, OCTOBeR 1, 2025

The Underworld
Hades

The King of the Dead sat alone in the dining room, picking at the last piece of pie made from Freya's cherry-apple hybrids. The palace cook was especially good at pastries. The crust was light and flakey, the filling fit for a god, but Hades barely noticed this culinary perfection. Persephone should have been in touch by now to give him the harvest update and an idea of when she was coming home.

Damn nature, it never came out the same way twice! The digital device Hermes had sent him a couple of decades ago was a means of monitoring Earth's weather, but the preponderance of climates and sub climates made the task irksome and boring. He privately cheered for global warming.

Hades set down his fork and rang the dining table bell. Anatole arrived in seconds.

"Sir?"

"Any word from the Queen?"

"No, sir. Nothing."

His heart heavy with loneliness, Hades said the unthinkable.

"Join me for a drink?"

Anatole regarded him, stiff-shouldered and wide-eyed. "Sir?"

"Have a seat, man! You've been standing on ceremony for, what, five hundred years?"

"Six hundred seven years, four months and twenty-three days to be exact, sir."

"And you've been on your feet the whole time?"

"Not precisely, sir."

"Doesn't matter, take a chair." He reached for a bottle. "Red okay?"

Anatole hovered alongside him and took the bottle from his hand. "This is highly irregular, sir." The valet topped off Hades' goblet.

"Damn it, Anatole, stop hopping around and sit! I want to talk to you about something."

Anatole frowned. He perched on the edge of the chair Hades pointed to.

"Sir?"

Hades' thoughts whirled for a topic of conversation. The latest tally of souls in each of the three provinces? His projection of who'd win the annual football championship in Tartarus? Hot gossip about the palace servants?

"The white spot over Elysium," he said, inspired. "Any new developments? When was the last time you checked?"

"Monday, sir, per our regular schedule. Nothing new to report."

Hades poured wine for his valet and pushed the goblet toward him.

"Drink."

Anatole eyed him warily.

"I *insist.*"

"This is most irregular, sir." Anatole raised his wine glass for one refined sip.

Gad, the man was stiff, but there was no one else to talk to if you didn't count the Furies.

"Care to make a wager?"

"I think not, sir."

"Oh, come on!" Hades bellowed, annoyed. "Not for anything big, just for fun."

Anatole said nothing, his expression skeptical.

"How about this? If you win, I'll hang up my own togas for a week. If I win, I'll keep a month of your pay."

Anatole sighed. "As you wish, sir."

Hades slapped his palms together. "Good!" They hadn't had a wager in years. "Each of us will pick the date we think the Queen will return. Whoever's closest wins. Now drink!"

Anatole took another sip. "Will that be all, sir?"

"No, that will not be all, sir! You're going to finish your glass and we are going to finish this bottle. Understood?"

Hades didn't like the rise of Anatole's eyebrows, as if he knew something his master didn't.

"Yes, sir."

"I'll go first," Hades said magnanimously. "I wager Queen Persephone will return to the Underworld on October 17."

Anatole removed a pad and pencil from his pocket and recorded the date. "Very good, sir."

She'd never been later than that, or had she, maybe that once? Sometimes the details escaped him, ever since he'd accidentally brushed his toga against the Chair of Forgetfulness when he'd trapped Theseus there so long ago. Dratted Heracles had somehow gained entry to the Underworld and freed the trespasser. The ancient memory made his blood boil.

"Now you pick a date, Anatole."

"November 14, sir."

The prompt reply troubled Hades. Something about Anatole, but he couldn't quite remember what.

"Will that be all, sir?" Anatole rose and tucked the pad and pencil into his pocket.

"Yes," said Hades, forgetting he'd insisted Anatole finish the bottle with him. The valet padded away. Alone, it suddenly came to him, the thing that troubled him about Anatole. Anatole, Hades now recalled, was psychic.

Thursday, October 2, 2025

City of Mount Olympus
Monique

Monique lay on her back on the ultrasound table. Her bladder threatened to burst under the pressure of eight glasses of water. She hardly noticed the indignities of the lubricant jelly and the wand, her eyes fixed on a monitor. It displayed patches of black and marbled gray she couldn't put a name to.

The technician, a young small-g with a white coat over her toga and a tag reading Anya Blakeslee, removed the wand and rolled her stool back. "I can't quite get the image we need. Too much water in your bladder. Can you pee out about half of it and hold the rest, please? The restroom is through there." She pointed to an interior door.

Are you fricking crazy? Of course I can't! Monique wondered if the technician had ever had an ultrasound herself. How could she have, and request this impossible feat?

Approximately one-quart lighter Monique resumed her position on the table, her angry bladder barely under control. It felt like the baby (or possibly, babies) were using it as a trampoline. In slid the wand, the technician moving it this way and that as the black and gray images swirled on the monitor. The technician extracted the wand again.

"Wait there, please," she said. Her bland expression suggested no details. "I want the doctor to see this. Won't be a minute."

Monique watched the second hand on the clock above the door. It swept through three minutes before they returned. She was gritting her molars so hard she feared they'd break. Did no one in this Zeus-forsaken clinic understand urine was about to leak from her eyes?

In went the wand. The technician manipulated the instrument to show several views of a mass that maybe had something like a head.

"See there?" the technician said to Apollo, answered by his, "Hmmmm." They repeated this routine several times, Apollo working his stethoscope over Monique's belly. She was about to scream from discomfort when Apollo said, "That's sufficient, Blakeslee."

After she'd (praise Heaven and Earth) relieved herself and dressed, Monique joined Apollo in his office. He was seated and wore an avuncular expression.

"That must have been a trial." He gestured to the chair across from him.

She sat, determined not to sound as bitchy as she felt. "Not my favorite way to spend the afternoon, thanks."

"Hah! Glad you're keeping your sense of humor." He rested his arms on the desk and leaned forward. "Blakeslee spotted one baby with the ultrasound."

Something in Apollo's face told her he had more to say.

"I call that good news," she said, waiting.

"Monique," he said in a gentle tone, "I must tell you, I've never seen anything like this. There is definitely a child growing in your body, definitely a heartbeat. But it's…"

Her hands clasped her belly. "Tell me!"

Apollo's expression turned grave. "There's a nebulous quality to it. That's the only way I can describe it. The heartbeat is continuous, but the form of the child has a way of dissipating and coming back together."

She could form no words. Had she harmed the baby without realizing it?

"Monique." Apollo came around the desk and sat in the chair alongside her. He took her hands, ice cold, in his. "I'm not here to judge you. No one on Mount Olympus is a paragon of virtue, but it's time for more details. Monique, I need to know who, or what, is your baby's father."

Salt Lake City, Utah
David

David Bernstein lay on his bed, staring at the walls of his old room. The walls stared back. The pennant and posters seemed to ask *Who are you?*

He and Cleo were leaving tomorrow, for a week at the Grand Canyon and then on to Seattle for an extended stay with Jim and

Candy Smith. David was curious to see the underground tunnel that replaced Ralph's old haunt, the Alaskan Way Viaduct. He was considering writing a paper on it for his Masters of Architecture program if the structure lasted that long; its predecessor, the Viaduct, had been demolished after less than seven decades.

"I should be so lucky," he said to the walls.

Thelma had confined everyone to quarters this morning. It was Yom Kippur, the culmination of the Days of Awe starting the Jewish New Year, known as the Day of Atonement. He was in a crappy frame of mind for reconciling with God for sins against Him, or, as David the immortal now interpreted it, saying he was sorry to everyone he'd been a jerk to in the old year. He thought about Monique and how he'd used her or vice-versa. His relationship with Cleo had soured. She wouldn't get off her Ari Cantor kick, though she hadn't found a thing about him on the Internet. He'd snapped at her more than once.

Thelma's triple knock sounded on the door.

"Come in."

"Detention is over. You hungry?"

The Bernsteins did a short version of the ritual fast, serving the break-fast meal at noon instead of at the end of the day.

"As usual." He rolled off the bed and got to his feet.

Atonement was considered a private matter. No one talked about their own reflections, but Thelma was giving him her Concerned Mom look. "You think you can be nicer to your friend?"

Her question made him feel like a ten-year-old. He looked at Thelma without answering.

"Never mind, then. None of my business."

David studied the walls of his room again. The decorations seemed to be from an alien culture. Did Cleo understand the unmoored pain that came from not knowing one's origins? No, he was pretty sure she didn't.

He ran his fingers through his hair and headed for the dining room. The scent of Thelma's kugel sparked a glimmer of enthusiasm. David managed a smile for Cleo, even though she looked smug. Atonement probably wasn't a skill she'd cultivated as the beautiful and intelligent daughter of a wealthy family.

The traditional meal (for their family, anyway) worked its magic. The slightly sweet creamy noodles reminded him of when he was on his own but before he knew he was the son of a Goddess. How many times had he eaten generic macaroni and cheese and fantasized it was Thelma's kugel?

"Great kugel, Mom." He held out his plate for seconds.

"Thank you, David." Thelma lifted a generous helping from the pan. "More coffee?"

"Yeah. I'll get it." He rose, coffee pot in hand, and topped off the others' mugs first. Cleo's expression softened. Yeah, he could be nicer to her.

"So, your Grand Canyon adventure starts tomorrow," said Milton, "then on to Seattle. Ever been to Seattle, Cleo?"

She blotted her lips with her napkin. "No, but I've wanted to go there for years. David's told me so much about it." She nudged her knee against his under the table.

"So much to do there," Thelma said. "Beautiful scenery, lots of music, lots of theatres. Hey, I saw on a news program that a touring company of *Fiddler on the Roof* is coming to Seattle. Let me order you some tickets."

David's anti-coddling sentiments kicked in. "Thanks, Thelma, but—"

"I insist. I'll do it right after lunch. If you drag your feet they'll be snapped up before you know it." She shifted her eyes from David to Cleo.

Cleo smiled. "Thank you, Thelma, I've never seen a play with mortal actors."

"And not just a play, but a musical! Such wonderful songs. You'll learn a lot about Jewish culture without knowing it, it's such a masterpiece."

David exchanged a look with Milton. No use trying to stop Thelma when she was enthusiastic about something.

"Thanks." David forced a smile. He'd seen the damn thing ten times at least. What was the point of Jewish tradition, anyway, since he was destined to live forever? The faith his unknown father had insisted he be raised in was just another mortal relic, like the list of Herod's servants tucked away in his backpack.

FRIDAY, OCTOBER 3, 2025

The Underworld
Hades

The King of the Dead wished he were. His valet, Anatole, was such a small man; it was hard to remember he had a hollow leg. The day of their wager he'd summoned Anatole back and commanded him again to drink. At Hades' unwavering insistence they'd met each other glass for glass, through three bottles of the good red before he lost count. This morning his mouth was as dry as a desert and tasted like well-worn sandals. He eyed the water pitcher beside his bed—empty. Hades reached for the bell pull. The throbbing in his head quadrupled. For a moment, he feared he'd vomit.

Anatole, impeccably dressed and every hair in place, appeared in the archway.

"You rang, sir?"

"More water, Anatole."

"Yes, sir."

"And one of your special tonics," Hades added, though the memory of drinking the mixture of raw egg, tobacco, Worcestershire sauce and Zeus knew what else made him wince.

"Very good, sir."

The valet collected the empty pitcher and exited. Hades rolled on his side. He opened the nightstand drawer and extracted his digital pad. The device showed the date as October 3.

The valet returned with a murky looking concoction on a golden tray. Hades held up the digital pad. "Anatole, there's something wrong with this thing."

Anatole set the tray on the nightstand. "In what way, sir?"

"The date's off. It's October second."

"October third, if I may be so bold, sir."

"What the—you mean, I slept through an entire day?"

"So it would seem, sir." Anatole handed him the glass. "Your tonic, sir."

Hades pinched his nose and downed the noxious concoction in one gulp. His pounding head cleared and his stomach groaned hollowly. "I'm as hungry as Cerberus."

"Without doubt, sir."

"Have the cook make up some scrambled eggs and sausages. And plenty of butter on the toast. With marmalade."

"Immediately, sir."

Alone, Hades tapped a message to Persephone on the digital pad. *Lonely as Hell, please come home soon.* The device, designed for the upper world, couldn't find a signal at first. The message flitted away just as Anatole returned. He pushed a rolling cart, topped with a full water pitcher and a gold-domed plate on a breakfast tray.

"Your repast, sir."

Hades allowed Anatole to adjust the pillows behind his back and settle the breakfast tray over his lap.

"Will that be all, sir?"

"One more thing." The details of their wager ebbed faintly in his mind. "What date did you pick for the Queen's return?"

"November fourteenth, sir."

More than a month away. "And I said it would be the…"

"Seventeenth of October, sir."

Two weeks from today. He hoped.

"That'll be all, Anatole."

"Very good, sir."

Hades dug his fork into the scrambled eggs (seasoned with cheddar cheese, just the way he liked them) and chomped a marmalade-slathered hunk of toast. Calories surged into his ravenous body like an electrical current, made him feel like a new god. He'd just finished the last sausage when the digital pad chimed. Hades wiped his greasy fingers on a napkin and tapped the blackened screen. Persephone's reply was one short line.

Delayed again this year, no later than November 5.

"Damnation!" Hades pitched the crystal marmalade jar across the room where it smashed against the onyx-faced fireplace. Already he'd lost.

WeðNesðay, OctOBeR 8, 2025

Yakima Valley, Washington
Persephone

Persephone looked out across acres and acres of vineyard, every vine picked clean of grapes. The fieldwork portion of harvest was over for the year. Crates of fruit were stored in temperature-controlled warehouses all over the Yakima Valley, famous for apples and peaches as well as wine. Happily, this region had been spared the worst effects of shifting climate. But next year? It all seemed up to chance.

She adjusted her headdress, a new wreath woven from local vines, and sighed. In less than a month she'd return to the Under-world—and to Hades. Why hadn't she stretched it to December, embellished the effects of climate change on the unpredictable growing season? The Underworld was a lonely place, unless you were dead. No one to care for or confide in. Hades wouldn't have children, no matter what she wanted. Hundreds of years would pass in a blink and there'd she be, a barren crone with only Cerberus for company.

Persephone tore the wreath from her hair and threw it into the sky with such force it disappeared in the clouds. It was absolutely crazy making, blessing the world's agricultural bounty and not having a child of her own! She'd hovered, unseen, watching the harvest workers. Some had children with them. Healthy, beautiful children to cheer them at the end of each back-breaking workday. An empty chamber in her heart ached. She longed to steal a child but the ones available were mortal. They'd only last a few paltry decades.

The Goddess cried and rain began to fall. Cerberus was probably the only one who missed her, or at least the snacks she slipped him on the sly. Hades *said* he missed her, but if that were true wouldn't he leave his precious kingdom and risk the loss of a coin or two to see her? Why, all those millennia ago, had he roared through a field in his chariot and abducted her as she innocently picked flowers, special flowers he'd put there by magic to enchant her? He never made her enchanted flowers anymore.

Persephone brushed the tears from her cheeks and ascended. It was a long flight to Europe. There she'd join Demeter to debrief for this year and plan for the next. They'd have their usual mother-daughter retreat at a resort in the Alps to reward themselves for a job well done, report to Ares at Mount Olympus, and part. Mother would cry when Persephone descended to the Underworld. Mother had always said marriage wasn't easy. Mother was divorced.

FRIDAY, OCTOBER 10, 2025

City of Mount Olympus
Hera

Normally, Hera looked forward to meeting with Veronica in the CEO suite. The top floor of headquarters was an airy oasis where skylights urged the best efforts of healthy, green plants.

Today she didn't feel the love. They'd just gone over the third quarter Department of Marriage financial reports, loaded with favorable variances. The old Hera would have crowed about her department's achievements. But that had all changed.

Veronica set aside the profit and loss statement. "Are you feeling okay, Mom?"

Hera assured her daughter she was as healthy as an ox. The truth was far too embarrassing: Aphrodite's transformation from enemy to collaborator had proved surprisingly depressing.

"Glad to hear it," Veronica said, though she looked skeptical. "Attendance is beyond capacity for the *Deep Marriage* seminars. I'd like you to move up the timeline for the next installment to keep the momentum. Have you selected a theme yet?"

Hera's forced smile drooped. She'd Skyped with Candy last week. The mortal married couples had responded fabulously to the gift bag component and were begging for more. Sure, the Napoleon and Josephine edition she and Zeus had sampled had added excitement to an evening, but Hera had discounted it as mere novelty. She'd been counting the days until the contract with Love, Inc., expired. Now Candy was recommending an extension of their joint venture.

"No, no theme yet." There was a drumming sound nearby. Hera glanced down and stilled her fingertips from beating on the desktop. "Do you have anything to drink?"

"I have herbal tea," Veronica said primly.

"I *need* wine."

"Mother! It's morning."

Veronica reminded Hera she was the boss and professional behavior was expected from all employees, especially department heads. Hera's eyes longed to roll.

"The Department of Marriage has made great strides in the last decade," Veronica said. "The current trend can take it to an even higher level. You hit on something brilliant with the gift bags, Mom. You need to go with the flow."

They kissed cheeks and parted. Hera grumbled to herself in the elevator. Gilda had forgotten to replenish the departmental supply of Chardonnay. She bypassed her own tenth floor turf and descended to the mezzanine. The cafeteria didn't serve wine until noon. She'd go to a nearby dive for a bracer.

A for-hire chariot set her down in front of Grape and Grain, open 24/7. She blinked in the dark interior, scanning the joint as her eyes adjusted. It smelled of spilled wine, tobacco smoke and dirty restrooms. Occupancy was light. She claimed a vacant table near the back. If anyone she knew came through the door, she'd duck beneath the table before they saw her.

A slovenly young woman with her hair in disarray, probably the latest style, took her order. When the waitress walked away, someone spoke from a neighboring table.

"Fancy seeing you here."

Hera recognized the sarcastic tone.

"I could say the same of you. Drinking your troubles away, dear daughter-in-law?"

Streaks of mascara stained Aphrodite's cheeks. Hera had never considered her archrival capable of crying.

"That's one way to put it." The Goddess of Love raised her glass and took a long pull of wine. "Damn Monique and her expansion plans! Not to mention the baby," she muttered under her breath.

Aphrodite drained her glass. She signaled for another when the waitress brought Hera's Chardonnay. "At least no one can accuse us of drinking alone," she slurred.

Hera wondered how long Aphrodite had been there. Wine splotched the front of her hot pink toga and one of her fingernails, always impeccably polished, was broken. The Goddess before her was not the resilient enemy she'd striven to best over the millennia. To her amazement, Hera realized she actually gave a damn.

TUESDAY, OCTOBER 14, 2025

Seattle, Washington
Cleo

Cleo Petra gazed out the guest room window. Ferries passed each other on Elliott Bay. The weather had been perfect since their arrival last Friday, sunny days and crisp autumn nights. Candy and Jim Smith were thoughtful hosts. They'd even left a box of chocolate truffles on the nightstand. After three days in Seattle, Cleo Petra knew she'd be happy to live in this mortal city for as long as it existed.

A familiar tap sounded on the half-open door. "Come in."

David stepped into the room. He'd insisted she take the bed while he camped out on Jim and Candy's sofa. "Ten years ago you would have seen the Alaskan Way Viaduct out there."

"You sound like you miss it."

"Yeah, I kind of do. It's where I first met Ralph, the same day I found out I was immortal. Wanna go someplace?"

They'd already visited the University of Washington campus where David had earned his double bachelor's degree. Seattle's light rail system had carried them there in minutes. Most of the riders were taking and posting selfies to the *Green World Works* website. Crazy how it seemed to be everywhere. They'd also visited Seattle Center. David pointed out city landmarks from the observation deck of the Space Needle, the futuristic tower Clifford Essex had inhabited before structureling work went digital. When David got hungry he took her to the Food Court and introduced her to a mélange of mortal fast food.

She nodded toward the window. "We haven't been to the waterfront yet."

"Yeah, we could do that."

They stopped by Jim's office on the way out. His oversized oak desk was strewn with papers, the digital pad most people used pushed to one side. "Just can't work with a screen as well as a printout," he'd explained yesterday.

"Back for lunch?" Jim asked.

"Nah. I'm treating Cleo to fish and chips," David said. "Want me to bring some back for you and Titus?"

"Thanks, but we'll stick to our zwieback."

Jim was single parenting it, responsible for their toddler while Candy presented regional seminars on *Deep Marriage*.

Cleo and David shrugged into their windbreakers; garments David had insisted they buy the day they'd arrived, and rode the elevator to street level.

"That's where I had my espresso cart," he said, pointing across Third Avenue.

Cleo laughed. "So you've said." *For about the tenth time.*

"Just want to be sure you remembered."

At the corner they turned downhill, toward the waterfront. The steep sidewalks pitched her forward. "They call Seattle the City of Seven Hills, like Rome," David said. "The mortals messed with these hills a lot in the last couple of centuries. The waterfront is all fill."

By the time they reached First Avenue the grade was gentle. David pointed ahead to a tastefully landscaped green space with a few benches and tables. "That's where the Viaduct used to be, the part where I first saw Ralph. Those," he pointed to two paved lanes between the park and the waterfront, "are for ferry traffic and emergency services." They crossed the street and leaned against a railing overlooking Elliott Bay. To their left, a ferry blasted its horn and cast off. Piers with warehouses were built over the water to their right. A gigantic Ferris wheel dominated the skyline a few piers away.

David took a deep breath "Smell that? I love the salt air. Feel the vibration underfoot?"

"The infamous tunnel?" Cleo guessed. Veronica had mentioned it several times. There was a problem with the seawall that protected the tunnel from the bay, something that kept Clifford away from Mount Olympus.

"The same. You hungry?"

She'd learned to say yes whenever David asked this question, usually begging off with a cup of coffee while he downed a burger or a slice of pizza. They headed toward a blue and white striped awning that shaded an open-front food stand. Customers were three or four deep.

"Best fish and chips in town, maybe in the world." David

pointed to the letters *IVAR'S* painted above the stripes. "Okay if I order for you?"

She waited at a blue metal table, her seat facing the sidewalk. Lots of mortals passed, on lunch break she supposed. Two extremely tall men caught her eye. One wore a shiny turquoise suit with padded shoulders, the other one—

"Clifford!" Cleo stood up and waved. "Clifford Essex!"

~ * ~

After downing their fish and chips, David and Cleo met Clifford and Poseidon at the dock where *Ms. Zeta* was moored. "Cool," David said when Clifford showed them the wheelhouse's complex instrument board. After a brief tour they adjourned to the main cabin, what Clifford called the saloon, where two computers were installed: one to monitor the digital technology embedded in the seawall, the other linked to a camera capable of moving from the water's surface to the floor of Elliott Bay.

"Poseidon's here for the monthly check-in," Clifford explained. The God of the Sea had excused himself to change for his dive. "The camera does a fine job, but there's no substitute for someone with his expertise making on-site observations. In case of emergency, life vests are under there." He pointed to a padded bench along a bulkhead. "David, you can help me cast off. Cleo, if you'd bring in the fenders?"

David stepped onto the dock. The distance from the dock to the tapered bow was wide. He'd have to jump. The engine started; vibration and the smell of diesel exhaust. Clifford brought in the stern line from on board and gave the signal to free the bow line from its cleat. With a quick prayer to Heaven and Earth, David let it fly and scrambled on board. His shin barked the toe rail. He limped to the cockpit.

Clifford steered *Ms. Zeta* into the bay. "Capital to have two more sets of hands. David, you can keep us in position while Poseidon makes his dive. Cleo, if you'd assist me on the computers?"

"Great," said Cleo.

Clifford walked David through the gears, throttles and gauges. He'd been on boats before but had never piloted one. It didn't help that, unlike a car, the boat turned in the opposite direction of the steering wheel.

"Easy once you get the hang of it," Clifford said.

Poseidon emerged from the aft cabin. His shimmering wetsuit made him look like a rainbow trout with limbs. Cleo coughed and turned away, probably to suppress a laugh. Poseidon had flirted with her earlier, calling his turquoise zoot suit his "paternity suit" because women couldn't resist him in it. She'd yet to tell Poseidon she was his granddaughter.

Clifford instructed David to keep *Ms. Zeta* in neutral and ducked into the main cabin. Poseidon sat backward on the cockpit railing and flipped fins-over-head into Elliott Bay. The incoming ferry rocked *Ms. Zeta* with its wake.

"All well out there?" Clifford called from the cabin.

Ms. Zeta drifted toward the seawall. "Yeah," David shouted back, turning the wheel away from land before he remembered he needed to do the opposite. He was drenched in sweat by the time he corrected his steering—too far. Bow pointed into the bay and stern drifting toward the seawall, he shifted into first gear. Clifford was instantly alongside him.

"Good instinct," Clifford said. He took the wheel and piloted the boat back into position. "Hang on, now, won't be but a few minutes." Clifford ducked back into the cabin.

High on stress, the minutes pass like hours. At last Clifford returned. David joined Cleo in the cabin and plopped in the chair at the computer Clifford had abandoned.

"See anything interesting?"

Her face glowed in monitor light. "Clifford says no, but it's great to be at a computer again. Look." She entered a command that lowered the camera down the seawall. "See the glow? It's pretty faint, but if you squint…"

There was a slight swirling pattern in the concrete.

"That's the part they're worried about, but Clifford says it hasn't changed for a couple of months." She rolled her chair back from the monitor and sighed. "I hate to admit it, but I'm starting to miss my projects at work."

No wonder thought David. They'd gotten along better since they'd left Utah, friends, at least. It seemed eons since they'd kissed. He kicked himself for not letting go of his identity obsession and trying to get back on track with Cleo, but he just couldn't shake it. Their time together was running out. In a few weeks, Cleo would be around charismatic guys like Hermes again, and there were plenty of old creeps like Poseidon, eager to snap her up. Did she even care about him, except as a friend? Maybe he'd lost his chance. Maybe it was already too late.

Thursday, October 16, 2025

City of Mount Olympus
Monique

Monique chose the stairs for her descent instead of the elevator. Nausea was coming on with the slightest disturbance these days. Even the sway of a lift could set her off.

Her meeting with Hera had gone well. Both sides were satisfied with the success of the gift bags as part of the *Deep Marriage* program, though Hera had seemed preoccupied. She'd also eyed Monique's baby bump.

Briefcase in one hand, the other gripping the metal pipe railing, Monique waddled down echoing concrete steps, past doors marked IX, VIII, VII, VI. She met not a soul. Winded, she stopped on a landing between the sixth and fifth floors to rest. She set down her briefcase and lay a hand on her belly. It was large enough to challenge the seams of the maternity toga she'd bought the day of her ultrasound. The baby was growing at an alarming rate. Still, she couldn't bring herself to accept Apollo's conclusion: that it might have been fathered by a supernatural force. Apollo's diagnostic equipment had to be at fault.

Monique resumed her descent. Unwelcome footfalls ascended from below. She'd just grasped the fifth-floor doorknob to duck in and hide when Hermes rounded on the landing. His eyes fell from her face to her bulge. His jaw dropped.

"Heaven and Earth."

"Long time no see." She'd stopped leaving him messages after her consultation with Apollo.

Hermes ran a hand through his greying mop. "Mine?"

"Possibly."

"You told me you had protection."

"Things happen," she said with a casual shrug, though her heart pounded.

"Don't give me that." He gripped her arm and pulled her toward him. "What kind of funny business are you up to, Monique? If you think you can force me to marry you, you're sadly mistaken."

She wrenched away from him. "In your dreams! The last thing I want is a husband. Lots of immortal women have babies on their own."

Monique brushed past him and continued her descent, one slow step at a time. He came alongside her.

"If it's mine, I want to know. A baby needs a mother and a father."

"That'll be news to Pan," she snapped.

"I was only two thousand at the time. What did I know about kids?"

She stopped and watched him stumble past her to the next landing.

"This isn't a joke, is it?" he said as he scrambled back.

"That's for me to know and you to find out. Leave me alone, Hermes." The baby somersaulted, propelling her forward. All she wanted was to get out of the building and to her own office, shut the door and figure out how she'd cope if she really did give birth to a monster.

Friday, October 17, 2025

Hera

One week had passed since Hera had loaded Aphrodite into a hired chariot in front of the Grape and Grain and sent her home, stone cold drunk.

Today Hera sat behind her desk, waiting for Aphrodite who was ten minutes late. She rose and strolled to the reception area outside her private office, poised to ask Gilda to call and see if Aphrodite had forgotten the appointment, when a disheveled collection of hot pink toga, bronzed legs and platinum blonde hair wreathed in alcohol fumes stumbled in from the hall.

"Good, you made it," Hera said. "Hold my calls, Gilda." Her executive assistant regarded her quizzically. Hera gestured for Aphrodite to go into the office ahead of her and mouthed *it's okay* to Gilda.

Coffee service and baklava waited on the low table between two comfortable armchairs. They settled across from each other. Hera infused warmth into her smile. "Thank you for coming."

"I suppose it's about the damn gift bags." The lines any five-thousand-year-old might sport showed clear and deep on Aphrodite's forehead, around her eyes, alongside her mouth.

"No, not about the gift bags." But that's what had started Hera thinking. After millennia of competition and enmity, neither one of them could derive pleasure from the success of their business collaboration. One of them had always been up, the other down and plotting revenge. After serious self-examination, Hera realized she was afraid of her lifelong rival becoming a friend.

She poured two cups of coffee and slid one toward Aphrodite. "I need to talk to you about something that happened a long time ago. Remember the Judgment of Paris?"

Aphrodite smiled. A slash of hot-pink lipstick stained her teeth. "Hah! You and me splashing around au natural in the spring of Ida and Athena shivering on the bank in her chemise, all of us waiting for Hermes to bring Paris. What kind of joke was that? Zeus asking a mortal to judge which of us was the most beautiful? I think

Hermes cooked up the plot so he could see us naked."

Hera stuck to her purpose and withheld the first comment that came to mind, that Aphrodite had been one of Hermes' lovers centuries before then.

"I've been thinking about the contest lately and I wanted to ask you, does anything peculiar about it come to mind?"

"Hah! You're still mad that I won! I still have the golden apple."

Hera's teeth gritted under her smile. "I got over that centuries ago." She sipped her coffee, hoping Aphrodite would do the same. "But a funny thing occurred to me recently. Why is it we're always in competition with each other, yet neither of us has a grudge against Athena?"

"Are you kidding?" Aphrodite picked up a diamond of Baklava and bit it in half. Pastry crumbs sprayed her chin. "She's not in the same class. Too maidenly to take her clothes off when she takes a bath."

Hera averted her eyes to avoid the unattractive sight of filo dough churning in Aphrodite's mouth. "Let me put it another way. Have you ever noticed most of the problems between us were started by someone else?"

Aphrodite swallowed; eyes wide. "You mean we're being *used*?" She vaulted from her chair and started pacing. "Heaven and Earth, have people been making fools of us and we didn't even realize it?"

"Looks that way," Hera said smoothly. "Whatever shall we do?"

Aphrodite made a fist. "Revenge!"

"Exactly. And you know what the best revenge is, don't you?"

"Flay their skins and boil them in oil!"

"Vivid, but no. The best revenge is living well, and that's what we're going to do. I've had a bag made up for each of us—"

"Oh no, not another Zeus-forsaken gift bag."

"Not in the least." Hera reached under the table and produced two large, zippered shoulder bags, one red the other hot pink. "These are gym bags. Finish your coffee, Aphrodite, we're going to Zumba class."

The Underworld
Heracles

Heracles stepped from Charon's barge, a flat open vessel with a high prow, onto the far bank of the River Styx. He stole toward the gate to the Underworld, marrow bones in hand. The hell hound's serpent tail thumped as he approached.

"There's my Cerberus. There's my boy. Good fellow!"

Three dog heads whined with pleasure. Their fearsome-toothed chops streamed waterfalls of canine drool.

"Treat for you, boy. Sit!"

Mouths grimaced. Three pairs of red eyes implored.

"Not until you sit."

The beast reluctantly sat on its haunches and raised its forelegs.

"Good boy!" Starting with the head on the left, Heracles proffered three fist-sized beef bones. Three ear-shattering crunches in quick succession, three long-throated swallows. The tail thumped again.

"Ahoy!"

Charon's voice, a unique pitch of gravel and foghorn, gave the agreed-upon warning.

Heracles dashed for the barge and stuffed as much of his bulk under a bench as he could manage. Charon covered him with a tarp. He barely breathed, ears sharp to hear what was happening. Two sets of sandaled feet, one pair with heavy tread and one with light, approached the riverbank.

"Your Royal Highness," Charon growled. The barge rocked slightly, the old seaman doubtless pulling his forelock and bowing in reverence.

"Many passengers today?" Hades voice was as deep as a bull's.

"About average, my King. We seem to be past the bottleneck."

When Heracles had taken over as escort to the newly dead, tens of thousands of souls had responded to his call, many of them agitated. *Where's Hermes? What's been keeping you? I demand a discount for waiting so long!* One soul said he'd been dead since April. Working six nights a week, Heracles had almost caught up with the backlog and was down to moonlighting on Monday, Wednesday and Friday.

"Humpf. I suppose this means the end of the windfall?"

"Seems so, Your Royal Highness."

A playful bark emanated from the area of the gate.

"What's wrong with him?" boomed Hades. "Anatole, go see to the blasted dog."

"Yes, sir." The lighter pair of feet retreated. A pause ensued.

"Well?"

"It appears Cerberus wants to shake, sir."

"Shake?"

"Yes, sir. Shake paws, sir."

Heracles smiled under the canvas. *Good boy!* They'd been working on "shake" all week.

"Heaven and Earth! Is there no order in this place?" Hades' heavy tread pounded toward the gate. "Look at him, he's as plump as a partridge! Explain this, boatman!"

"Couldn't say, Your Royal Highness," Charon said in as humble a tone as foghorns and gravel allowed. "Maybe a case of gas?"

Charon always had a quick answer, Heracles would give him that. For a few pieces of gold he'd even told Heracles about the network of secret entrances to the Underworld, ones he controlled through a syndicate that charged a fraction of the usual fee, most of which went into his own ragged pocket.

"Gas? Bah! Back to the palace, Anatole. I'll scour the butcher's bill and get to the bottom of this."

The footsteps receded and died.

Heracles chuckled. He rolled back the canvas and extracted himself from under the bench, weary from his extra duties but glad just the same. His bonus made Hebe happy, the marrow bones made Cerberus happy and he'd have quite a tale for Persephone the next time they were hiding out together at a family party. Better still, he'd learned a dozen ways to sneak into the Underworld. Though Heracles wasn't sure how he'd use this information to his advantage, he knew that someday, somehow, the chance would come.

END OF MONTH FOUR

MONTH FIVE

October 20-November 14, 2025

THURSDAY, OCTOBER 23, 2025

City of Mount Olympus
Elle

It would have taken dynamite to blast Elle out of her desert humanitarian work but Apollo's summons back to Mount Olympus was one she was compelled to answer. They sat in his New Mycenae office, door closed, studying the prints of ultrasound images from an unnamed patient. In the millennia she'd served as a midwife, she'd never seen anything like it.

"You're sure it's a baby?" She traced the static curls of gas with her finger. In some but not all images, an outline that could be interpreted as a human head appeared.

"It's in a womb and there's a beating heart so yes, I've concluded it's a baby."

Elle twisted an ear stud, perplexed. "And you think it's viable?"

"There's no reason to think otherwise. I've seen some unusual pregnancies in my time. When Leda was carrying Helen and Polydeuces they were shaped like swans until the third trimester. And you remember Io. Providing prenatal care for a woman transformed into a cow is not something I'd care to repeat."

"But the babies were human when they were delivered," she said, drawing on ancient memories. "Do you think that's possible in the current case?"

"Anything's possible." Apollo stood and opened the door. "Ready to see the patient?"

He showed her to an examining room. A youngish, dark-haired woman in a hospital gown sat uncomfortably in a chair, as if it were difficult to keep her balance.

"Monique," Apollo said to the woman, "this is Ilithyia. She's the consultant we discussed on your last visit."

"Cousin," the woman said. She held out her hand. It was cold to the touch.

"It's good to see you, and please, call me Elle." Elle recognized Monique from some family party or other. The patient was

Aphrodite's daughter, someone Elle had never given much thought. "How are you feeling today?"

"Tired. Not bad, but tired."

"Nausea?"

"In the mornings, mostly."

Elle smiled. "That's normal."

She took Monique's blood pressure (high normal range) and listened to her heart. When she set the stethoscope on Monique's belly something like a tympani thundered in her ears.

"Whoa!" She rolled back on her stool. "Strong heart. Let's get you on the examining table."

Once Monique was settled, Elle placed her hands over the fetus. She closed her eyes to concentrate, to feel the shape of Monique's belly and the pulsing within. The beat wouldn't localize, a swirling diaspora of muscle and blood. A chill ran through her, like one she'd felt at her sister Veronica's bedside when Veronica had been struck blind by a terrible force of darkness. She opened her eyes and looked grimly at Apollo.

"You can dress now, Monique," the doctor said. "We'll be back to talk with you in a few minutes."

They returned to his office and closed the door.

"Your opinion?" Apollo said once they were seated.

"I know what it is, but I won't say its name."

She told him of her experience at Veronica's bedside.

"Another colleague of mine has dealt with this force," Apollo said. "I think we should bring him in on the case."

She assented.

"Meanwhile," he said, rising, "we need to explain the seriousness of the situation to the mother, for her sake as well as the child's. If you can get her to talk about the father, who or what he is, it will help us determine the best path of treatment."

Elle's dark mood plummeted. Her title, Goddess of Childbirth, weighed like a millstone around her neck. She belonged in the desert delivering aid, not here tending the mother of a demon, but when Apollo himself called upon her to assist with a pregnancy she was bound to obey.

FRIDAY, OCTOBER 24, 2025

Seattle, Washington
Candy

Jim met Candy at the penthouse door with a warm embrace and a glass of wine. "Sit down, sit down," he coaxed, leading her to the living room. "I'll get Titus and let Cleo and David know you're here."

Candy sank onto the sofa, kicked off her mortal-wear pumps and wiggled her toes. It had been a long couple of weeks, leading seminars in all the major West Coast cities. Enrollment had increased by seventy percent since the introduction of the costume gift bags. She strongly suspected most of the new enthusiasts paid little attention to the *Deep Marriage* lectures, their thoughts straying to the "Connubial Playtime on Your Own" slot in the schedule.

Jim returned, Titus cradled in his arms.

"Hi stranger," she said, reaching for her boy.

"Ma-ma!" he chirped and tugged her hair.

She lured him into a game of peek-a-boo. So much time away, and this trip she'd missed time with their guests, too. A rare opportunity lost, as few of their immortal friends visited Seattle.

Cleo and David entered the room.

"Hi." Candy started to rise.

"Please don't get up," Cleo said. "You must be exhausted."

Jim arrived with a tray, a bottle and three more wine glasses.

"A toast to the return of our traveler," he proposed when the glasses were filled.

The others swarmed to the sofa to clink glasses. Jim sat alongside Candy. "What's new out in the big world?" he said.

Cleo and David took the oversized armchairs opposite. They looked so young. Cute couple, Candy thought, though she wasn't sure how together they really were. There was a hesitation between them that made her wonder.

"Oh, you know how the mortals are," she said with a wave of her hand. "I'm sure you've heard the latest gossip from Mount Olympus?"

"Now, Candy," Jim warned. She knew he didn't like it when she talked about other immortals but what she'd heard was too good not to share.

"Oh, but this is fun. Hera told me she and Aphrodite are going to Zumba class."

"Wow," said David.

"Together?" Jim said in an astonished tone.

"Straight from the boss's mouth," Candy said. "She didn't say how it happened, but I'll bet it's from getting friendlier through their new business arrangement. Oh, and then there's Monique."

Jim laughed. "Don't tell me she's taken up Zumba, too?"

"Maybe so. But Hera says Monique's pregnant."

David set his wine on the coffee table and excused himself.

"You okay?" Candy called after him. "You look pale."

"Stomach," he replied.

Cleo, too, looked sick. "We've been spending a lot of time on the waterfront," she said hurriedly. "Too much fish and chips."

"But not tonight." Jim rose. "I'll get David some seltzer and give the sauce a stir. Your favorite dinner," he said to Candy.

"Thanks, honey." She adored his homemade lasagna. "So great to be home," she said to Cleo. "Now tell me everything you've done while I was away."

David returned, more subdued than usual but he said he felt better. Cleo took his news with odd coolness, but Candy was so happy to be home she didn't dwell on it. They passed a perfect evening until a few minutes past ten when a message from Apollo arrived. Jim, at his earliest convenience, was ordered to Mount Olympus.

City of Mount Olympus
Aphrodite

The Goddess of Love danced joyfully to the hip-hop beat. She copied the moves of Sadie (nee Saxonia but she'd updated her name), the Zumba instructor. Sweat sheeted Aphrodite's face and chest, trickled down her back underneath her hot-pink leotard. She grinned into the wall-length studio mirror, admiring her own fluid and graceful moves. Hera puffed in the row behind her, sometimes falling a beat behind but more than credible for someone sixty-six hundred. Arms, legs, hips, torso, jumping, sliding, and gyrating on happy feet! They totally rocked in the One Hour Body Works five thousand and over class.

All too soon the cool-down music played. Sadie led them through a slow routine and some stretches, clapped her hands and yelled, "Outstanding, ladies!" as she did at the end of every session. Aphrodite felt warm and relaxed all over. How was it possible she'd only started this new course in life a week ago? Non-ritual dancing had never crossed her radar before now, and it was a blast!

Free! That's what her mind said as she showered and changed into her toga. Free of the business, Monique's baby and everything else that weighed on her. All this because Hera had taken the time and trouble to get her off her drunk but perfect butt and get a grip!

Hera joined her in front of the locker room mirror, brushed her silver mane smooth and applied fresh lipstick. "Time for a little something on the way home?" she asked.

"You bet!" They'd split a plate of antipasto, sip one and only one glass of wine apiece and talk things over, as they'd done on Monday and Wednesday. Never in her wildest dreams had she imagined her mother-in-law could be a resource instead of a nemesis.

At Club Dionysus, Hera led the way to what had become their usual table in the bar section. "Whew!" The older Goddess plopped into a long-legged chair at the high, round table. "Sadie really put us through it today. What's new with you?"

"The baby. It's…" Aphrodite paused, upset by what she didn't know as well as yesterday's news. "Are you sure you want to hear this?"

Hera smiled reassuringly. "There's not much in this world I haven't seen, twice."

Ganymede arrived with two large glasses of water and took their order. Aphrodite sipped, relishing the rush of rehydration as she considered how to share the latest.

"You know she wouldn't tell me who the father is."

Hera nodded and leaned forward.

"She still hasn't, but she did tell me there's something different about the baby. She wouldn't say wrong, but I don't think it's good. Apollo brought in a specialist for a consultation yesterday, but Monique hasn't told me what happened." Frustration pulsed through her. "I wonder if she's told the damn father, whoever in Tartarus he may be?"

The wine and antipasto arrived. "When's the baby due?"

"No one's really sure." Aphrodite gulped a mouthful of red, more than she'd meant to.

"Apollo's not sure? I find that hard to believe."

"All I know is what I've been told." She tapped Hera's glass with her own. "Cheers."

"Kids," Hera returned. "They can be stubborn." She nudged the plate toward Aphrodite. "Have some olives."

The Kalamata olives were a house specialty, pitted and stuffed with Feta cheese. Aphrodite savored the salty goodness and licked her fingers. "Seems like it's always me who does the talking," she said, eyeing Hera. "Anything you want to talk about?"

Hera laughed and shared the latest installment of Veronica's pique at Clifford. "She's so used to being in charge of everything, it's hard for her to set boundaries," Hera rationalized. "She even lectured *me* a couple of weeks ago, if you can believe it."

"You can tell her from me that, with lovers, enticement works better than dominance." Aphrodite rolled her eyes. "Most of the time, anyway."

They laughed.

"How's your traveler? Heard anything from David?"

The flicker of anxiety crossed Hera's face so quickly she almost didn't catch it.

Hera shrugged. "Not a word. You know how kids are."

"Hera." Aphrodite set her hand on her friend's. "I'm really sorry I interfered, giving him a clue about his father." Hera started to pull her hand away, but Aphrodite held on. "Listen to me. I owe you. I mean it. I'd still be staggering around drunk if you hadn't intervened. The identity of David's father is your secret to keep. From now on, what happened in Tiberias stays in Tiberias, okay?"

They sipped their wine, eyes locked.

"Thank you," Hera said at last, breaking the silence. Ganymede arrived with the bill. "My turn." Hera plunked down her Bank of Olympus platinum card and left as soon as she'd signed the receipt, though an inch of Chardonnay remained in her glass.

Thursday, October 30, 2025

City of Mount Olympus
Pan

Pan flew into the capital city of the gods on his own power. His return from the mortal desert took a matter of minutes, thanks to the warp speed training he'd received for his undercover military assignment. The last nest of warlords had fallen to Operation Tigers to Butter, killing each other over the last Rolex watch and the first of a new generation iPhone. In a debriefing with Elle's top aide (Elle, herself, being called back to Mount Olympus last week) he'd received hearty congratulations for a job done quickly and well.

His crowning contribution had been creating the digital illusion of a warlord's encampment in strategic locations throughout the desert, complete with nightly revels and occasional beheadings. Pan had lured blood-thirsty bandits to these sites and, cloaking himself once his targets were distracted by their lust for power and riches, fitted them with virtual reality gear and real weapons. All he had to do then was stand back and let nature take its course. It was an idea he'd developed in an exchange of messages with Hermes one night when he was cloaked and hiding out from a routine bloodbath. Hermes had sent projection beacons via drone and placed them at coordinates determined by Elle and Pan. Now that he was back on Mount Olympus he'd track down Hermes and thank him for his invaluable assistance. But first he was due at the Department of Armed Forces.

He ascended the gold-railed staircase, his filthy and fragrant mortal-style uniform drawing sharp reactions from those he passed but Pan was too preoccupied to care. He'd forwarded his ETA and they were waiting for him upstairs: Athena and Ares, the top brass.

It was thirteen hundred when he arrived at the elevators. The post-lunch crowd parted for him when the doors of an upward bound car rolled open. Tempted as he was to believe they were showing a military hero his due, their sniffs and expletives said otherwise.

The car stopped on the ninth floor. When the doors parted he faced a six-piece brass band. They struck up a march. People cheered and threw confetti. Two beautiful young women who seemed immune to his smell each took an arm and escorted him to Athena's office. The band marched behind them. Some sort of expansion magic had been worked; Athena's office stretched to the size of a reception hall. A red carpet, lined with cheering immortals from every department, ran to a platform at the far end. Chants of "Pan!" and "End Hunger!" alternated from side to side.

Pan stood, open-mouthed. A hand gripped his elbow.

"Time for a hero's welcome," Ares said in his ear. The God of Agriculture led Pan down the red carpet toward the platform where Athena, owl on shoulder even on this occasion, waited. The Goddess of War and Wisdom wasn't known for her radiant smiles, but she beamed one now.

"Hail, kinsman," she shouted, arms spread wide. Pan stumbled up to the platform. Athena took him by the shoulders and kissed him on both cheeks. She raised her hand to silence the brass band and jubilant cheers.

"Today we gather in honor of Pan, and his inimitable contributions to the War Against Hunger."

Cheers surged again. Athena again urged the crowd to silence and waved two people dressed in white togas edged with gold onto the platform. Veronica held a large gold key. Zeus carried a red velvet pillow topped with something shiny.

"In recognition of extraordinary valor," Zeus said in a voice that vibrated through the hall, "we present Pan, God of Shepherds and Flocks, with the Olympian Cross."

Athena took the medal from the pillow and pinned it over Pan's heart. His knees went weak. This honor had been given only once before, ages ago, when Heracles, single-handed, had repelled a band of chthonic monsters that were trying to seize the City of Mount Olympus.

Veronica spoke next. "Pan, in acknowledgement of your dedication, bravery and nerve," a few giggles rippled through the room, but Veronica merely smiled, "we give you the Key to the City of Mount Olympus."

"Speech! Speech! Speech!"

A tear rolled down Pan's unshaven cheek.

"It's been my honor to serve."

A roar of approval thundered. Someone handed him a glass of champagne. Pan stared at the sea of immortal faces. Overwhelmed, he cloaked himself and abandoned the grateful mob for the quiet of the city's best bath house.

SATURDAY, NOVEMBER 1, 2025

City of Mount Olympus
Hermes

 Hermes rolled toward the fashionable New Mycenae district in his custom sports chariot, a bright blue two-person rig pulled by a thoroughbred stallion. It wasn't a swanky brunch or a game of racquetball he'd been summoned to: Apollo had commanded Hermes to present himself to discuss his monitoring of The Power.

 The Trickster was annoyed. He had more interesting assignments to attend to. Athena's operatives in the mortal world had unearthed some scandalous tidbits about a powerful fossil fuel magnate and were designing their sting tactics. That project was worth pursing, unlike the pointless security duty he'd walked away from. For too long he'd monitored the detention cell, had reviewed every recorded second of surveillance personally. There was nothing out of order, not a blip, not a bleep. Why wouldn't Apollo accept that nothing had been missed?

 He drove his chariot around the last corner and glided into a parking spot in front of Apollo's clinic. "Whoa, Alexander." The stallion stopped along the curb.

 "Not long, boy, I hope." Hermes slipped a lightly provisioned feed bag onto the horse's nose and over his ears. A "closed" sign was displayed on the door, though the hours painted beneath it showed the office was open on Saturday. Apollo waited on the other side. He let Hermes in. An antiseptic smell assaulted Hermes' nostrils.

 Two others were in Apollo's private office, Hermes' half-sister Elle and Jim Smith, the psychological counselor who'd discovered The Power hiding in an antique intercom ten years ago. Apollo gestured Hermes to a vacant chair and took a seat behind his desk.

 "Thank you all for meeting with me this morning. Simply put, we have a crisis on our hands. It's urgent we come together as a team and share our findings regarding," he paused and lowered his voice, "The Power."

 The spoken words chilled Hermes. The other three were pale,

their expressions grim.

"Jim," said Apollo, "you were the first to observe the subject of our investigation. Please tell us about your experience."

Hermes listened to Jim's story of the black aura hovering around Stella, the deranged crone who'd been The Power's secret keeper, during his recent visit at Olympus Rest. Elle was next, telling about the supernatural force she'd felt while examining a pregnant woman. Hermes thought of Monique. He'd called her since their encounter on the staircase, but she hadn't called back. His own report was brief. "Nothing unusual to report."

Apollo leaned forward, elbows on desk, his chin resting in his hands. "I'll pose two questions. First, are the black aura and the supernatural force in the woman's womb related? Also, is the entity we suspect of causing these abnormalities intelligent enough to conceal the fact it's escaped from its cell?"

The second question made Hermes' head spin. If It possessed such super-intelligence, could a mere immortal even begin to assess Its capabilities? What was Its motive in shrouding a crazy old woman or, bizarre as it seemed, creating a baby? Could It shift into a humanoid male form and stage a seduction? If that was not possible, how else could It impregnate a woman, if Elle's conclusion was correct?

They brainstormed the questions, Apollo writing furiously on a whiteboard while they all contributed ideas. Moving forward, everyone was tasked to ponder Apollo's two questions and report any new observations: Jim would visit Stella, Elle and Apollo would reexamine the expectant mother, Hermes would continue to monitor security.

Hermes' head was pounding by the time he removed Alexander's feed bag and took up the chariot lines. Pan had invited him to dinner at Club Dionysus this evening. He was tempted to cancel and spend the rest of the night in the seventh basement, staring at security monitors. He'd been too cocky, washing his hands of the project. What had he missed? Jim's and Elle's observations indicated The Power was out in the world again. Security, somehow, had failed.

Failure, again. Pan had become a hero in spite of him, not because of him. Monique was pregnant and wouldn't talk to him, though he was certain the child was his. Roderick Waller had outclassed him in ideas for curbing climate change. If he failed any more, he might as well go to a tattoo parlor and have "Loser" emblazoned on his forehead.

MONDAY, NOVEMBER 3, 2025

Jim

It was as familiar as an old coat, visiting Stella in the Olympus Rest common room—a moldy, itchy coat with holes in it that no longer kept out the chill. She was kicking his butt at *Stratego!* and he was getting nowhere. Her aura was a dull green-grey instead of the typical purple hue of an immortal, plus a gold super-corona befitting her Big-G ancestry. The black shroud had yet to make an appearance.

He purposely tapped one of her bombs with a sergeant.

"Boom!" she cackled.

He was pursuing an indirect approach to find out if she knew anything about the supernatural pregnancy. So far he'd asked (though he knew the answers already) if she had any children of her own (no); if she'd share with him a favorite childhood experience (buzz off!); if she'd ever had to change the diapers of her younger siblings (I was in hiding, idiot!).

She captured his flag. Again.

"Long live red!" Stella cried, holding her flag playing piece aloft.

"And blue dead again," he said, "without a son and heir."

Stella's copper-colored eyes sparkled. "That's what they all think," she said, her voice an octave lower than its regular tone. A faint black outline surrounded her.

"It's the end of the line, Stella," he ventured.

The black outline thickened and pulsed.

"You'll see," Stella said. "You'll *all* see." She sagged back in her chair as if exhausted. The outline vanished.

"Care for another game?" Jim said.

"Fool," she murmured.

Maybe so, but now he could answer both of Apollo's questions: Stella's black aura was definitely related to the baby and The Power was definitely coming and going at will.

WEDNESDAY, NOVEMBER 5, 2025

Elle

Elle regarded her patient with as much calm as she could muster. The results of Monique's physical examination were consistent with prior ones, but in less than two weeks the baby, whatever its species, had grown larger by half.

"Still experiencing nausea?"

"Not much."

"Good. How's your energy?" Elle glanced at Apollo to make sure he was listening. He was, of course. It was difficult to contain her own nervousness.

Monique sighed. "I seem to need a lot of sleep right now. I'm training someone to take over at work for a few weeks when the baby comes."

"A wise plan," said Apollo. He'd told Elle about Jim's recent appointment with Stella, how she'd hinted in an otherworldly voice about an heir. Now it was Elle's turn to investigate this notion from the other side.

"I'm sure the father will want to help with the baby," Elle said. Monique turned her face toward the wall. Elle took Monique's hand. "We've talked about complications," she reminded her patient. "This is a very unusual pregnancy. You may need help we can't envision until the baby arrives."

After a long silence Monique murmured, "It might be one of his experiments."

"Whose experiment, Monique?" Elle urged.

"He likes to invent things," Monique said, "the baby's father, he's—"

Monique broke off in a scream and writhed so violently Elle and Apollo had to hold her down to keep her from falling off the table.

"Mine!" Monique cried, her voice so deep and vibrant it shook the room. "Mine!"

FRIDAY, NOVEMBER 7, 2025

Elle

They'd moved Monique to a private room at Olympus Rest. The being she carried had grown alarmingly in the two days since. The measurements indicated that, if it were a human of some kind, it was nearly at term. Aphrodite, Monique's closest relative, waited in the hall; she had no idea who the father might be.

Apollo looked up from their patient who lay, sedated, on a hospital bed. "She needs rest." Monique's arms and legs were strapped down to prevent her from harming herself. Her cheeks bore deep scratches, inflicted by her own fingernails. "We can watch her on the monitor, outside."

Elle dimmed the lights. Apollo closed the door softly behind them. In the hallway, Hermes and Jim Smith had joined Aphrodite. Apollo looked at each in turn.

"Anything new to report?"

Jim looked drawn. Hermes gestured toward the monitor. "That's Monique."

"You, Hermes?" Aphrodite burst into an odd, anguished laugh. "You're the father?"

Jim Smith cleared his throat. "I've checked Stella's records. The timing of her last violent episode coincides with Monique's seizure on Wednesday. Stella's in restraints. She can still spit, though." Jim wiped a spot near his left eye. "I've instructed her attendants not to sedate her as you requested, Apollo."

Apollo turned to Hermes. "Any security irregularities on Wednesday, the day of Monique's seizure?"

"None."

He was visibly trembling. Elle lay a hand on Hermes' arm. "You believe you're the baby's father?" she said.

"I never should have taken her there," Hermes murmured. He told them about the tryst in The Power's cell.

Jim grabbed Hermes by the shoulders and shook him. Instead of resisting Hermes flapped like a ragdoll. "What in Heaven and Earth did you think you were doing? You of all people should understand the stupidity of tempting that—that *thing*."

"You've impregnated my daughter with a monster!" Aphrodite flew at Hermes, her fingernails poised to strike his eyes. Apollo caught her by the waist and swung her away the instant before contact. Elle seized the confusion of the moment and placed herself between Jim and Hermes, pushing them apart.

"In a way, we have Hermes to thank," Apollo said, keeping tight hold on Aphrodite. "His involvement is the missing piece of the puzzle, don't you see? The Power needed him to act as a host. I believe Monique's baby was fathered by them both."

Aphrodite twisted away from him and backed down the hall. "I'm going straight to Zeus about this," she spat. "He's still the most powerful God on Olympus!"

She turned and ran. Jim started after her.

"Wait." Apollo grabbed Jim's arm. "Let her go. We can use Zeus' help."

Elle's brain whirled. She looked at Monique's image on the monitor screen. How could they deliver a baby that was part—

A ragged scream tore the air.

"Heaven and Earth!" Elle threw open the door and ran to Monique's side. She clasped one of the rigid, restrained hands and lay her other hand on the patient's forehead, gently pressing Monique's head onto the pillow. Hermes had Monique's other hand. Tears streamed down his cheeks. Apollo's hands lay on Monique's belly that pulsed up and down like it was filled with hyperactive pistons. The door slammed shut. A chill filled the room. All went black.

~ * ~

Alone in the hallway, Jim Smith tried the door handle. It was locked. He sensed the concentration of energy in Monique's room. He'd heard her scream but now no sound came from within. That shouldn't be possible. None of this should be possible.

Terrified for those locked in the room, he paced. Zeus would arrive soon, but he might not be soon enough. Jim turned on his heel and ran down the corridor, toward the wing where Stella was confined.

He entered a scene of chaos. Stella had broken free from the restraint holding her right arm and was swinging it violently. One attendant bobbed and weaved to avoid her blows; the other, a sturdy male, was crumpled against a wall. He appeared to be unconscious.

"The Power has arrived!" Stella screamed. Her hand formed a fist and pointed to the ceiling. "It will crush you all!" Her pupils were so severely dilated her eyes were black.

Jim pulled the conscious attendant away from Stella's bedside. "When did this start?"

"Couple of minutes ago," the attendant said. "She cold-cocked Robinson over there before we noticed her arm was free."

Time pressed hard. Was The Power using Stella to channel its energy to Monique's baby? If he could distract Stella for a few seconds the energy might falter.

"Stella, listen to me." Jim lunged forward and gripped her arm. He tried but failed to push it down from its raised position. A wild, lonesome cry rose around her.

"It's Jim Smith, Stella," he shouted over the din. She stared straight ahead, didn't blink when he waved his free hand in front of her face. "Looks like you've won at last. Your father, Cronus, would be proud, but he's dead, of course."

Her eyelids twitched.

"Victory must feel hollow without his praise," Jim ventured, "like all those times I've let you beat me at *Stratego*."

Stella blinked.

"Funny, The Power didn't save Cronus from Zeus. Almost like Cronus was being used, don't you think? Once It was done with him, It let him die."

"Lies!" Her arm unlocked and cut the air so forcefully Jim could barely stay on his feet. "My father passed The Power to me! At last I'll avenge myself on Zeus and the rest of you!"

"If you survive," Jim countered. Every muscle strained to fight Stella's arm. "It won't need you anymore when It has an heir."

An animal scream ripped from her throat and echoed around the room. The wild, lonesome sound ceased. Stella went limp. She fell back in her bed.

"Heaven and Earth," Jim swore. "Stay with her," he ordered the attendant and dashed from the room to find out what was happening to Monique.

Zeus and Aphrodite were in the hallway, their palms pressed against Monique's door, faces set in grim determination.

"Energy transfer," Zeus said through gritted teeth.

It was training Jim had received as a Continental Manager, to be used in emergencies when mortals were trapped in cave-ins or underneath the rubble of earthquakes. He moved between them and planted his palms against the metal. *Open*, he said in his mind, eyes closed in concentration. The wild, lonely sound keened on the other side of the door. *Open*.

~ * ~

Monique gripped Elle's hand so hard it felt like the bones would break. "Breathe!" she coached, unable to see her patient in the darkness.

"It's crawling on me!"

Hermes' voice came from the other side of the hospital bed. "Hold on!"

A chilling cry rose alongside Elle. "It's cut my hands." Apollo's voice, a monotone of shock. Why in the name of Heaven and Earth wouldn't the lights come on?

"Breathe," Elle said again, struggling to keep her voice steady. Disembodied shrieks filled the room and rose to an ear-splitting pitch that threatened to strike her deaf. In the darkness a glow appeared, four luminous patches on the door. The sound of tearing flesh and Monique's scream shredded the air. A baby cried. Monique's hand went limp.

"Monique, can you hear me?"

No reply.

Six patches glowed on the door now. The metal shivered and clattered to the floor in pieces. Three people stood in the opening. A dazzling light shimmered around them, then dissipated.

Zeus entered the room. "Heaven and Earth! Is everybody all right?" Aphrodite pushed past him to Monique. Jim lingered in the doorway, staring. The baby lay on its mother's chest in a pool of blood. Monique's belly looked as if it had been ripped open by an enraged bear.

Elle, on autopilot, searched the supply drawers for suture, needles and antiseptic. A quick glance showed Apollo's hands were slashed and bleeding. Her own hands shaking, Elle began to sew up Monique. The baby whimpered in Aphrodite's blood-smeared arms.

"Will she be all right?" said Hermes.

"Her pulse is weak." Apollo said. In her periphery, Elle saw his bloody hand on Monique's wrist. "Respiration shallow but steady. Too early to assess if there's permanent damage but we're not looking at the Rare Event."

The Rare Event. The thing that, by definition, should never happen to an immortal but, on rare occasions, did.

"Stella!" Jim shouted. The slap of his sandals receded down the hall.

Elle worked until the jagged wound in Monique's midsection was sutured. The scar would be much worse than one from a conventional C-Section but her internal organs, thank Zeus, had been spared.

Aphrodite spoke. "What do we do with him?"

The newborn in her arms was a normal-looking boy. Head, limbs, fingers, and toes. Nothing suggested supernatural parentage. Elle reached for him.

"I'll clean him up." She smoothed a towel on the counter and gently swabbed off blood, shreds of skin and amniotic fluid. One unusual feature was now evident: the baby had two navels.

~ * ~

Jim arrived at Stella's room winded, his hand pressed against the stitch in his side. The lights were dim. Both attendants were conscious. One made entries on a clipboard, the other watched the monitor. The arm restraint Stella had destroyed had been replaced. She appeared to be sleeping.

"How is she?" he said when he could draw a full breath.

The wiry attendant gestured at the monitor. Some lines were nearly flat. Others pulsed anemically. "Coma. Alive but not responsive."

"How long has she been this way?"

The other attendant consulted his clipboard. "Ten minutes, maybe a little less. I was unconscious when it started. Jack here," the man gestured to the wiry attendant, "gave me the time."

"Started when she fell back on her bed," Jack confirmed.

Jim looked from one exhausted face to the other. "You guys must be whipped. I'd be happy to sit with her if you need a break."

"Thanks," said the clipboard guy, name of Robinson, Jim remembered. Robinson touched a smear of dried blood on his temple and winced. "Mind if I go first, Jack? I should stop by the infirmary and get this cleaned up."

"Fine with me."

Robinson walked out. Jack returned to his work. Jim pulled up a chair on the other side of the bed and placed his hand over Stella's. It was cold, the skin blue-gray.

"What have you gotten yourself into this time, old girl?" Monique, Heaven and Earth be praised, had escaped the Rare Event, but would Stella?

~ * ~

As soon as Zeus observed Monique's baby had been born, he ran from Olympus Rest and flew over marble streets toward Olympus, Inc. As he soared through the air he messaged Veronica he was on his way to discuss an emergency. Intuition told him not all of The Power resided in the baby.

Veronica met him in front of headquarters. By the time they were in the elevator he'd briefed her. They arrived on the top floor and stopped at the executive assistant's desk.

"Alexandra," Veronica said.

The young woman with short hair and a simple but expensively made toga looked up from a document she was reading. She eyed Zeus, her expression quizzical.

"The budget can wait. Take the rest of the afternoon off."

Alexandra's brow creased but she cleared her desk and left without a question.

Veronica strode to her own desk. Zeus took a seat opposite. Clouds, newly gathered on what had been a sunny November day, muted the skylight overhead and cast Veronica's face in gloom.

"Let me recap," she said, her voice staccato. "Monique was impregnated by The Power." Veronica flinched when she said the words but proceeded undeterred, counting each point with her fingers. "This happened when she and Hermes had an assignation in the containment cell. The baby was born within the last hour. The Power performed a sort of Caesarian section to free the baby. Monique is badly injured. The baby is humanoid in form. You believe The Power, or part of It, is now at large."

"Call it a hunch, but yes."

Her eyes flashed. "And no one breathed a word to me." She shook her head as if to reset her thoughts. "What do you recommend?"

"Assemble a team to track It down and either recapture It or lure It back to the vault."

"Who do you want?"

"Artemis is the best hunter. Heracles has experience with the chthonic deities." Zeus shivered to speak the name of the ancient subterraneans who thrived on bloody sacrifice. "I believe The Power is one of them."

"I'll reassign Heracles immediately." Veronica tapped a few words into the digital pad on her desk. "Artemis is in Africa, leading our efforts against game poachers. Her second-in-command is excellent and can run the program in her absence. I can get her here in a day or so. What about Pan?"

Zeus had already considered Pan but rejected using the recently minted hero. "Too close to the situation. The baby is his brother to some degree."

A chime emanated from Veronica's pad.

"Heracles will meet you in Security, seventh floor basement, half-an-hour." She looked up from the message. "I'll let you know what arrangement I make with Artemis."

Zeus took a precious second to feel pride in his daughter. Veronica's intelligence and emotional strength didn't falter in this crisis, though her own brutal trial with The Power couldn't be far from her thoughts.

"Veronica. Ronnie," he said, reverting to her family name, "what measures will you take for your own protection?"

"Don't worry, Dad," she said, though her eyes were filled with it. "I don't believe It has anything to gain from attacking me."

Zeus hoped she was right. The Power had reclaimed Stella, but she'd been Its willing accomplice in previous tragedies and was doubtless an easy access point. He'd ask Jim to look in on Veronica in coming days, to be on the safe side.

"Better go," Zeus said, rising. "I'll have Dean Phineas cover for me on campus." Hera wasn't going to like him doing what he knew he must, but then, he didn't like it either.

SATURDAY, NOVEMBER 8, 2025

Zeus

Zeus had been impatient to start. Instead of waiting for Artemis and forming a cohesive strategy with his full team, he'd jumped on Heracles' suggestion to search for Dark Things in dark places.

"That's what chthonic types like," Heracles had said. "Caves, cellars, undersea grottoes, the bottoms of wells. Where it's dark, that's where you'll find 'em."

They scoured the subterranean sites of Mount Olympus, plus an ill-lit bar or two, but came up empty-handed. Discouraged, Zeus called it a day.

Hera greeted Zeus at the condo door. Servants' night off, he remembered. All smiles, she took his arm and led him to his chaise in the den.

"Rough day?" Hera poured him a goblet of wine from a full bottle. She'd been drinking less, he'd noticed, since she'd started her exercise class.

"Not my favorite kind of work." The wine washed the day's dust from his throat.

She poured a glass for herself and stretched out on her chaise. "Are you ready to tell me what this is about, besides working with Heracles? Hebe told me that much."

Heaven and Earth. He and Veronica had agreed, the less known about the crisis the better. The minute word of The Power hit Mount Olympus, panic would spread. It had a history of working secretly and selectively. If It had gone to ground, chances were good It would keep to Itself for a while.

"Heracles should keep his mouth shut." What kind of security chief told his wife about his assignments? "I love him, of course, but sometimes I wish you hadn't made him immortal."

Hera's hand tensed around her goblet. "If I hadn't, Hebe would still be living with us."

It was an old feud between them. Though any Big-G god could make any mortal immortal, Hera was the only one to defy

Zeus' ban on doing so. Though she had a point about Hebe. The Goddess of Youth, now aged four millennia, was a perpetual nag and spendthrift. Not even a small-g god had stepped forward to claim her hand when she'd come of age.

Hera poured her wine back in the bottle. "I need some air." She hoisted herself off the chaise and strode through the archway.

"Sorry. I'm sorry!" Zeus started to follow her, then let her go. His feet were killing him after a day on the beat.

The front door slammed. Zeus kicked off his sandals and powered up his digital pad to see if there was news of Artemis.

MONƏAY, NOVEMBER 10, 2025

Pan

Pan perched on the edge of Monique's sofa. He held his alleged half-brother in his arms. Pan had never liked babies, wouldn't be here if Hermes hadn't begged him to come.

"I was a terrible father to you, I know, but now's my chance to do it right for P. B."

The initials didn't stand for a name. They described part of the baby's lineage: Power Baby. In appearance, his unnatural roots barely showed. His head was tufted with fine hair the color of Hermes' and his eyes were shaped like Monique's. As long as they kept his tummy covered, concealing the two navels, no one would guess the bizarre third rail of his parentage. Unless they saw him eat. The four-day-old baby had a voracious appetite. Cases of baby formula lined the living room, also a supply of rubber nipples. The little brute chewed through dozens a day in spite of having no teeth.

"I'll just check on Monique." Hermes tip-toed to the bedroom where P. B.'s mother recuperated.

P. B. gurgled and waved his tiny fists at Pan. The nasty glint in his eyes was unmistakable. This dude was bad news.

Hermes was gone a long time, probably had to do something for Monique. Pan had looked in on her when he'd first arrived and was shocked by her appearance. Her expression was listless. Her long, thick hair was white.

Burp me!

The words growled in his head. Pan stared at the baby. The words came again.

"Okay, okay!"

Pan put a towel over his shoulder the way Hermes had shown him and hoisted the baby against his chest. Two pats of his hand on the tiny back and the little bastard blew chunks all over the wall. Pan laid P. B. on the sofa beside him and removed the sodden towel from his person. Whatever it was that had leaked through to his toga reeked of month-old garbage. P. B. cooed, in duet with the vile chuckle dancing in Pan's head.

Hermes emerged from the bedroom and softly shut the door behind him. "I'm back. Everything okay?"

The besotted gaze Hermes beamed at P. B. sickened Pan. Thank Heaven and Earth Veronica had implemented a family leave policy so no one else had to see Hermes being such a dork.

"Yeah. Everything's fine." No way was this guy going to believe his infant son was a budding force of evil, in spite of the facts. Hermes had confided that not even Zeus could figure out where The Power had gone after P. B.'s birth. Pan suspected it lay on the couch beside him.

Tuesday, November 11, 2025

Seattle, Washington
Clifford

Clifford scanned the computer screen for pressure equalization readings. The seawall that protected the highway tunnel from Elliott Bay was holding, just. Poseidon and his assistants worked from the water side while Clifford and Heinrich ran a reinforcement program within the seawall. More was needed to ensure the wall's integrity and protect the lives of the tens of thousands of commuters who used the tunnel daily. Though the personal cost was high, Clifford bowed to the inevitable solution.

"Structurelings," he said under his breath, "the good old-fashioned way."

It had been years since Olympus, Inc., had reinforced architectural structures with the dispersed molecules of specially trained immortals. In most applications the conversion had worked perfectly. This seawall was a potentially lethal exception.

"How much longer do you think it will hold?" Heinrich said.

Clifford rubbed his aching temples. "Weeks, if we're lucky."

"A mere blink."

How many workers in the Architectural and Computer Services Department would still be capable of old-style structureling technique? Of the thousands world-wide, who had the strength, skill and experience to master this crisis?

One name came to mind, but first he'd consult with Veronica. Not only would she have to approve his plan; she'd also have to help him implement it as only a full Big-G could do. Clifford took up his digital pad, selected the secured message app that went only to Veronica and tapped in his text. While he waited for her reply, he scrolled through his contact list and stopped on Ralph.

City of Mount Olympus
Zeus

Zeus and his team conferred in the cell that had housed The Power. A tall, middle-aged woman of athletic build knelt in the center of the cell, examining the cube that had contained It. After several minutes, Artemis rose and brushed the knees of her sand-colored camouflage trousers. Her analytical expression deepened her resemblance to Apollo, her twin.

"Both you and Hermes cast charms over the cubicle to reinforce the seal?"

"That's right."

Artemis nodded gravely. "Clearly it wasn't enough, but that's always a risk when dealing with something new. After ten years of confinement I don't believe our quarry will return."

Heracles, who'd been leaning against the cell wall studying his cuticles, came to life. "We've looked all over the city. Sounds like we're out of luck, unless you have some bright idea."

Heaven and Earth, Zeus hated working with these two. Heracles, easily offended for all his might, had been sniping at Artemis ever since she'd arrived on Monday.

"Just thinking like a hunter," Artemis returned coldly. "The Power," she said the name with no trace of fear, "came out for a reason. We believe the reason is Monique's baby."

They'd met P. B. yesterday. Pan was there, trying to hold the wiggly, snorting being he referred to as the little bastard. The cold, black stare the baby aimed at Zeus had chilled him to the core.

Artemis paced the front of the cell, hands clasped behind her back. "The Power wanted a child, an heir. It will want to raise Its heir in order to continue Its work. At some point, I believe The Power will make a grab for P. B. As such," she paused and looked at Zeus, then Heracles, "I believe P. B. is the ideal bait."

"Bait?" said Heracles dully.

"As in trap." Her eyes gleamed. "If we can determine the best place to contain The Power, a place from which it can never escape, I believe we can lure It there with P. B."

Zeus digested the idea. "Interesting, but where will we find such a place?"

Heracles said, "I know one."

"Yeah, right," said Artemis.

"Come on." Zeus intervened before they started carping at each other. "We have work to do." He led the way to the lobby, out of Olympus, Inc., headquarters and hailed a chariot.

"Where to?" said the driver.

"Athens U." And a charmed conference room where they could discuss their plans without fear of being overheard.

WeɒNeSɒAY, NOVemBeR 12, 2025

Persephone

The Queen of the Underworld sipped her Mai Tai, ruing each second as it slipped away. Persephone had stalled as long as she could but Demeter, her own mother, had ordered her to go back home on Friday. Tonight they were out on the town, dining at Club Dionysus.

"You can't stay up here forever, honey." Demeter reached across the table to pat her hand. "We have a schedule to keep. If you stay topside any longer, we're going to have to postpone spring. You wouldn't want that, would you? All those lambs waiting to be born, all those farmers getting cabin fever when they should be planting crops? We can't put our own wishes before the world's food supply, Sepphie."

"I know, I *know*!" Persephone winced at the sight of her own chipped nail polish. She always turned dowdy at this time of year, couldn't be helped when Earth's bounty was fading.

Demeter placed a hand over her heart. "I suffer, too, when you go underground."

Oh, don't I know it! Persephone gulped the rest of her Mai Tai and signaled Ganymede for another, her only defense against Mother's and Hades' guilt competition. He'd keyed a digital fit when she told him she'd be another week, ten days at the most. The message she'd sent him about wanting a baby had gone unanswered.

"That's strange."

Demeter's words derailed Persephone's funk.

"What?"

"Look over there." Demeter pointed to a tall, round table near the bar where two women sat. "Your Aunt Hera and Aphrodite. What in Heaven and Earth are they doing together? They've hated each other for millennia!"

That wasn't the only strange thing. Though Hera and Aphrodite wore their signature colors of red and hot pink, respectively, they were dressed is sweat suits. Very nice, obviously tailored sweat suits. They were sharing a bottle of wine, picking at a platter of antipasto and, strangest of all, smiling.

Ganymede arrived with a fresh Mai Tai for Persephone and a double shot of corn whiskey with a water back for Demeter.

"Compliments of the house," he said with a bow. "Dionysus thanks you for overseeing a difficult harvest."

Persephone basked in the recognition. Hades never praised or rewarded her. Sure, he said he couldn't wait for her to come back but she knew him too well. He was too miserly to show his love in a tangible way, would never foot the bill for a special welcome home feast. He'd probably tell the cook to make her deplorable, economical meatloaf. The only one who'd be happy to see her was Cerberus, and only because she brought him treats.

"We'll do a little shopping tomorrow. That will lift your spirits," Demeter said. She raised her shot glass and clinked it against the Mai Tai in a toast.

"Yes, Mother." Hades had cancelled her Bank of Olympus platinum card after a mild shopping spree last year—two marked-down summer togas and a new pair of sandals. It didn't matter anyway. Everything she wore in the Underworld looked drab. Maybe it was just as well Hades hadn't said anything about a baby. Who would be cruel enough to confine a living, breathing child in the Underworld?

~ * ~

Aphrodite touched her goblet to Hera's and savored a sip of Dionysus' Best Red, a full-bodied wine with a hint of cranberry.

"You are far too good to me."

Hera smiled. "You and I are two of very few immortals whose children have been plagued by," she leaned forward and whispered, "The Power. It's more than the mind can absorb, I know. I'm so glad Monique's recovery is progressing."

Aphrodite nodded. Apollo believed the physical damage Monique had sustained in childbirth would heal completely, but she would never forgive Hermes for his role in this disaster.

"I hear the baby's strong and healthy."

"Very."

Hera set down her glass. "Want to talk about it?"

Did she? Who wanted to talk or even think about what to do

with her grandson who was twenty-five percent evil? What kind of claims would his paranormal half-father make on him when he grew up?

Aphrodite shook her head. "No, but getting me out to Zumba class helps." She again clinked her goblet against Hera's. "Thanks."

Funny how things turned out sometimes. Last month they'd accidentally run into each other in a dive bar and now they had a regular Wednesday night date for dinner after Zumba. Her competitive enmity for Hera had been mere habit. Their individual realms of Love and Marriage didn't necessarily have to fight with each other; there was room to peacefully co-exist. Monique's gift bags had brought them where they were today. Poor Monique.

"I have to get the baby away from her," Aphrodite said. "She says she wants to keep it but I know her. I've seen her. She doesn't have the strength to raise that…thing."

Hera topped off Aphrodite's goblet. "It reminds me of the old days." she said. "Like the time I sent Heracles on his Twelve Trials, or the mess Hermes started with Helen of Troy."

"He's on my list," said Aphrodite. Hermes could grovel and wait on Monique all he wanted; it wouldn't change the danger he'd brought into their lives. She prayed to Heaven and Earth nothing worse would happen.

Hera's eyes narrowed. "Someone's finally tricked the Trickster. I hope the rest of us don't go down with him. Cheers."

She tapped her glass against Aphrodite's and threw back the contents like a pro.

ᴄhuʀsᴅᴀy, ᴎovembeʀ 13, 2025

Seattle, Washington
David

David Bernstein tugged at his turtleneck. The lobby of the beautiful old theatre had steam heat and he was sweltering. What was it, the hundredth time he'd attended a production of *Fiddler on the Roof*?

Cleo drew many admiring looks in the skimpy red dress Candy had lent her. She dawdled over her wine. It was five minutes to curtain when she set her empty glass on the tray of a passing waiter. Cleo took David's hand as they descended the aisle steps to their seats in the center section. In heels she was a full head taller than he, made him feel like he was a little kid going to a play with his mom.

"Why did Thelma have to give us tickets to this?"

"Try to relax and have a good time," Cleo whispered. "And keep your voice down. Mortals get edgy when people act irrational in public."

"I know, I know!" he hissed back. "I was one of them."

"I haven't been to the theatre for ages," she continued. "For Zeus' sake, let's have some fun for once on this trip."

Her lack of sympathy wounded him but he'd be damned if he'd let it show. The good manners Thelma Bernstein had drilled into him surfaced. He stepped gallantly aside and gestured for Cleo to take the inner of their pair of seats, placing himself on the aisle. She didn't say a word, just buried her nose in the program. Fine, he could shut her out, too. David flipped past the Artistic Director's greeting on the first page and beyond the advertisements to the cast list. After a quick scan he closed his program.

"What's the matter now?" Cleo murmured, frowning.

"Not very authentic. Hardly any of these people have Jewish-sounding names."

She made a clucking noise with her tongue. "Get over yourself, David. Most of them probably have stage names. For all you know, Dean Prescott," she pointed to the headshot of the actor playing Tevya, "could have been born Harold Schwartz."

"You've got an explanation for everything."

The auditorium lights began to fade.

Cleo put a finger to her lips. "Shhh!"

Conversations hushed. Crinkling programs settled in laps. The heavy red curtain rose, revealing a painted backdrop and a few set pieces to indicate the town of Anatevka. A wiry man with a violin moved gracefully around the stage, pantomiming the melody of the title song as played by the concertmaster in the orchestra pit. The actor named Dean Prescott entered as Tevya. He spoke lines so familiar David found himself mouthing along. But as the play unfolded, he was overtaken by its magic. Cleo laughed out loud at the words Tevya's five daughters sang about their hopes and fears of the matchmaker and gripped his arm when the full cast masterfully performed "Sabbath Prayer."

"He's really good," she whispered during the celebratory scene between Tevya and Lazar Wolf, the one that exploded into a raucous rendition of "To Life." "Not the main guy, the other one," she clarified.

David flipped through his program, pausing at the bio of Saul Crispin. "No wonder. That guy really is Jewish."

When the houselights came up at intermission David was relaxed and happy. They headed to the lobby and enjoyed another glass of wine. Cleo was like a kid, speculating about how the story would end. *Very cute*, he thought, for the first time in days.

The storyline grew somber in the second act. They both dabbed their eyes when the ensemble mourned the loss of their home, Anatevka.

"Bravo!" They stood with the rest of the audience, applauding.

The curtain rose and the actors returned to take their bows, first in groups of supernumeraries, followed by a rapid progression of individuals who'd played specific characters. Lazar Wolf was allowed a few seconds to bask in elevated applause. The actor Saul Crispin smiled, doffed his hat and bowed deeply to the audience.

"Weird," said David. "I didn't recognize that Crispin guy before he took off his hat, but he sure looks familiar. Must have seen him somewhere when I was living in Seattle, I guess?"

Cleo had stopped applauding. She stared at David.

"David, Saul Crispin looks like *you!*"

David's knees buckled. Cleo grabbed his arm to steady him.

Could it—how could it possibly be? Whoever the Mystery Dad of Jerusalem was, he'd died millennia ago. No way could his genes have made such a good copy thousands of years later. Saul Crispin, once he'd dropped the guise of Lazar Wolf, was pretty close to what David saw in the mirror every morning.

"It's a fluke, it's gotta be," he said weakly. But why would Thelma Bernstein have insisted on giving them tickets to this performance if there wasn't some special reason?

"He's got to be your father's descendant," Cleo said. "You don't look like Hera, except for your coloring. Clearly the man had killer genes."

After three curtain calls the cast was allowed to retreat. The audience lumbered up the aisles and into the lobby.

Cleo took his arm. "Maybe we can meet him?"

"I don't know," David mumbled, torn. He'd zeroed out so many times on this quest he barely had the heart to try again.

"You don't have to say anything about your dad." She nodded toward a curtained opening with *Cast only, please* posted above. "Just tell him how much you enjoyed his performance. Come on, I'll go with you."

She pulled him sideways through the departing audience members and they ducked behind the curtain into the restricted area.

David stumbled in the sudden dark. "I can't see a damn thing."

"Wait a minute," Cleo whispered. "Our eyes will adjust and then—oh, look at the floor. Let's follow the glowing arrows."

Cleo led the way through what seemed to be a subterranean warren until David realized they were somewhere under the highly raked auditorium seats. Stripes of glow tape marked a stairway ahead.

Up they climbed. David's heart pounded in his ears. No way could it be this simple, finding a trace of his long-lost father in Seattle, where he, himself, had lived for seven or eight years. The Crispin guy probably wouldn't look anything like him once his makeup was off. He might not talk to them anyway and who could blame him? Actors probably had crazies bothering them all the time.

It was lighter at the top of the stairs. A long room lined with mirrors and makeup tables was to the left. Dozens of actors were shedding costumes, removing hair pieces, and swabbing off their faces. None of them looked like Saul Crispin. A wall full of half-open doors was to the right.

"He must be in one of those," Cleo said.

David stepped back but she tugged him forward.

"We're not supposed to be here," he said through clenched teeth.

"In this chaos? No one's even noticed us. Come *on*."

He felt like a peeping Tom, peering into rooms no larger than closets to get a look at the occupants. Seeing most of Golda's ample bosom reflected in the first room's mirror fried his nerves. Ten rooms in all. By the time they reached the last one, David could barely breathe.

A gray beard lay on the makeup table, left of Saul Crispin's elbow. In the corner leaned a stomach-shaped piece of body padding. A pile of stained tissues were heaped to his right, another one in his hand, wiping the last traces of greasepaint from his forehead.

Cleo tapped her knuckles on the doorframe.

"Mr. Crispin?"

The actor leaned toward the mirror as if to study their reflections before turning, his smile warm but weary. "I don't believe I've had the pleasure…."

Crispin's mouth dropped open. David made a brief, guttural sound and stared.

"Come in, the two of you," Saul Crispin said after a pause that gaped across millennia. "And close the door, please."

They crammed into the tiny space and shut the door. Crispin rose and looked David in the eye.

"What's your name, young man?"

"D-David. David Bernstein."

Saul Crispin sagged backward and rested a hand on the table to steady himself.

"I believe I've met your parents, the Bernsteins. It was a long time ago, before you were born. I…."

Cleo squeezed David's arm.

"Ladies' room," she said. "See you in the lobby."

She slipped through the door and closed it softly behind her.

David tried three times before the word would come out.

"Dad?"

~ * ~

The three of them adjourned to the bar at the Palomino Restaurant, one block from the theatre. Saul Crispin recommended something called the Corpse Reviver from the martini list. David ordered a round.

"Thank the gods Thelma Bernstein didn't send you to a matinee." Crispin shook his head. "I don't think I could have made it through the evening performance if I'd met you in between."

David couldn't keep his eyes off his dad. He gripped Cleo's hand to remind himself she was there, too.

"I can't believe Hera wouldn't let you see me after I was born."

"The only thing I could get from her was a promise to raise you in the Jewish faith. My own mother would have killed me if I hadn't insisted."

"I can't believe you're still alive," said Cleo. "We thought you were mortal."

"That's how I started." Saul smiled a rumpled smile. "Hera granted me immortality as a parting gift, I guess you'd call it."

David's jaw dropped. "She can do that?"

"Your mother is a powerful woman. She did the same thing for Heracles, though the circumstances were different. Finding a husband for Hebe was a tough sell. Hera told me none of the other gods would take her."

"Wow," said David, picturing his irritable half-sister and seeing the truth in the situation.

Their waiter arrived with a tray of long-stemmed glasses, serving Cleo first and Saul second as he worked his way around the tall-legged table. David studied the liquid in his martini glass. It had a slight orange tint, reminiscent of rust. He sipped tentatively. The taste of gin was a mere echo underneath flavors of orange and licorice.

"Mmmm," said Cleo. She set down her glass after two sips. "Smooth."

"My end of day treat when I'm working," Saul said. The lines in his forehead relaxed. "All my life I've been in the entertainment business. My mother was Jewish. My father was a Roman soldier and pretty high up. My two elder brothers joined the army but I was small and weak as a child, so I was trained in music. When I met Hera I was singing at a banquet at Herod's palace in Tiberias."

"Wow!" said David. "Were you the flute player we read about in the census scrolls?"

Saul Crispin laughed. "My flute playing is marginal. Mostly I sang. Through my father's connections I became part of Herod's retinue. Not a bad life, but it wasn't a livelihood that could support a wife and family, so I never married. I was twenty-three when Hera came to Tiberias. Anyone who wanted to stay on her good side agreed she was no more than thirty." Saul's smile warmed. "She was beauty personified and had a boatload of treasure. None of this was lost on Herod. He did what he could to seduce her, in spite of having his own wife and, well," he looked apologetically at Cleo, "pretty much whoever else he wanted on the side."

"Whatever," Cleo said agreeably.

David sipped the last of his martini and signaled the waiter for another round.

"Hera drove a hard bargain, as you might expect. Somewhere in her string of refusals she persuaded Herod to lend me to her household. You can guess the rest."

David's tongue felt thick. "And then she dumped you."

"Yes. She dumped me."

Saul drained his glass. When the waiter arrived with fresh drinks Cleo pointed at the bar menu and ordered three artisan pizzas.

David studied Saul's deeply sad expression. "At least you get to be immortal."

"An immortal who is forced to live amongst the mortals." Saul gripped David's shoulder. "Think about it, David. What do you think Zeus would do if I went anywhere near the City of Mount Olympus?"

"Uhm, well, maybe now that Veronica's in charge—"

"You have no idea what my life's been like, do you? No idea at all." Saul crossed his arms, exhaled mightily, and flopped back in his chair. "Everyone I knew when I was mortal died while I was suspended at age twenty-three. I met new people, sure, but could I ever marry or have a family of my own? Not even a mistress wants a lover who doesn't age while she marches from maiden to crone. I had to move every few years, so my prolonged youth didn't become obvious."

"There must have been some good times, though?" Cleo said, her voice soft.

"It might sound like an enviable existence to have worked with Seneca and Shakespeare and George Bernard Shaw, but those times were the tip of the iceberg. So much darkness in between."

They sipped their drinks. No one said anything until the pizzas arrived.

"Kind of strange," David said after eating a slice. "We kind of have the opposite ends of the same experience, me being immortal and not knowing it and you, well. Weird that Thelma got us tickets to your show."

Saul's face got the strangest expression.

"You okay?" David said.

"Not as weird as you might think," Saul said slowly. "She recognized me when I was doing a show in Los Angeles. I wasn't acting then, just singing."

Cleo dropped David's hand. "You! You're Ari Cantor!"

"Thelma Bernstein made up some story about being with the press and talked my manager into letting her visit my dressing room. That woman is determined," he said with a chuckle. "She told me about you, how smart you were and how you were starting college that fall."

"No way!" David said. "We were in L. A. decades ago. I don't remember it, but from what Milton said—"

"She never told Milton." Saul lowered his voice and leaned in. "Any idea how many times you entered college during your lifetime, David? Has to be ten, at least. She told me they'd started moving you every four years or so. The last two years in whatever school system and the first two of college, with a few decades off here and there. Believe me, it's a lot of work moving around so much."

He stared at Saul for a long time. "You knew about me?"

Saul shrugged. "Yes and no. Sometimes she'd send a picture of you but no return address. I tried to track her down off and on, but it was hard to find people in those days if they didn't want to be found. No Internet then and I've avoided all that stuff on purpose so there's less chance someone will start wondering about me and my extended middle age."

"I couldn't find anything about Ari Cantor online," Cleo said. "Good!"

"Someone else knows who you are," David said.

Saul signaled the waiter to bring more water. "Oh? And who is that?"

"Aphrodite. She told me to look for you in Tiberias."

"Herod's blonde friend." He thrust out his chest and batted his eyelashes coquettishly. Cleo giggled. "But she wasn't there at the same time as Hera. How would she know?"

"She's met David. How would she not?" Cleo said.

Something inconsistent rattled in David's martini-boosted brain. "Isn't it kind of strange," he said, "I mean, I don't really agree with immortal morality, but—"

"Oh, brother," Cleo muttered.

David glared at her. "What I mean is, why is it such a big deal for Hera to have a child out of wedlock? Aphrodite has dozens, maybe hundreds of them and no one seems to care."

"It's more to do with Zeus than with Hera," Saul said. "Another round?"

Cleo said no but David said sure. Saul signaled the waiter for two more Corpse Revivers.

"You see it with mortals all the time. The more important the husband is, the more closely his wife is scrutinized. That's why she had the Bernsteins hide you. She was afraid Zeus would tear you to pieces to avenge his pride."

David thought of the last time he'd seen Zeus, for a friendly game of chess. "Wow."

The drinks arrived. Cleo stole a sip of David's martini and said, "Where's the next stop on your tour?"

"San Francisco, then Albuquerque, then home. New York, that is."

The waiter hovered nearby. David looked around. All the other tables were empty.

"Guess we'd better call it a night."

They gulped their martinis, and the waiter brought the bill. David insisted on picking up the tab in spite of Saul's protest. Soon they were standing on the sidewalk. David shivered inside his lightweight suit jacket, words failing him.

Saul folded him in a hug. "Hey, son."

Tears spilled down David's cheeks. "Can I see you again?"

When they pulled apart, Saul was crying, too.

"Here." Saul handed him a business card. "I'm back in New York the second week of December, ten days off before rehearsals start for the new show. We can do Chanukah?"

"Wow. I mean, sure."

Saul patted David's shoulder. "Good boy." He turned to Cleo, made a courtly bow, and kissed her hand. "A pleasure, young lady. Take care of each other," he said to them both, then turned and strolled away.

David took Cleo's hand. They watched until Saul turned a corner and vanished. "Wow," he said, his breath steaming in the cold. "Wow."

~ * ~

Cleo shivered under her glittery shawl and red cocktail dress. "Come on." She tugged David in the direction of the Parthenon Building. "I'm freezing."

"Oh. Sure. Sorry." His voice was a monotone.

Cleo slipped an arm around his shoulders. She wondered if he was in shock, finding a man he'd thought was long dead. His quest had ended. Poor baby must be laboring under all kinds of emotion.

Soon they were out of the cold. He looked so small, reflected in the Parthenon Building's polished elevator doors. Cleo hugged him close and rubbed his back. "It's okay," she said.

When they reached the penthouse they were both crying. The apartment lights were dim.

"Tea?" she said, dabbing tears from her cheeks.

"Sure."

David followed her to the kitchen. Candy had left a note on the kitchen island.

Gone to bed. Jim home tomorrow.

Cleo filled the kettle and lit the burner. "Chamomile okay?" she said, opening a cupboard.

David slumped onto a stool. "Sure."

She felt way out of her depth as to how to help him. Tonight's discovery was a miracle, but it was a lot to deal with, too. So was the possibility he'd fathered Monique's baby. With effort, Cleo pushed past the anger welling inside. She made the tea and handed him a mug.

"Thanks."

He wrapped his hands around it but didn't drink.

Cleo sipped her tea and thought. David needed her help. It

wouldn't be right to leave him alone tonight. She put the tea mugs in the sink and circled behind him to remove his sports coat. "Come on." She took his hand. "You're sleeping with me."

~ * ~

David awoke in Jim and Candy's guest room. He lay on his side. Something weighty rested across his ribcage and his back was warm. He turned over.

"Cleo?"

She was dead asleep, her silk pajama top buttoned in place. She'd sung to him last night, he remembered now, the same lullaby Thelma Bernstein sang when she was gardening or folding laundry.

He carefully lifted her arm and got out of bed, his throbbing head a reminder of last night's martini binge and the incredible meeting with Saul Crispin. David's shoes had been placed under a chair by the dresser. He still wore the turtleneck and jeans he'd had on last night.

Water. That's what he needed and lots of it. David tiptoed from the room and headed for the kitchen where he found Jim, seated on a stool at the kitchen island, a double-Americano halfway to his lips.

"Hey," David said softly. "Welcome back."

"Thanks." Jim looked as beat as David felt. He must have flown back from Mount Olympus on his own power.

David opened a cupboard and found a glass. "How are things in the Big-G City?" he said as he watched the water rise to the rim.

"Hard. Very hard. You remember Stella, Veronica's former Executive Assistant?"

David recalled Stella's cruel copper eyes. "Who could forget her?"

"She's in a coma. Has been since the baby was born."

"She had a baby?"

"No, Monique's baby."

Shit. With everything else that had happened, he'd forgotten about Monique.

"Is Monique okay?"

Jim sighed wearily. "It was a traumatic delivery, to say the least. She'll be confined to bed for I don't know how long. Turned her hair white."

"Heaven and Earth!" His sour stomach clenched with guilt.

Jim looked at David quizzically. "She has the best care available. Elle checks in on her daily and Hermes is there around the clock to take care of the baby."

"Hermes?" The notion of that prick being helpful struck David as implausible.

"Well, he is the baby's father, one of them anyway." Jim cleared his throat. "Uhm, forget I said that. I'd love to tell you the whole story and get it off my chest, but it's classified."

David didn't press for details. "So. You're back."

"By order of Veronica Zeta. Flew in at warp speed." Jim downed the rest of his Americano. "Something unspecified. She wants me on call 24/7." He stood and carried his cup to the sink. "Guess I'll wake Candy up and say hello. Hey, would you mind making her a double mocha?" Jim nodded toward the top-end home espresso machine on the kitchen counter. "No one makes them better than you."

David would have done anything, he was so relieved to be off the hook with Monique. He powered on the machine and made Candy's mocha and a cappuccino for Cleo. He was frothing the milk for his own latte when it hit him: in the last twenty-four hours, his personal life had shifted from miserably unresolved to worry-free.

Jim returned for Candy's drink. "Thanks," he said, then started laughing.

"What?"

"You must really enjoy making espresso," Jim said. "You're grinning from ear-to-ear."

David returned to the guest room, hands laden with brimming-full mugs. He knocked on the door with his knee.

A sleep-logged voice said, "Come in."

"Can't. My hands are full."

The box spring squeaked. Feet thumped the floor. Cleo, cutely rumpled in her pajamas, let him in.

"Thanks," she said, taking the cappuccino he proffered. Cleo sat on the bed and patted the spot alongside her. "Mmm. This is so good, and I sure need it," she said after a couple of sips. "I haven't slept so hard in years."

David felt fizzy inside. When their mugs were empty, he took Cleo's hand.

"Thanks for taking care of me last night."

"It was nothing."

"It was everything," David said, his heart firing his words. "Cleo, look at me." She turned to him, so beautiful, so kind. "Cleo, I love you."

"I love you, too, David."

He touched his lips to hers and the rest of the world disappeared.

Saturday, November 15, 2025

Clifford

The four of them stood on top of the seawall, facing Elliott Bay. Clifford wished Mum had stayed at the hotel but there was no talking her out of it.

"I lived without your dad for a long time. I won't give up one second with him now," Briana had stated.

Veronica completed the foursome. Tears had shone in her eyes last night when they'd reviewed Clifford's calculations. The result held: it was the best short-term solution for securing the seawall.

Only Ralph seemed in good spirits. He embraced his sweetheart and tapped a kiss on her forehead. "I'll be back before you know it, Brie."

The sight of them parting made Clifford's heart constrict. "Are you ready, sir?" He extended his hand. Ralph's powerful grip compressed Clifford's bones.

"I'll buy you a pint when I get back," Ralph said, grinning. He turned to Veronica. "Ready when you are, Ms. Zeta. I'd like to face the bay, if you don't mind."

With the wave of her hand Veronica stopped the movement of every mortal being and every mortal conveyance, including the Bainbridge Island ferry preparing to dock at the waterfront terminal. Seagulls were suspended in mid-air. The Seattle Great Wheel stopped its rotation. An unnatural silence hovered.

Veronica faced Ralph, arms raised and palms flexed toward him. Slowly she circled her hands. Ralph was covered with shimmering light. Clifford shuddered in visceral recall when his father's body dispersed into glittering flecks. The shining cloud spread thin and sank into the seawall concrete.

Briana sniffled. Clifford knelt on the seawall and looked over the edge.

"I can see his eyes, Mum," he said. "Listen." Ralph's telekinetic voice, a heavier version of what he sounded like when reconstituted, registered in Clifford's brain.

Be a good boy and don't eavesdrop while I talk to your mother.

Clifford and Veronica walked a few yards away to give the couple privacy. Veronica's hand slipped into his.

"Jim Smith is on call 24/7 until we figure out a permanent solution," she said, pointing to the penthouse atop a Third Avenue skyscraper. "I asked him to—"

"Cliffy! Come quick, love, something's wrong!"

Mum had him by the arm. She tugged him to the edge of the seawall.

I can't hold it, boy! I need help!

Clifford turned to Veronica. Brilliant, brave woman that she was she understood precisely what was required. Her palms flexed. Tears streamed down her face.

"I love you, Clifford Essex."

Veronica's hands circled slowly, dispersing his molecules into a cloud that shimmered, sank, and filtered into the seawall.

I love you, too, Veronica Zeta.

~ * ~

Veronica Zeta, digital pad in hand, tapped a brief message to Jim Smith. Briana stood beside her, as still as if she were made of stone. Veronica slipped an arm around her future mother-in-law. "We'll do everything we can to get them back," she said. "I know it's hard, but please try not to worry."

She could barely stop herself from cursing the mortals for their arrogance and stupidity. Reports and calculations prepared by the mortals themselves had concluded the option was not structurally sound. Nevertheless, a handful of wealthy individuals had greased palms and pushed the plans through. Even the tunnel boring machine's repeated breakdowns and the discovery of sink holes hadn't stopped the project. If the seawall failed and took the tunnel with it, the fill on which Seattle's waterfront rested would dissolve into Elliott Bay.

Veronica listened for telekinetic communication from Clifford or Ralph. A faint voice colored with a British accent whispered *I'll always love you.* If the seawall failed before they could be removed and reconstituted, they would die. It was one of the few ways an immortal life could end.

"Ms. Zeta." Jim Smith materialized alongside them. "I came

the instant I read your message. How I can help?"

She brushed her hand across her face. Time to wipe the tears and manage the crisis.

"We need to establish communication with Ralph and Clifford. Their voices are faint. Can you transform yourself into a sea mammal and try to contact them under water?"

Transfiguration was a skill Jim had developed to counsel structureling clients before their work was computerized. His body rippled, shortened and eased into the shape of an oversized seal. He rocked and pulled himself to the edge of the seawall and dove into Elliott Bay.

Veronica removed the stasis spell from mortals, vehicles, birds and the rest, setting the scene in motion again. She wiggled a pinkie to stall enough cars to block the tunnel entryways. Tires squealed and horns blared. She took up her digital pad and messaged Heinrich, who watched the monitoring devices on board *Ms. Zeta*:

Advise if seawall strength has increased.

The answer arrived. *Percentage of improvement small but trending upward.* Veronica prayed to Heaven and Earth they'd have enough time to find a solution.

~ * ~

Jim Smith twitched his whiskers. He'd made two dives so far, first to establish Ralph and Clifford were still conscious (two pairs of large, open eyes were etched in the seawall), then to get a status. Ralph said the seawall wasn't breaching, it was being sucked under by a newly formed sinkhole. Clifford added the odds of stabilization were extremely low.

On the third dive he eyed the forms of Poseidon and two small-g sea gods bracing the wall at its base. Jim cut briskly through the water toward Poseidon. In the yelping telekinetic dialect his form dictated, he relayed the information given by the structurelings.

Damn the mortals, the God of the Sea thought back. *I say we let go and let 'em die.*

You're not in charge here, Jim said, whiskers bristling. *Tell me what solutions are available and I'll report to Ms. Zeta.*

Damn few solutions, Poseidon snarled, *short of someone burrowing under and expanding themselves to fill the sink hole.*

You guys can do that?

Not them. Poseidon tilted his head toward the small-gs. *Me.*

Jim's taut, slick skin shivered. He shot back to Veronica and Briana who knelt at the edge of the seawall. Jim delivered his message. Veronica rendered her decision. He sped off to relay her orders.

In Two Worlds
Pan

Pan entered the lobby of Monique's condo building and pushed the elevator button.

"Crazy. This is absolutely crazy."

Zeus had come by his hut on the outskirts of Mount Olympus late last night, accompanied by Artemis, Heracles and an insane proposition. They ordered him to kidnap P. B. Athena would probably yank his medal if she found out.

Artemis supplied his cover story. He'd offer to take the baby for a walk, load P. B. into his buggy and wheel him into the elevator. The parents wouldn't be a problem: Monique was bedridden, and Hermes was rummy from sleep deprivation. He could make his getaway before they could say baklava.

He knocked on Monique's condo door. Elle answered. She looked whipped, bags under her eyes and her short hair going in every direction. The deep tan she'd acquired from working in the desert had faded.

"Home health check," she said instead of hello.

"P. B. doing okay?" Pan said with feigned concern.

"Oh. Him." She waved a hand toward the living room. "Take a look for yourself. His mother's the one I'm here to see. Should be able to remove her stitches by Monday," she said on her way to Monique's bedroom.

Hermes sat on the sofa, P. B. in his arms. "How's Daddy's little man?" He waved a bandaged finger in the baby's face. Pan didn't have to guess the origin of the shiner under Hermes' left eye. Mean little brute.

"Hi."

Hermes looked up, a saccharine grin on his mug. "Look, P. B., big brother's here!"

P. B.'s face wrinkled like an ancient apple. Drool sheeted down his chin. His tiny fists punched the air.

"Thought I'd take him for a walk," Pan said, cutting to the chase. "You look like you could use a break."

"Oh, this?" Hermes touched the shiner with his fingertips. "Just a little love tap. I can hardly feel it now."

Pan wheeled a chariot-shaped buggy out from behind the cases of baby formula. "Fresh air will do him good. A couple of spins around the block for fraternal bonding."

This pretty notion brought a tear to Hermes' eye. *Get a grip*, thought Pan as the repentant father swaddled P. B. to within an inch of his miserable little life and filled two bottles with formula for the trip. "So hungry, this one," Hermes said, fussing like a nursemaid. The scene made Pan want to puke.

Soon they were in the elevator waving bye-bye. Pan ditched the buggy in the lobby. P. B. screamed when Pan picked him up and hustled him to the kidnapping party who waited outside.

"Here." Pan shoved the squalling bundle at Zeus.

Zeus stepped back. "You need to take him to his destination."

"What? You're joking, right? You guys are the ones who wanted him!"

"We're busy," Artemis said. She studied the street as if a sniper were loose. "Keep hold of the baby and follow Heracles. Zeus and I will bring up the rear."

"But—"

"It's here!" Artemis pointed between the condo building and the one next to it. "It just dodged into the alleyway. Looks like we have the right bait."

Bait?

Heracles sprinted ahead. Zeus shoved Pan from behind. "Move it, kid!"

"But—"

"No time to explain. Don't lose Heracles, he's the one who knows the entrance."

Pan, with P. B. pressed tight to his chest, slapped the soles of his sandals on the marble streets for all he was worth. Falling behind with every stride, Pan followed Heracles through alleyways and intersections until they reached the path encircling the City of Mount Olympus. Heracles vaulted over the path. Pan flew after him. P. B.

laughed. When they landed on the other side, Heracles had rolled a boulder away from a vast hole in the ground. He waved them forward.

"Jump!"

Adrenaline coursed through Pan so violently he felt like his skin would burst. Clutching the delightedly shrieking P. B. to his breast, he charged to the hole and jumped. For a moment there was no daylight. Heracles hurtled past him and landed somewhere below. Pan hit something that broke his fall with a meaty slap.

"Caught you! Welcome to Tartarus." Heracles set him on his feet. P. B. clapped gleefully. "No time to waste. Follow me!"

The mouth of the hole above filled with blackness. Inside his head, Pan heard a raspy voice shout *Mine!*

Heracles grabbed P. B. and ordered Pan to get on his back. He raced at incredible velocity through hewn rock tunnels that glowed red. The internal voice grew fainter. *Mine! Mine! Mine!*

They came upon a vast cave. A bonfire raged in the center. Heracles kept close to the wall, away from a sea of pale fighting forms that shouted, "Preston North End!" and "Aston Villa!" Until now, Pan had assumed the Pit of Football Hooligans was a myth. He accidentally made eye contact with one of the inmates.

"Fresh meat!" the soul cried. "After them!"

"Damn," said Heracles. He accelerated as if a switch had been thrown.

The raspy inner voice interrupted its *Mine! Mine! Mine!* chant to shout *Out of the way, fools!* A roar like thunder reverberated behind them, accompanied by the whimper of a thousand trampled souls.

Heracles slowed down. "Duck!" he shouted and bent double to clear a low arch.

They stumbled out of the cave. Heracles righted himself and charged toward a shining black castle in the distance.

Pan looked back. A heavy pool of black seeped from the mouth of Tartarus.

"Hurry!"

Sweat sheeted Heracles' neck. Pan could barely keep hold when the Champion of the Gods soared into the air. In minutes they landed on the palace steps.

"Get down," Heracles ordered. He handed P. B. to Pan. "Up the stairs, through the entrance, fifth door on the right. Stand behind the big chair but don't touch it, either of you. Hold the baby up so he can be seen. I'll delay It for as long as I can."

Heracles assumed a fighting stance. Pan clutched P. B. and scrambled up the shining black staircase, hoping he had the wits to count to five. When he passed through the entrance archway an ear-splitting alarm shrilled. Stunned, he staggered to the right past one door, two, three, four. The fourth door swung open.

"Pan!" cried a woman with a mass of flaxen hair. "Why didn't you tell me you were coming? I would have told the cook to make breakfast for three. Oh, and look what you've—"

He shoved Persephone back into the room and yanked the door shut.

Take that! rasped the voice in his head, followed by an audible groan from somewhere behind him. Fearing for Heracles as well as himself, he sped to the fifth room, ducked inside and slammed the door behind him.

Pan blinked. Dim wall-mounted torches outlined furnishings —a chaise lounge, two carved stone chairs and a third chair as big as a throne, decorated with mysterious symbols wrought in gold.

A hiss came from the door. Black liquid, barely distinguishable in the gloom, oozed underneath. Pan wrapped his hands around P. B.'s torso, lifted him in the air and slid against the wall behind the sinister-looking chair. P. B. wriggled perilously close to the back. "Don't touch it!" Pan said through gritted teeth.

"Mine! Mine! Mine!"

The raspy voice, no longer in Pan's head, echoed around the room. He peeked out. The pool of black shivered toward the chair.

"Mine! Mine! Mine!"

Defying gravity, It slid up the legs and into the seat, edged up the back, was inches from enveloping P. B.—

"Huh?" The voice abruptly lost its edge. "That's strange, I know I have something important to do, but..."

The voice trailed off. Pan lowered the baby into his arms. He crept around the front of the chair. It looked like it had been uphol-stered with black leather.

"Excuse me," said the leather. "Could you tell me please...oh, what was it again? Oh, drat, I can't remember."

Persephone burst through the door.

"I cannot believe you brought a baby in here, Pan!" She

snatched P. B. from him and cradled the little brute in her arms. "That's the Chair of Forgetfulness, goat brains, not a toy!"

Persephone strolled out, beaming down at P. B. and making ridiculous cooing noises about Persephone's Little Manikin. Heracles entered the room moments later, Zeus and Artemis behind him. The three of them advanced toward the big chair, their expressions quizzical.

"Hi," said the black thing covering the chair. "I don't believe we've met?"

"More guests!" Everyone turned. Persephone and P. B. stood in the doorway. They made a lovely picture if you could forget he was twenty-five percent evil. "The cook is going to have my head, and I don't know what's keeping Hades. Some stupid emergency in Elysium. He should have been back hours ago." She glanced down at P. B., wrinkled her nose, and made a face. "I don't suppose anyone brought a diaper bag?"

Seattle, Washington
Poseidon

The God of the Sea left his small-g assistants to deal with the sink hole and emerged from Elliott Bay for a strategic session aboard the research vessel. Veronica was a smart girl, though it chafed him to admit it. She'd immediately seen the wisdom of having him expand into the sinkhole to stabilize the seawall. The crisis reminded him of the old days, when there were monsters to slay and curses to repel. Who knew if he'd succeed at something no one had ever attempted? Making himself into immortal Bondo to save the mortals was a young god's game. Fit though he was, did he still have that kind of strength?

"Let's go over the sequence one more time," Veronica said. "On my signal, you'll descend to the sinkhole and begin the expansion process. You," she nodded to Jim, who had resumed his human form, "will go with Poseidon and report back to me when the process is complete. Ralph and Clifford will remain disbursed in the seawall until we determine it's stable." She looked at Heinrich, the computer jockey who monitored the vital signs. "Then we're on to Phase Two, reconstituting Clifford first and assessing the impact."

Veronica pushed her chair back from the table. The light hit her just right to highlight the dark circles beneath her eyes. "That's all we have to go on for now. Questions?"

Poseidon said, "Let's do it."

He headed for the aft cabin to tug on his wetsuit, window dressing for whatever mortals might be watching when he dropped back into the bay. When he emerged, a large seal waited on the deck. Ralph's girlfriend, the British job, knelt on the seawall.

Veronica stepped out into the cockpit. "Ready?"

Poseidon nodded. Jim barked twice for yes.

"On three," Veronica said, eyes on the stopwatch she held in her hand—for what reason he couldn't fathom. "One, two, th—"

He flipped over the railing and swam down, down, down, waved at his small-g assistants and continued down as the bay dropped sharply off, the seal alongside him. Poseidon breathed the water, his lungs converting it to oxygen. At the murky gray bottom lay the sink hole. The crater had widened perceptibly since he'd examined it minutes ago. Not sure whether he could reverse the incantation, he floated to the center of the hole and employed Big-G expansion magic. He'd saved hundreds of sinking ships this way, but with the Earth, itself? Poseidon half-swore, half-prayed to Heaven and Earth his luck would hold.

~ * ~

Jim watched, fascinated, as Poseidon's body spread in all directions. His molecules were iridescent turquoise. A radiant glow illuminated the gap as it filled. The signal they'd agreed on was a single telekinetic word. When the molecules stopped moving, *Safe* echoed in his head.

His seal body lightened as he ascended, the pressure of tons upon tons of water lessening as he passed the small-g sea gods and the vast, fine-etched eyes of Clifford and Ralph in the seawall. His nose broke the water, eyes seeking Veronica in the cockpit of the *Ms. Zeta*. He barked twice for yes. She gave a thumbs up and ducked into the cabin.

The Underworld
Hades

Hades had been cursing to himself all morning. Persephone was home at last, and what was the first thing he had to do? Run off with Anatole to observe changes in the ceiling of Elysium.

"Over there, sir," the valet said, pointing. "The color's changing again, can you see it?"

"Kind of green for a sky." In Elysium it was the rule to call it that, even though it was masked rock, painted blue. Something wet plopped on Hades' shoulder. He eyed the nearby trees. "Damned birds."

"Would you care to use the binoculars, sir?"

Hades adjusted the focus. The blue-green patch sparkled. An indentation divided the patch lengthwise. It reminded him of something.

"Anatole, does whatever that is look like a gigantic butt?"

Anatole cleared his throat. "It had crossed my mind, sir."

"I'm going to get to the bottom of this." Hades handed the binoculars to his valet and raised his arms ceiling-ward. In minutes he hovered below the dripping turquoise bum.

"What's the meaning of this?" Hades shouted, dodging saltwater drops as best he could. "You're not allowed to come in if you don't pay your fare!"

There was a long silence. Inside his head a familiar voice said *Hades?*

The God of the Underworld emitted a low growl. Poseidon and his big butt were going to get a stiff repair bill for pulling this stunt.

City of Mount Olympus
Apollo

Apollo sat alongside Stella's hospital bed. He strummed his lute, lulled by the anemic lines on the patient's monitor. He'd promised Jim he'd keep watch over her when Jim had been summoned to Seattle. Her condition hadn't changed since then.

A beep broke his stupor. Stella stirred. On the monitor, every vital sign showed normal levels.

"What's up, doc?" Stella croaked. Her perpetually straight lips curved upward.

Skeptical, Apollo took her wrist and checked her pulse. Normal. He checked her pupils. Normal. The expression in the copper eyes was soft in a way he'd never before observed.

"Welcome back, Stella," he said. "You gave us quite a fright."

"I did?" She pushed a button to raise the bed to a sitting position. "What happened? I don't remember much, except being in some kind of convalescent home."

Her last visitation from The Power must have scrambled her memory. "How do you feel?" Apollo touched his hand to her forehead. No fever.

She twisted her torso tentatively. "A little stiff."

"Hungry?"

"Hungry as a war horse."

Apollo rang for an attendant and ordered a small serving of pulverized ambrosia.

"Jim Smith will be glad to hear you're feeling better," he said.

"Nice of him," Stella said, "but I have to tell you, he's terrible at board games."

Hera

Hera paced the penthouse den. Zeus had left at dawn and now it was afternoon. He'd told her to contact Veronica if she didn't hear from him by tomorrow. Impatient and worried, her mind strayed to old times, when Zeus had been an unabashed philanderer. He'd told her he was working with Heracles and Artemis. Hopefully their presence would keep him safe and out of trouble.

An electronic ping sounded. Hera rushed to the coffee table, picked up her digital pad and selected the message app. Much as she despised these things, they were handy in an emergency. She eagerly scanned the top of the "in" folder for Zeus' address.

It was from David. She read the message three times, stunned. *I've found him.*

The device fell from her hand, landed on the marble floor and cracked in two. How was this possible? She'd told no one about gifting Saul Crispin with immortality, had sworn Saul, himself, to secrecy on pain of retribution. Now David knew her terrible secret. He was traveling with the Petra girl. Did she know, too?

There was only one way to minimize the damage. She had to come clean with Zeus.

Elle

Elle looked down at her patient. Monique slept deeply, aided by a valerian-based preparation Elle had injected into the IV drip. Since the birth of P. B., the new mother had been able to take intravenous nourishment only, her internal organs dangerously stressed after the violent delivery.

Monique stirred. Her snow-white hair, slick against her scalp, was a knotted tangle on the red silk pillowcase. Hermes had offered to comb out the ratted tresses, but Monique refused to let him touch her. He was so desperate to help Elle almost pitied him.

She'd been more than three weeks away from her humanitarian aid responsibilities. Though Halah had assured her the Woman-Front camp was operating at full throttle, she longed to get back to the work she cherished. The sick room, even the City of Mount Olympus, was stifling after her time in the desert. Once the stitches were out there'd be physical therapy. Apollo had engaged a specialist for this, but he wanted Elle to monitor Monique for another week to ten days, to be on the safe side.

A soft moan brought her back to the present. Elle touched the back of her hand to Monique's forehead. The danger of infection and fever was still present.

"Sleep well?" Elle said, removing her hand from her patient's cool brow.

"Yes, thank you." Monique's voice was raspy, vocal cords mending from her screams during the birth. "Will Mother visit today?"

Aphrodite had stopped in earlier and sat beside the bed while Monique was sleeping. "She'll never be the same, will she?" the Goddess of Love had said, though Elle sensed she didn't want an answer.

"She's coming this afternoon."

It would be a long convalescence. The Power could inflict hurt in ways medical science didn't fully understand, hidden wounds under the skin. Apollo had ordered Monique to take a six-month leave.

"How's the baby?"

Monique asked this question several times a day, though she'd yet to hold P. B. Elle had barely ducked away in time to avoid the swing he'd taken at her when she'd bathed him this morning.

"Strong as a little ox."

"That's good." She drifted back to sleep.

Monique was weak now, but as she gained strength and independence Elle was certain a prolonged leave would frustrate her patient. She needed time away from the City of Mount Olympus and Love, Inc., but she also needed something to do. Elle tiptoed to the impromptu nursing station she'd set up in Monique's walk-in closet and powered up her digital device. A limited amount of humanitarian aid work might be the best kind of medicine. Jocelyn Chadwick was sure to have some practical suggestions.

Seattle, Washington
Clifford

The pressure changed in an instant. Clifford was so startled by the shift he'd almost missed the seal Jim shooting by. The seawall was gaining solidity.

Ralph's telekinetic voice sounded in Clifford's mind. *Feel that?*

Yes, Clifford replied. *I'm cautiously optimistic it's stable.*

Poseidon's doing?

Must be. Poor bloke; hope he's all right.

Jim swam by again, slowly this time. He paused in front of their eye molecules. *The seawall has stabilized. Veronica says hang tight; she wants to give it an hour to be on the safe side. I'll watch Poseidon. If everything holds, Veronica will rematerialize Clifford, first.*

No! Clifford thought with unaccustomed vehemence. *Ralph first. Mum's going bonkers up there.* Briana's tearful reassurances had been floating down to them nonstop.

No time to discuss. Jim spiraled down, down, down.

Fiancée or no fiancée, Ms. Zeta's the boss, Ralph thought.

Clifford's molecules bristled. Ever since the engagement party Veronica had treated him as if she didn't trust his professional judgment. *I've been in charge of this project from the beginning,* he thought back.

Ralph heaved a long telekinetic sigh. *If you haven't noticed, son, this is an emergency. Whatever's wrong between you, keep your mind on the job and deal with the rest of it when we're out of this mess.*

Clifford wanted to reprimand his father for thinking out of turn but didn't. Ralph was right.

The hour passed glacially. Veronica contacted him regularly from the research vessel, her telekinetic speech as flawless as everything else about her. At last his molecules were summoned out of the seawall and reconstituted in the cockpit. She stood in front of him, cool and focused, and handed him a towel.

"Join us in the cabin when you've changed," she said. "You're the best one to run the diagnostics." When he returned from the aft cabin to the cockpit, snug in a dry sweat suit with the Olympus, Inc., logo embroidered on the breast, she was on her knees, looking over the railing. She turned toward Clifford, a perplexed smile on her lips. "Jim says there's been a breakthrough." She tilted her head toward the water where a large seal bobbed. "Go ahead with the diagnostics. I'll explain later."

Clifford wondered bitterly if the girl genius had solved the problem he'd been pursuing, off and on, for years. He also realized she hadn't expressed anything at all about his being back, safe and in one piece.

The Underworld
Zeus

Zeus pushed his chair back from the dining table. Heaven and Earth, Hades lived well. The impromptu brunch they'd been served on plates of gold was excellent and Persephone was a charming hostess, though she'd made some vexed remarks about Hades' whereabouts.

"With all the complaining he does about being lonely, and I just got back yesterday!" she said to Heracles, who was seated to her right.

Persephone cradled P. B. in one arm. They'd tried to explain to her he was the Son of Evil, but she wouldn't believe them.

"How can you say such things about this precious face?" she cooed at the bundle.

Zeus had taken a good look at P. B. before they'd sat down to eat. Though he couldn't pin it down, something had changed in the baby's demeanor. He'd even reached for Pan, smiling toothlessly and drooling down his chin as if he loved his kidnapper.

Hades stomped in. "What the—" He glared around the table at each of them in turn. "Seph, what are all these people doing here? You know we can't afford to entertain."

She rose from her chair and marched toward him. "And where were you when the chthonic monster was chasing the baby?"

"What baby?" he roared.

Persephone gathered P. B. to her bosom. "*My* baby!"

Zeus put his head in his hands. They'd achieved the impossible, had successfully captured The Power, but this domestic drama could be their undoing. Recovering himself, he exchanged glances with his team. Heracles shrugged. Artemis rolled her eyes. Pan cleared his throat. The heroic God of Shepherds and Flocks got up and joined the couple.

"Actually, he's my baby. This is my little brother, P. B."

The baby clapped his hands and reached for Pan.

"Give him back," Hades ordered Persephone. "We can't afford the marrow bones you order on the sly for Cerberus—don't think I didn't notice—let alone a baby."

Persephone stamped her foot. "I won't! It's so lonely down here I can hardly stand it, especially when you go running off on some stupid errand—"

"For your information, we're having an emergency. Poseidon's sparkling hind quarters are filling a hole in the ceiling of Elysium."

"You've been drinking!" Persephone wailed. She didn't notice Pan slipping P. B. out of her arms and tiptoeing to the door.

"Wonderful brunch," Zeus said, signaling Artemis and Heracles to go. "Can't thank you enough for your hospitality." The five of them, P. B. riding contentedly in Pan's arms, flew back through Tartarus with Heracles as guide, past the bruised souls of the football hooligans and up the hole just outside the City of Mount Olympus. They arrived at Monique's condo building, Zeus so weary he could barely stay aloft. He thanked Artemis and Heracles for their assistance and discharged them from duty. Pan accepted his offer to explain the kidnapping to Monique and Hermes.

Hermes was in the lobby.

"Oh! There you are. You'd been gone so long I came down to look for you. My boy must be starving. Not sure why you left the buggy." He wheeled it out from behind the potted palm where Pan had stashed it. Hermes took P. B. and laid him in the miniature chariot. "There you go, little man. Let's go see Mom."

Though not invited, Zeus and Pan followed Hermes into the elevator. The condo was the usual mess, boxes of baby formula and who-knew-what jamming the living room.

"Monique!" Hermes called, pushing the buggy toward the bedroom. "Our son is home."

The bedroom door closed behind him.

Zeus looked at Pan, who was looking at him.

"He's not mad, not even scared," Pan said.

"No."

Hera had told him about The Power leaving Veronica when she'd been Its victim and blinded her—a black cloud had risen from her body and she immediately recovered her sight. Maybe it was possible that—no, it was too far-fetched—but if The Power, itself, had forgotten who It was, perhaps everyone who'd been injured by It had forgotten Its evil, too?

"Come on." Zeus nodded toward the hallway. "They'll be okay on their own."

Back on the street, Zeus commended Pan for his bravery. After an "ah shucks" moment they hailed chariots and went their separate ways. By the time Zeus let himself in the penthouse door, all he wanted was a hot bath and a cold beer.

Harp music reverberated in the hallway, a favorite recording of Hera's that he, too, liked. He found her in the den, prone on a chaise lounge with a cold pack on her forehead. He perched alongside her and took her hands. "My dear." No wonder she was ill. He'd been driving her crazy with secrecy this past week.

She removed the icepack from her forehead and opened her eyes. "Brace yourself. There's something I need to tell you while I have the courage."

S.D. Matley

Seattle, Washington
Veronica

Veronica Zeta, alive with energy, sent Jim to Poseidon with a message to keep up the good work. The crisis, for now, had been resolved. A tremendous exertion of self-control had kept her from breaking out in laughter when Jim gave Poseidon's report that a leak in the ceiling of Elysium had caused the sink hole. Someone named Anatole was scurrying around down there now, assembling a repair crew. It really wasn't funny at all, but the image of Poseidon's rear end plugging the hole burst the dam of tension she'd labored under the past few days.

She didn't bother to hide her smirk when she joined Clifford and Heinrich in the main cabin. Clifford looked at her oddly, his mouth a flat line. Exhausted, she supposed. He hadn't done old-style structureling work for years and must be feeling it. Her thoughts immediately shifted to Ralph. She leaned over to study Clifford's monitor.

"How's he doing?"

"Well enough, but you should have left me in there."

His words were brusque, but she cut him some slack, given what he'd been through. "I had to make the best choice for the team."

"*My* team." He touched a finger to a place on the monitor. "See that?"

Of course she did, hadn't she been the one following the readings to determine if it was safe to remove Clifford from the seawall? Veronica bit the inside of her cheek to control her temper.

"Yes." She shifted into ego-soothing mode, a tactic she despised but if Clifford was going to behave stupidly, she'd treat him that way. "Tell me what it means."

"It *means* the seawall is stable," he said, as if she were the one being stupid.

Heinrich rose. "Ms. Zeta, would you mind watching my monitor for a few minutes? I really need a break."

She'd been so absorbed in the crisis she hadn't realized he'd been glued to his spot for hours. "Yes, of course." As soon as Heinrich left, she took his seat and snarled, "What's *your* problem, anyway? You know how jobs can shift when there's a crisis. I was the one who took Ralph's place when he abandoned the Viaduct and nearly killed all those people fifteen years ago."

"That's right," he snapped, his British clip more pronounced than usual. "You're Little Miss Perfect, aren't you? Know how to do everything better than everyone and can't stay out of other people's business. So silly of me not to realize you were the one to solve the seawall problem, not some common bloke like me."

"Is that what you think?" Bile rose in her throat and she had the sudden impulse to punch him. "You don't suppose it had any-thing to do with Poseidon and…"

It was more than she could take. She burst into laughter that rivaled a hyena's, Clifford scowling while she tried to spit out, "…his butt!"

He grabbed her shoulders. "Heaven and Earth, Veronica, what's the matter with you? Get a grip, old thing!"

"It's a leak in the ceiling of the Underworld," she gasped. "That's what's causing the sink hole. And Poseidon, he's…he's…"

She collapsed on Clifford and laughed some more, unable to deliver the punch line.

"Oh dear." His arms encircled her. "I'm afraid you need some time at Olympus Rest."

She straightened up and wiped the tears from her cheeks. "No need to fuss. After we get Ralph out, dinner would be fine. Now, let me tell you from the start."

Clifford listened to her complete report. There was a long silence.

"Whoever would have figured that out?" he said at last.

"Exactly." She tapped a kiss on his cheek.

Clifford cleared his throat. "So, dinner you say? Where would you like to go?"

"You pick." She kissed him again. "I trust your judgment."

City of Mount Olympus
Zeus

Zeus had downed two cold beers and split a bottle of Char-donnay with Hera by the time they'd worked it through. He was aghast at her abuse of power. In the end, he asked two questions.

"What were you planning to do with him, once you'd made him immortal?"

"Get rid of him, of course!" Zeus pitied her red eyes, but he was upset, too. "It's not like I had experience in jilting lovers, like some people I know."

That one hurt and he said so. She gruffly apologized. He felt like a fool asking the second question but in the interest of clearing the air he persisted.

"Hera, is this person, this Saul Crispin, better-looking than me?"

The question seemed to bewilder her. "No, of course not. Nobody is, you know."

It was a start. Zeus retired his wine goblet and excused himself to the shower. It was a custom unit with an extra-large enclosure. Jet-pressured water piped in at four levels, as well as overhead. He stood in the center, relishing the pummel of hot water on his flight-weary shoulders. Steam rose. His head began to clear. The shower door opened.

"You forgot the soap." Hera, in the outfit nature had provided her, stepped into the steam to join him.

Hermes

Babies mature rapidly. Hermes had heard so, somewhere. If you weren't around them every day, you'd miss all sorts of developmental miracles. He'd never before paid attention to his children when they were babies. Now he wished he had.

Something remarkable had happened to P. B. during the course of the day. A hardness about the infant had fallen away, a hardness Hermes hadn't acknowledged though he knew it was the source of his own black eye.

"You're really something special," he said to the baby. P. B. cuddled and cooed in his arms.

Monique had changed today, too. For the first time since the birth she could sit up in bed, though her face registered pain when she moved. He felt horrible about the damage she'd suffered, couldn't forgive himself for the dangerous stunt that had caused it.

Aphrodite had come for her afternoon visit. He'd been sent

from the room when she arrived, but now she was gone. Hermes poked his head out of the kitchen, where he'd retreated with P. B. The bedroom door was closed. He knew he wasn't welcome but turned the knob anyway.

The first thing he noticed was her hair. Long, white tresses lay smoothly in front of her shoulders. She must have let Aphrodite work out the tangles for her. Hurt, he forced a smile.

"Good visit?"

"Yes." If the rasp in her voice hadn't been from injury, he would have found it sexy. She raised her arms, a grimace revealing her pain. "Give me the baby."

Hermes instinctively pulled back and pressed P. B. to his chest. It was the first time Monique had asked for their son and it frightened him.

"Please." Hermes carefully set P. B. in her lap and steadied the baby until her arms encircled him. "We need to talk."

Certain he wouldn't like the conversation, Hermes pulled up a chair. For a long time Monique gazed down at the baby. At last she looked up. Her eyes, quite beautiful eyes he had to admit, looked sternly into his.

"I'm going away soon."

"What?"

His heart twisted. He hadn't expected her to want him now, possibly not ever, but leaving?

"I'm leaving Mount Olympus. Apollo believes I'll recover more quickly away from here and after what's happened…."

Ashamed, he looked away.

"I don't blame you, Hermes, if that's what you're thinking. We were both drunk and we were both stupid."

"But the boy—"

"I'm taking him with me."

"Where the Tartarus can you take him, Monique? He's still…he's still…."

No one in their right mind would take a child of The Power into the mortal world.

Monique bared P. B.'s tummy. "It's fading."

Hermes sat hard against the back of his chair. He'd noticed the second navel had shrunk the last time he changed P. B. He'd even mentioned it to Elle.

"I'm very, very tired of men, except for this one," Monique said, cuddling the baby. "We're going to the mortal desert to help women apply for business micro-loans through WomanFront."

"So," he said when realization struck. Elle hated him; Hermes was sure of it. She'd do anything to separate him from Monique and P. B.

"The desert is no place for a baby," he protested. "What if you're attacked by bandits?"

Monique smiled faintly. "Not a problem, since Pan took care of it."

With my help thought Hermes bitterly. The desert Elle served would still be attractive to gangs of thugs if he, himself, hadn't made the scarecrow beacons per Pan's specifications. He knelt at the bedside.

"What can I do to change your mind?"

She stared at him, didn't say a word.

"Right." He stood and reached for P. B. She turned away from him to shield the baby, groaning with pain until she settled. "I'll bring his bottle."

A large piece of his heart broke as he left the bedroom and closed the door behind him. Fate was not going to let him be a real father, not for now, anyway. All those little changes he'd just become aware of were going to happen somewhere else, damn it to Tartarus. P. B. was going to the worst drought region on Earth, a drought he, Hermes, had caused and had yet to solve. Would Earth and mortals and gods survive to see P. B.'s two hundredth birthday?

Suddenly, dialing back climate change had visceral meaning. After months of confusion, Hermes' destiny was clear. Roderick Waller's *Green World Works* social media campaign was yielding positive results. Athena's people were poised to sting a fossil fuel giant. Cleo would be back from leave by the end of the year. With that team and incredibly good luck, maybe, just maybe, he could save the world.

Appendix
Cast list, alphabetic by first name

Anatole – Valet to Hades.

Aphrodite – Daughter of Zeus by Dione. Goddess of Love and all that goes with it. Married to Hephaestus. Former mistress of Ares and many others. More children than she can count, notably Monique Raison, CFO of Aphrodite's commercial empire, Love, Inc.

Apollo – Son of Zeus and Leto, twin brother of Artemis. God of Music and Medicine. Owns and operates Olympus Rest convalescent home, has a private medical practice and records instrumental albums from time to time.

Ares – Son of Zeus and Hera. God of War and Agriculture but, once released from The Power's grip, now focuses only on Agriculture. Invented "Grecian Formula" hair treatment, though he no longer uses it himself.

Artemis – Daughter of Zeus and Leto, twin sister of Apollo. Goddess of the Hunt. Currently assigned to fight poachers in Africa.

Athena – Daughter of Zeus and Metis. Goddess of War, Wisdom and Diplomacy. Director of Armed Forces, Olympus, Inc.

Brianna – Retired structureling. Mother of Clifford Essex.

Candy Smith – Spokesperson to the mortal world for Hera's Marriage and the Media program. Vivacious and volatile. Married to Jim, mother of Titus (a toddler).

Cleo Petra – Rising girl genius at Olympus, Inc. Executive assistant to Hermes.

Clifford Essex – Director, Computer and Architectural Services, Olympus, Inc. Formerly a structureling. Fiancé of Veronica Zeta. Son of Ralph and Brianna.

David Bernstein – Son of Hera and some Jewish guy she seduced a couple millennia ago. Raised in secrecy as a mortal, discovered his immortal status while working as a barista in Seattle, Washington. He is currently enrolled in a master's program at Athens U.

Demeter – Goddess of the Harvest with a special interest in grains. Ex-wife of Zeus. Mother of Persephone.

Ilithyia (**Elle**) – Eldest daughter of Zeus and Hera, Goddess of Childbirth. Presently works delivering medical and food supplies to war-torn villages in a mortal desert. Lots of piercings. Her nickname is pronounced "L" (like the French word for girl).

Hades – God of the Underworld. Stern, wealthy and miserly. Married to Persephone.

Hebe – Daughter of Zeus and Hera. Goddess of Youth, but this is getting trickier with each new chin. Her most impressive power is running up credit card debt. Married to Heracles. Children Alexiares, Anicetus (adult male twins) and Aster (a toddler).

Hephaestus (**Hef**) – Eldest son of Zeus and Hera. God of Volcanoes, blacksmith, and builder of robots. Married to Aphrodite. Owns and operates the only motorcycle in the City of Mount Olympus.

Hera – Goddess of Marriage, Director of Department of Marriage and Family at Olympus, Inc. She's recently launched the highly successful program "Marriage and the Media." Married to Zeus with 5 children. Also mother to David Bernstein, the fruit of her one known marital indiscretion.

Heracles – Son of Zeus by mortal noblewoman Alcmene, via some impressive trickery. Began life as a mortal and performed Twelve Trials, which is another story altogether. After he died, Hera made him immortal and also made him marry Hebe. Works as chief security officer in the City of Mount Olympus.

Hermes – Son of Zeus and Maia. The Trickster. God of Travelers, Athletes and Inventors. Director of Digital Devices and Robotics at Olympus, Inc. Moonlights as escort of the recently dead to the

Underworld.

Hestia – Goddess of Home and Hearth. A virgin, by profession. Considered by many to be the most stable of her siblings.

James Ares (Jim) Smith – A psychological counselor, both for Olympus, Inc.'s Immortal Resources department and in private practice. Son of Poseidon. Married to Candy, father of Titus.

Jocelyn Chadwick – Former US Secretary of Defense, CEO of humanitarian aid NGO WomanFront Strategies. Mortal.

Massimo – Friar, scholar and friend of the Petra family.

Milton Bernstein – David Bernstein's foster father, former servant of Hera.

Monique Raison – Daughter of Aphrodite and Reynard, a French immortal associated with foxes. Chief Financial Officer of Love, Inc.

Pan – Son of Hermes and one of the Pleiades (aka, the Seven Sisters) but which one is unclear. God of Shepherds and Flocks. Given to drunkenness and debauchery.

Persephone – Daughter of Zeus and Demeter, wife of Hades. A Goddess of Harvest and Queen of the Underworld. Spends 9 months of the year aboveground and 3 months below.

Peter Petra – Cleo Petra's father.

Poseidon – God of the Sea. Physically fit, as promiscuous as the mortal blues singer Scream' Jay Hawkins and has the offspring to prove it.

Ralph – Retired structureling, father of Clifford Essex.

Roderick Weller – Rising boy genius at Olympus, Inc.

Saul Crispin – An actor with an interesting past.

Stella – Eldest child of Cronus and Rhea whom none of the others knew about until she revealed her identity and her relationship to The Power. Before then, served as Zeus' executive assistant at Olympus, Inc. Resides at Olympus Rest, an upscale sanitarium owned and operated by Apollo.

Thelma Bernstein – David Bernstein's foster mother, former servant of Hera.

Titania Petra – Cleo Petra's mother.

Veronica Zeta – The youngest child of Zeus and Hera. Presently CEO of Olympus, Inc. Affianced to Clifford Essex and adoptive mother of a large, orange cat named Bill Gates, Jr. Survivor of near-fatal attack by The Power.

Zeus – Former CEO of Olympus, Inc., now Provost of Athens U and Athens Tech. Married to Hera, with children Hephaestus (Hef), Ilithyia (Elle), Ares, Hebe, and Veronica Zeta. Many other children with many other romantic partners.

About the Author

S. D. Matley writes long and short fiction. "Beyond Big-G City" is the third book in her contemporary fantasy/mythology series featuring the Greek Pantheon. She prefers occupations that start with the letter "A": author, actor, and (formerly) accountant. Matley calls Washington State home; she resides in the southwest corner with her four-legged feline housemates. More at http://susandmatley.com.

More Books by S.D. Matley from WolfSinger Publications

Small-g City – S.D. Matley

Seattle is on the brink of disaster, but nobody knows it! Nobody except Ralph, a "small-g" god from Olympus, Inc.

Ralph suffers from extreme job burn-out, and no wonder—his job is to reinforce Seattle's notorious raised highway, the Alaskan Way Viaduct, by disbursing his molecules throughout the unstable and hazardous structure.

But Ralph's molecules are feeling the pull of reconstitution. Will he survive one more agonizing rush hour without resuming his humanoid form and emerging from the viaduct, sending thousands of commuters to their deaths? And what about the familiar shadow hovering over him? If Zeus (Olympus, Inc. CEO and the Biggest of Big-G Gods) is spying on him, all Tartarus is sure to break loose!

Big-G City – S.D. Matley

Veronica Zeta, youngest child of Zeus and Hera, is at last CEO of the immortal owned and operated corporation, Olympus, Inc. The biggest project on her agenda is creating world peace, but first she must depose her bloodthirsty brother Ares, God of War. To do so, she must deploy a supernatural force called The Power, which can demand a terrible price.

Zeus, former CEO and Ex-Lord of the Universe, struggles with identity issues after his retirement. The bright spot in his life is babysitting his toddler granddaughter, but his marriage with Hera is foundering and he longs for someone to confide in.

Hera's new campaign, a mortal lifestyle series of books and seminars called Marvelous Marriage, is a huge success. The face of this project, small-g goddess Candy Smith, has become a media celebrity. Hera, Goddess of Marriage, revels in the market share she's stealing from the "adult" industries owned by her rival, Aphrodite.

But Aphrodite, Goddess of Love, is ready to fight back! Employing a photo-shopped tabloid cover photo and a box of enchanted chocolates, she disrupts the personal life of Candy Smith and goads Hera into executing her own sabotage plan.

The lives of these Olympians collide when Veronica succeeds in deposing Ares, and pays for deploying a large dose The Power with blindness, anguish and, possibly, death. But how can an immortal die? The answer lies in an old family secret, daringly unearthed by Zeus in the eleventh hour.

Get ready for more adventures with these fantasy books from WolfSinger Publications.

Fanny & Dice – Rebecca McFarland Kyle

"I'm leaving Hell for good, Eurydice…"

When she heard those words, Eurydice had a choice: remain in Hades' realm or escape to Earth with her kinswoman, Persephone.

She knew the Earth wasn't what they'd left. Demeter hadn't summoned Persephone to bring Spring for quite some time…and the last dead crossed the River Styx many years before. She hadn't expected to arrive in a world where trains rode across the prairie on metal tracks instead of chariots and men settled disputes with six guns instead of swords.

Eurydice will face perils both immortal and mortal, from gun and axe to her own heart…

The Lawman's Daughter – Paul Miller

Raine receives a final, disturbing message from her father. The problem is, it was written after he was supposedly killed in battle. Now she must join the ranks of the inhuman Rift Wardens to try and uncover the truth.

What she finds is a dark plot involving some very powerful people, and stopping it could very well cost Raine her life.

Or, even worse, it could cost her soul.

The Last Sorcerer – Felicia Cash

Throughout the history of time, a war has raged between the forces of light and darkness.

As the millennia passed the blood lines thinned and powers waned. One year ago, the last great sorcerer disappeared in the process of killing the last of the Dark Dragons, and now the world is in the hands of only the weakly magicked.

But can you ever really kill a dragon?

Twila Aurelius and Morgan Stevens are two girls who are thrust into this time-honored struggle, pitted against the dark forces. With wit and friendship, and a little bit of dumb luck, they set out to put the world right again, even if it means fighting off werewolves with no more than a stapler. Evil sorcerers aren't the only threat, especially when the girls learn more about their own histories and those of their families.

Can friendship overcome history?

Can two girls overcome evil?

Maya, Resurrected – Kimberly Todd Wade

859 A.D. Yohl Ik'nal ("Heart of the Wind Place") is alone with her two starving children on their drought-stricken farm. Her husband and two grown sons have been drafted to fight in a distant war. Will they ever return? Yohl can't afford to wait. Her hungry children must be fed. It's time to dig up Yohl's past, for her mother was a princess, her grandfather a king. She still has relatives amongst the Maya royalty. They are her best hope for salvation.

Follow Yohl and her children as they travel Maya causeways, highways of the ancient world, through ravaged jungle and depressed homesteads to the capital city, itself on the verge of economic collapse.

Can the religious spectacle of human sacrifice provoke the Gods' beneficence? If the Maya ceremonies and myths fail, Yohl has recourse to the older, deeper traditions of the forest people.

She'll do whatever necessary to survive.

The Moleskin Cap - M. R. Williamson

Helen is trying to get over the recent loss of her mother. Seeing the struggle, her father sends her to live with her grandparents.

Now among the forests her mother loved, Helen connects with her mother's hobby, photography. With her mother's first camera, an old Nikon, she snaps a shadowy figure in the early-morning shade of a fir tree.

The resulting friendship not only pulls her from the destructive depression she was sinking into, but leads Helen into a world of magic and adventure and gives her a new purpose in life and a new reason to live.

Necromantic Shenanigans –
J.A. Campbell & Rebecca McFarland Kyle

From building Towers of Solitude in Colorado's mountains to freeing a bestiary held captive by a demon-possessed Scottish Laird, Elise and Hagatha Macrow are on the case.

Necromantic Shenanigans is a lucky combination of thirteen stories detailing the escapades of two necromancers, who fight crime and normalcy without ever donning a cape.

Seventh Daughter – Ronnie Seagren

Some people are destined from birth to do great things.

Gil Orlov is born in the shadow of totality of a solar eclipse, the seventh daughter of a seventh daughter. She is the culmination of a carefully planned genealogy begun by her great-grandmother. Gil's purpose, the goal of her family—defeating a Vision of the world in flames, reduced to a lifeless cinder.

But the power she should have is muted or lacking. Gil and her six sisters begin an arduous journey to a place of power high in the Peruvian Andes known as Killichaka—the Bridge to the Moon. They must make it to this ancient temple in time to complete a ritual during the totality of the 1937 solar eclipse. If they are successful, Gil's powers should be restored—giving her the ability to prevent the global disaster her ancestors warned of.

To succeed they must first survive the journey and locate Killichaka. Against them is the environment, the elements, their own doubts and fears as well as the 'Other' and a force that would gleefully see the world fall into chaos—an entity known as Supay.

Find out more about these and our other books at
www.wolfsingerpubs.com